"SIR HENRY, IT'S HAPPENED AGAIN!"

Sir Henry Merrivale opened his mouth, but closed it without speech.

"The Oak Room," Virginia explained. "From eleven o'clock on, Chief Inspector Masters was in the Oak Room with the doors and windows all locked on the inside. He went to sleep, but something woke him up. Before he had time to turn round he was hit on the head."

H.M.'s gaze strayed across the room. It was cold, but there was moisture on the forehead of Sir Henry Merrivale.

"Do you remember the cup-hilted rapier that hangs on the wall *outside* the door of the Oak Room?" Virginia continued. "Well, it was there. Lying at Mr. Masters' feet in the impossibly locked room, *was the cup-hilted rapier!*"

CARTER DICKSON

THE CAVALIER'S CUP

ZEBRA BOOKS
KENSINGTON PUBLISHING CORP.

ZEBRA BOOKS

are published by

Kensington Publishing Corp.
475 Park Avenue South
New York, NY 10016

First Zebra Books printing: September 1987

Printed in the United States of America

For
my daughter Julia
and
her husband, Richard,
but
not forgetting Gramp.

1

When Sir Henry Merrivale took up singing lessons, it was agreed that this new pursuit might wreak incalculable harm on innocent people. But few believed that it could ever have any bearing on the happy marriage of Virginia Brace, or on the wild problem at Telford Old Hall.

Our old friend Chief Inspector Masters had heard nothing of this hobby. Since he had not seen H.M. for fully six months, knowing H.M. to be at the latter's country house near Great Yewborough in Sussex, Masters was a happy man.

He was a happy man, that is, until one fine June morning not so many years ago. Masters was at New Scotland Yard, in the large office he shared with four other Chief Inspectors of the Metropolitan Police. But on this occasion only Masters (Criminal Investigation) sat in the stuffy room which smelled of damp and old stone, when his sergeant brought him an official form just filled in by a visitor downstairs.

"Oh, ah," said Masters, glancing first at the official form and then at a memorandum which had been delivered from the Assistant Commissioner. "Right you are, Bob. Show the lady up."

The name written on the official form was merely "Virginia Brace." But across the memorandum on the desk Masters had scribbled notes which told a different story.

"Lady Brace," he had written. "Wife of Lord Brace of Hove. Young, wealthy, sport, big bug."

The latter terms, it is hardly necessary to say, referred to Lady Brace's husband and not to Lady Brace herself. A minute later it became clear that "big bug," at least, could not apply to Virginia Brace in any sense of the word. Though Masters sometimes boasted that he never showed surprise, he could hardly restrain it.

The very pretty girl who entered his office, he would have sworn at a first quick glance, could not have been more than fifteen years old, despite her modish clothes.

First of all, even wearing her heels she was only about five feet tall. Her soft and silky light-brown hair fell to her shoulders and curled out a little in artless, young-girl fashion. Her eyes were large and grey, with luminous whites. She wore something blue, touched with white—Masters could not have told you what—and there were dimples at the corners of her mouth.

"Hurrum!" said Masters, hastily getting to his feet and giving what, for him, might even have passed as a bow.

"I'm awfully sorry to intrude, Chief Inspector," said the small girl, in a warm and sweet voice as feminine as herself. "But do you mind if I sit down?"

Masters, who ordinarily never stirred from his own

seat, nearly fell over his large feet in setting out a chair for her.

Now the building called New Scotland Yard has been skilfully constructed so that a blaze of morning sunlight falls straight in the eyes of the detectives, making them swear, rather than in the eyes of visitors as no doubt it should. Therefore Masters' first glance at Virginia Brace did not include everything.

It did not include a study of her figure, which was a fine one. It did not see that, for all its innocent and demure appearance, her expression held a quality of the impish. The small girl—quite unconsciously, it must be insisted; she could not help it—used her rather heavy-lidded grey eyes and pink lips in a way which would have inspired speculation in any man who had been married for fewer years than Chief Inspector Humphrey Masters.

A close observer would also have guessed that, deplorable as it may have been, this small girl hugely enjoyed the telling of low-minded jokes.

At the moment, however, the dimples at the corners of her mouth were not much in evidence. Lady Brace was badly worried and showed it.

"I didn't know what else to do except come to you," she confessed, as she sat down. "It's dreadful, and yet it's silly too. If it weren't for Tom—that's my husband—I shouldn't mind. But it troubles Tom. And whatever else happens I *won't* have Tom worried."

Masters beamed. Large and burly in dark blue, bland as a card-sharper despite the fact that his face was redder with the years and his grizzled hair more scant, he remained exactly as he had always been:

every bit as shrewd and, despite his apparent stolidness, every bit as apt to go off the deep end as Sir Henry Merrivale himself.

"Just so, miss," he soothed her, sitting back with his finger-tips together. "That is—just so, my lady! You tell me all about it, and I'm sure we can put things right."

Virginia had one of those fair skins which easily show colour. For a moment she hesitated in a helpless way.

"But that's just it. I don't know where on earth to begin."

"Begin at the beginning," said Masters, not unreasonably.

"Well! You see, Tom and I live at Telford Old Hall. That's in Sussex, not far from Great Yewborough . . . Is anything wrong, Mr. Masters?"

Masters cleared his throat.

"Hurrum! You don't happen to know a gentleman named Merrivale, do you? Sir Henry Merrivale?"

"I believe he lives at Cranleigh Court, about six miles away. But I've never met him."

Masters felt great relief. Virginia crossed her knees, and for the first time he noticed that this child's figure was very well developed. Hastily Masters averted his eyes and his thoughts.

"Then that's all right, miss. Beg pardon—my lady! You go on and tell me."

"At Telford," continued Virginia, drawing a deep breath, "there's a certain room that I've loved, really loved more than any other place in the house, since Tom and I were married ten years ago. Please, you mustn't look so surprised! I'm twenty-eight. Tom and I have been married for ten years, and we have a son nine years old. Well! As I was saying . . ."

Virginia began her story at one minute to eleven o'clock by Masters' wrist watch. At two minutes past eleven a wary, suspicious look had crept into the Chief Inspector's boiled blue eye. At four minutes past eleven he was clearing his throat several times. At six minutes past eleven he could restrain himself no longer, and burst out.

"No!" he said. "No, no, no!"

Virginia, a warm-hearted girl, was deeply and seriously concerned about him as well as puzzled.

"Mr. Masters, what have I done to you now?"

Though several shades of red passed across her companion's face, he managed—at least, partly—to get a grip on himself.

"Not again!" he said with some violence. "Oh, lummy, not again! I tell you straight, miss, I'm not as young as I once was. I can't stand any more of these things that couldn't possibly have happened, but did happen!"

"You never heard anything like this before," declared Virginia.

As events were to prove, she spoke the absolute truth. But Masters, with all the experience we know, may be forgiven for considering her remark a little naive.

"Anyway, you see my difficulty?" she asked anxiously. "Nobody was hurt. And, though the thing is worth I don't know how many thousand pounds, it wasn't stolen. It was only moved. Although nobody could possibly have got in there, or come anywhere near it, it *was* moved. The trouble is, what can the

11

police do?"

"Ah!" cried Masters, like a shipwrecked mariner who catches sight of a sail.

"The reason why I'm here," continued Virginia, "is very simple. Poor Tom thinks he did it himself. He thinks he walked in his sleep, and moved the cup himself! He's so worried about it, Mr. Masters, that he can't even *get* to sleep now. And when a man begins to brood about what he might do while he's walking in his sleep—I mean, that he might even commit a murder or something—well . . . !"

Small Virginia, who had been speaking so rapidly she was almost gasping, now paused for breath. Whenever she spoke of her husband, her grey eyes held an expression which showed that, though she might have been married for ten years, she was even more in love than she had been at the time of the wedding.

But Masters would not hear of the problem she presented.

The Chief Inspector, now on his dignity, held up a hand so much in the fashion of a traffic-policeman that it almost destroyed Virginia's gravity.

"Now, my lady, please listen to me!" he said. "There's only one possible explanation. You've said it yourself!"

"But, Mr. Masters . . . !"

"Now, now miss! I'm a police-officer, you know, and an old hand. I ought to know. Lord Brace walked in his sleep, and did move the cup himself."

"Mr. Masters, he didn't!"

Though the Chief Inspector half-hypnotized her with his most persuasive and fatherly air, which once or twice had caused old lags to give him the regrettable nickname of Soapy Hump, still the distressed girl refused to agree.

"Please, I tell you he didn't!" she insisted. "Do you think, after all these years, I shouldn't know whether Tom walked in his sleep or not? And he doesn't. He never has!"

"Now, now, my lady, you can't be sure of that. You can't be sure of that, can you? Eh? You occupy separate bedrooms, I daresay?"

Virginia opened her eyes wide.

"Good heavens, no! I think that's a silly idea!"

"You don't occupy separate rooms, my lady?"

"No. I should never dream of it, and I know Tom would kick up a frightful row if I did. Of course we're very old-fashioned. But then we both like being old-fashioned." Suddenly, for no apparent reason, pink colour appeared in the face of the small angel, and there was a pleasantly wicked twinkle in her eyes. "I mean," she added hastily, "Tom doesn't walk in his sleep, and he couldn't have moved the cup!"

"But you can see for yourself, my lady . . . !"

"I really am sorry to bother you," said Virginia forlornly. "You sound as though you didn't want to help me."

"It's not that, my lady! Gawdlummycharley—I mean, so help me, it's not that! I've got to be reasonable, that's all. I don't suppose," added Masters, with a hideous attempt at jocularity, "there's a ghost at this Telford Old Hall, is there?"

Virginia took this quite seriously.

"As a matter of fact, Telford *is* supposed to be haunted. But I never saw the ghost, and neither did

Tom. So far as the records show, nobody has seen it since the eighteenth century. But it's associated with the cavalier's window in that same seventeenth-century Oak Room—"

Masters, who was sweating, laughed much too heartily.

"Well, maybe the ghost went in and moved the cup. Ha ha ha. According to the facts, nobody else could have."

Virginia bit her lip and said nothing.

"Come, now, you can see how it is!" Masters boomed away. "And there's another thing you mentioned yourself. There's been no burglary, you tell me; not even any breaking or entering. How could the police interfere, even though we want to?"

"But what am I to do about poor Tom? You wouldn't think he had a nerve in his body, and yet he's scared to death!"

"I'm very sorry about Lord Brace, my lady. But there it is. After all, there are doctors who can cure these nervous disorders . . ."

"Mr. Masters! If my husband has any kind of nervous disorder at all, then I never knew it!"

"Ha ha ha," said the Chief Inspector, who was perhaps not quite himself. "You just take the advice of a man old enough to be your father, my lady. What your husband needs is a good tonic, for the liver maybe, and then he'll be as right as rain. When his eyes' back in condition again . . ."

"His eyes?" breathed Virginia. "Mr. Masters, did you ever see Tom play polo?"

"Eh?"

"He beat the Indian Army practically single-

14

handed. And with a revolver he can shoot the centre out of the ace of diamonds at twenty yards."

"That's very interesting. Yes, yes, very! But you're a sensible lady, I know. And you can see it still doesn't affect my position, miss. Ur! Beg pardon again; I mean, my lady!"

For the first time Virginia really smiled, in a sleepy but electrifying way.

"Why don't you just call me Jinny?" she suggested. "Everybody else does. I've been called that ever since I was a little girl in America."

"In America?" exclaimed Masters, badly jolted. "You're not an American, are you?"

"Of course I am," smiled Virginia. "Couldn't you deduce that, like Sherlock Holmes, from my first name? How many English girls are called Virginia?"

"Hurrum!" said Masters, fingering his chin. "Come to think of it, I did notice you pronounced some of your words a bit different, like. But I never thought anything of it. Why, miss"—though embarrassment flooded him, he spoke before he could stop himself—"you don't talk a bit like the people in films!"

Virginia remained grave.

"Comparatively few of us do," she assured him. "Mr. Masters, may I ask you a question?"

"A question, miss?"

"Yes." Virginia was apologetic. "I mention it, you see, only because all of us who live in this country are always hearing the same thing." Gently, she registered stupefied shock. " 'You're not an American, are you? You don't talk a bit like the people in films.' That's why I want to ask you the question."

Behind that sleepy smile, behind the flash of the provocative personality, there was not only attractiveness but high intelligence.

"No offense, miss! But what do you want to ask?"

"Well," said Virginia, "suppose you judged life here in England entirely by what you see in British films?"

Masters opened his mouth, but shut it again.

"Suppose," she went on in the same gentle, earnest way, "you judged it by such films as *Passport to Pimlico* and *Whisky Galore? Whisky Galore*, my father tells me, was shown in America under the title of *Tight Little Island*. What would you learn about your own country?"

"Now stop a bit, miss!"

Virginia looked sad.

"You would learn," she said, "that all persons in the British Foreign Office are amiable dim-wits with just sense enough to come in out of the rain. But that really isn't a very accurate picture of the Foreign Office, even under a Labour Government. What's more, you would learn that nobody in Scotland is ever sober or ever wants to be. You would learn . . ."

Masters' gesture silenced her, and she murmured another apology.

"Can't say *I* saw anything very funny in those films," growled the Chief Inspector. "Anyway, they were supposed to be comedies!"

"But is it so much different, though of course to a far lesser degree, even in serious British films?"

"Now, now, miss!"

"Surely it isn't? I mean, almost always you get the funny landlady, the doddering lord, the silly-ass

16

young man, the peppery Colonel Blimp who says, 'Gad, sir!' " Virginia restrained her delight. "Such people really do exist, lots of them. But we should be wrong if we said they were universal or even the general rule, shouldn't we?"

Masters passed a hand across his steaming reddish forehead.

"So help me, miss, I can't think how we got on this subject! I'm bound to admit I enjoy a good flick, but . . ."

"You enjoy the flicks?" softly asked Virginia, who had been leaning back in her chair. "Oh, that's wonderful! Tom and I have a fine projector at Telford, you know."

"So?"

"Yes. We both adore the Marx Brothers, especially Harpo, and we show those old films over and over again. Mr. Masters! If you'd honour us by coming down to Telford and finding out how somebody got in and out of a locked room without leaving a trace, we should love to show you classics like *A Night at the Opera* . . ."

"No!" shouted Masters, seeing the trap open before him and violently shying back. But again he corked himself, becoming persuasive. "For the first time, miss, much as I might like it, I can't interfere. It's impossible! It's absolutely im . . ."

This was where the telephone rang.

Masters, glancing quickly at the phone on his desk, already felt a presentiment of doom. Nor was he wrong. The voice at the other end of the line was that of Sir Herbert Armstrong, the Assistant Commissioner of the C.I.D. Though Virginia could not

17

know this, she easily guessed it must be somebody of importance, and her small hands were clasped together in a meek but fervent prayer.

"Yes, sir?" said Masters, freezing to attention. "Yes, sir, Lady Brace is here now." His boiled blue eye swivelled around. "Yes, I've heard it."

The phone spoke at some length. Masters closed his eyes, with a look not far from ferocity, but he answered with dignity.

"If you order me, sir, as a special favour to her ladyship—well, I've got no choice. But you'll admit, won't you, that I've had what you might call a pretty wide experience with locked rooms?"

The phone assented.

"Very well, sir. Just so. And of all the rooms I ever heard of as being locked, this one is the *most* smacking well locked! This time it's only a mistake, and I can tell you what the mistake is. I can . . ."

Suddenly Masters' whole demeanour altered, and he gripped the phone.

"Will you repeat that? Sir Henry? What about him . . . ?

"Sir, can I depend on that? I'll tell you why I ask. The old ba—the old gentleman is buried down at Cranleigh Court in the country. He won't answer the phone; he won't see anybody. I don't know what he's doing, except that he can't be getting into any mischief, because I haven't heard a single noise out of him for six months. He . . .

"Then that's understood, sir? I have your full authority to go down and rout him out, no matter what he says or how he carries on? Not at all, sir! The pleasure's mine! Glad to, glad to! Thank *you*,

18

sir! Good-bye."

Slowly Masters put back the receiver.

"Well, well, miss!" he said. "Well, well, well!"

Masters was exalted by a sort of bursting affability which nevertheless had a certain quality of the sinister, as though behind his back, figuratively speaking, he grasped a sharp knife which he fondly waited to plunge into somebody's gizzard.

The tactful Virginia had pretended to hear not one word of what passed. Taking from Masters' desk a copy of *The Poultry Fanciers' Gazette*, she had appeared to be lost in this with a rapt attention which, in actuality, she would have devoted only to a piece of fine literature on the oner hand or to a dubious French novel on the other.

"The fact is, miss," said Masters, rubbing his hands together in deep satisfaction, "I've got some news for you. If you'd still like me to, I now see my way clear to looking into this matter."

"Mr. Masters, I did so hope you would! It's perfectly marvellous of you!"

"Not a bit, miss, not a bit! Now tell me. Did you come up to town by train or car?"

"By car. I can give you a lift back, if you like."

"Thank you, miss. That'ud be very kind of you, and it'd save petrol for a police-car. Would you mind stopping on the way, so that we can see Sir Henry Merrivale at Cranleigh Court?"

Virginia breathed a perplexed little whisper of a laugh.

"No, not in the least. I—I don't want to seem inquisitive, but is this Sir Henry Merrivale a detective or something?"

19

"We-el, now! Yes, miss, in a manner of speaking, I suppose you could say he is." Masters lowered his voice. "And one of the best, too, though you mustn't ever tell him that."

"I'm afraid I still don't understand. Is he eccentric, or difficult to handle—anything of that sort?"

Masters' laugh was again hearty, but for a different reason.

"Don't you believe it, miss! Mind! I won't say there aren't some people, maybe, who might say he was hard to handle. But I can always handle him, by George!" The Chief Inspector looked at his watch. "After lunch, I think, would be the best time. Say two-thirty? Right! All the same . . ."

Now Masters, as we know, had a conscience. Once he had passed the first flush of his triumph, it began to gobble at him.

"All the same, it does seem a pity to spring the old man on you without a word of warning. Forgive me, miss, but where are you having lunch?"

Virginia, though fascinated, remained even more puzzled.

"At the Savoy, with my father. Dad's here for only a short time. Congress isn't in session, of course, but he's got to go back to America."

"Congress? Your father's a Senator, maybe?"

"No, a Congressman. You may have heard of him. He's William T. Harvey of the 23½ congressional district of Pennsylvania—Oh, dear!"

"Easy, miss! No call to be upset, now!"

"It isn't that. I'm afraid I've got to warn you about something too. If you meet Dad, for heaven's sake don't mention the Republican Party!"

"Oh, ah? Why not?"

"Because he's a Democrat."

Masters, whose mind grasped the word "Democrat" as being spelled with a small d, frowned and almost asked if it could be called unusual to find a democrat in a democracy. But he remembered the names of the two great American political parties. True, he was not definitely sure what each of them stood for—a confusion of mind, however, which in the past has sometimes been shared by Americans living in the United States.

"But I don't think you'll meet him," said Virginia, "because he isn't going down to Telford until this evening. Oh, now I remember! We're having lunch with his solicitor here, a Mr. Dennis Foster, and Mr. Foster's wife."

"Are you, by George!" exclaimed Masters, and snapped his fingers. "That'd be Mr. Dennis Foster of Foster & Mackintosh. Gentleman who was mixed up in the Bewlay murder case and married a young lady named Miss Daphne Herbert? That was back in 1945, I think."

"I don't know anything about a murder case, but Mr. Foster's wife is named Daphne."

Masters could now prepare to whet his knife with a clear conscience.

"Same gentleman!" he declared. "The fact is, miss, I was wondering whether we could find somebody to tell you about Sir Henry without—hurrum!—doing it myself. You just ask Mr. Foster; he'll tell you. Everything is fine!"

"Mr. Masters, it isn't fine! How many times must I tell you my poor Tom is worried to death!"

"Still and all, miss, there hasn't been a crime."

"No, but . . ."

"There hasn't been a crime," said Masters happily, "and there isn't going to be any crime!"

"I hope not."

"Just so. Now I wouldn't be honest with you, miss, if I didn't tell you straight: your husband walked in his sleep, and nobody got in or out of that Oak Room because the room really was locked up tight. That's the joke."

"Joke?"

"Ha ha ha," said the Chief Inspector. "I warn you, miss, Sir Henry's going to go scatty trying to find an explanation for it, when there isn't any explanation at all. Lummy! I wonder what the old boy will say about this one?"

2

Towards tea-time, on a drowsy summer afternoon, a car turned in between tall stone pillars and moved up a winding drive of white and finely crushed gravel towards Cranleigh Court, near the village of Great Yewborough.

Virginia Brace was at the wheel of the noble, powerful American car, whose dark-red sleekness winked with highlights under the sun. Though it had been necessary to push forward the sliding seat and put two pillows under Virginia so that her foot could reach the clutch, even Masters—who still had an unreasoning prejudice against women drivers—was compelled to admire the ease with which she handled the car.

Masters, bowler-hatted, sat beside her as the very image of stuffed-shirt. Their drive from London had been very silent, and Masters, uneasy, greatly feared he knew why.

"Lummy!" he had been thinking to himself, as mile after mile sped by without a word being spoken. "Mr. Foster's told her all about the old geezer—too much, maybe—and the little lady's shocked. Can't blame her, though."

Once or twice he had glanced sideways. Virginia, her soft light-brown hair bound in a coloured scarf against the breeze, her thin blue suit-coat put aside so that her soft bare arms gleamed white yet pink-tinged with health, seemed deep in (possibly shocked) thought.

So he had refrained from speaking.

But now, as they approached H. M.'s house, strange things began to happen even in the tough, cynical old heart of Chief Inspector Masters.

He realized, with something of a start, that he had not visited Cranleigh Court since just before the beginning of Hitler's war. As the car hummed up the drive between ancient oak trees and round in a half-circle before a fine, low-built house of dark-red brick in the late Tudor period, it was a scene straight from the ever-glorious days before that war.

The intervening years might never have existed. Westward, beyond the oaks and beeches of the small park, the Sussex Downs rolled away to a dim purple horizon along the Channel. Cranleigh Court, built by that Curtius Merrivale who was knighted by the first James and made a baronet under the first Charles, had suffered few architectural changes or monstrosities.

Though not large—as Telford Old Hall was large—it glowed with that beauty which will last as long as oak trees grow in English soil. And considering the character of the sinner who now owned it, it was remarkable for being a kindly house—beloved of birds, the hours ever warm on its sun-dials.

"Lummy!" thought Masters. "What's wrong with me?"

What ailed him was a bad attack of nostalgia. He would not have described it like this, calling it merely "a funny feeling, like." And had he known what it really was, he would indignantly have denied it.

Consequently, forcing the matter out of his mind, he decided to ask Virginia what she had learned about Sir Henry Merrivale. At the same moment, Virginia stopped the car in the drive before the front door. And she spoke first.

"Isn't it lovely?" she asked.

"What's that, miss?"

It had been agreed, by the way, that he should call her "miss." Masters literally and physically couldn't force himself to call her Jinny, as she wished, and he was always slipping up when he attempted to address her by any married name.

"This," explained Virginia, nodding towards the house and breathing deeply. "I've never been inside the grounds before. It takes all Tom and I have to keep up Telford, even though all the farms have gone and most of the park. I imagine it must be the same with Sir Henry." Again she sighed, in sheer ecstasy.

"But—oh, lord! Isn't it worth it?"

With great dignity Masters got out of the car, slammed the door, and went round to the other side to assist Virginia out.

"No, miss," he said sternly. "If you want my honest opinion, I'm bound to tell you it's *not* worth it!"

"Oh."

"There's a different order of things in England now, miss. Different, and much better."

"But, honestly, Mr. Masters—"

Her companion regarded her darkly.

"Forgive me, miss, but you're an American. You don't understand these things, or conditions in England."

Ten years before that time, an eighteen-year-old Virginia Brace, then Virginia Harvey, had driven an ambulance through the whole of the London blitz. Like five thousand-odd of her compatriots, she had refused to leave England when the late Cordell Hull frantically tried to round up his Americans.

That, or course, was when she had met the ninth Viscount Brace, a private in the Durhams. Perhaps as she now breathed the fragrance of grass or trees, and watched the windows of Cranleigh Court turn golden with late afternoon, she remembered wild nights of long ago: when every fire seemed ten times larger by night, when a lunatic *whack-whack* danced in the sky amid a glitter of white spark-points, when life ripped past like the nightmare bell on her own ambulance.

But perhaps she didn't remember it. In any case, Virginia saw no reason to mention the matter.

"Maybe you're right," she sighed. "Do you know, Mr. Masters, sometimes you sound so exactly like my father—that . . . !"

"Oh, ah? Then your father's a sensible man, miss."

"He *is* a sensible man!" declared Virginia, with surprising passion over such a comment. "He's highly intelligent and very well-read. That's why I wish . . ."

"Wish what?"

Whether she remembered it or not, one of Virginia's most cherished possessions—now kept in a sandal-wood box, together with the first bundle of love-letters from Tom—was a certain cablegram. It had arrived during those same banging dreamlike blitz days. Reaching her amid a barrage of other messages from her mother, from five aunts and two uncles, all urging her to refrain from being a crazy fool and keep out of what was not her quarrel, that cablegram had made Virginia's heart contract in a way surpassed only by her different feelings when Tom proposed marriage.

STICK TO IT, KID. IF YOU SKEDADDLED NOW I'D DISOWN YOU.

And it had been signed, THE OLD MAN. Unfortunately, it was a fraud. Congressman Wil-

27

liam T. Harvey had never sent such a cablegram, or at least swore he hadn't. His views about Great Britain, touching that nation's wish to have and keep a monarchy, might have been considered severe even by Colonel McCormick.

The cablegram, it appeared, had been the work of Congressman Harvey's romantic-minded secretary. But it might have been real, reflected Virginia. It might have been real!

Thus Virginia, dreaming outside the front door of H.M.'s sinister lair, suddenly realized that Chief Inspector Masters—usually articulate because all men found it easy to talk to her—had been preaching a strong sermon about the righting of social injustice.

". . . so you see, miss, that things have all changed, and a good job too! Why, you take Sir Henry himself! *He's* changed out of all recognition."

Here Masters observed that this pocket Venus looked surprised, even a little dismayed. "He has?"

"Yes, indeed, miss!" Masters cleared his throat. "Now, I daresay Mr. Foster told you a lot about Sir Henry? He's told you, maybe, how the old boy once wrecked an amusement-arcade in Charing Cross Road, and went about with a Scotch golf-teacher who nearly landed in the madhouse afterwards?"

"Oh, yes!"

"Well, miss," Masters soothed her, with smothering fatherliness, "you don't need to be a bit afraid of him now. He's a different character."

"How terrible!"

"Wrecking the amusement-arcade, you mean? Oh, ah! That was a bad business, and he'd 'uv landed in front of the beak if I hadn't squared it."

"No, I really meant . . ."

"Most of what he calls his cussedness has gone. Stands to reason! If I'm not getting any younger, you can be sure Sir Henry's a blessed sight older than I am. He can't keep it up. And how do I know that?" demanded Masters, a purely rhetorical question. "Because, as I told you, he's been peacefully down here in the country, probably collecting stamps or bits of pottery or anything else a man of his age ought to do, and there hasn't been a single noise out of him."

"Oh, well," said Virginia, with an air of philosophy.

Unwinding the coloured scarf from round her head shaking out the rich brown hair, she gave another sigh of what this time might have been inexplicable sadness, and glanced at the front door.

To the left of the iron-studded door, the button of a modern bell-push had been let into the old oak of the door-post.

"But aren't we here to see him?" asked Virginia. "Instead of talking about righting social injustices, and changing Sir Henry, and other depress—other things, oughtn't we just to ring the bell?"

"To be sure, miss! Here we are. The bell!"

Masters gave the electric button a long pressure, with a hop, skip, and jump of his finger for emphasis. He turned back with undampened good spirits.

29

"And, by George" he said. "Whoever answers that bell, it won't be a butler."

"It won't be? Are you sure?"

"Butlers!" grated Masters. "They're a what-d'ye-call-it, they're a symbol of all the bad old days." His face darkened. "I remember one chap in those days. Name of Benson. He was the Earl of Severn's butler, at Severn Hall in Gloucestershire, when Sir Henry gave me a little bit of help in solving a mystery about a bronze lamp. Ur!"

"Was Benson as offensive as all that?"

"We-el! Not what you'd call offensive, like. But, miss, you wouldn't believe it! F...m like a bishop, all buttery talk and long words. And yet he *encouraged* Sir Henry, egged him on as you might say, to be even worse than he was!"

"Still it must have been interesting."

"Not by a jugful it wasn't!" snorted Masters, giving the button another push so long that it might have roused irritation inside the hermitage of a saint. "Fair drove me loony, what with his thinking things were funny when they weren't, and yet never as much as smiling. We can thank the lord nobody's got a butler nowadays. Nobody can have one."

At this point the iron-bound door slowly opened. Masters, who for a third time had reached out towards the bell, stopped with his hand in midair.

In the doorway, indubitably, stood a real butler.

By tradition, at least, butlers are tall, portly, and of great stateliness. The man in the doorway, so impec-

30

cably dressed in short black coat, striped trousers, hard collar, and dark tie, was somewhat plump and certainly of very dignified bearing. But he was only of middle height, even a little under it.

Through thinning hair, now pure white, showed a healthy pink scalp. Age could not wither him. His fresh-complexioned face remained serene and un-lined.

But it was not the sight of a butler, *qua* butler, which made Masters stand and stare as though para-lyzed. It was ten seconds before he found his voice.

"I know you!" he shouted, and so far forgot his manners as to point a finger. "You're Benson!"

The butler gave a very slight inclination of the head.

"Yes, sir." It would not have been proper to express pleasure, but Benson's face showed the shadow of pleasure. "And if you will permit me to say so, Mr. Masters, it is most gratifying to welcome you to Cranleigh Court."

"But what in lum's name are you doing here? You're at Severn Hall! You work for Lord Severn!"

Benson coughed.

"No, sir. If you will recall, at the time of the bronze lamp affair, his lordship unfortunately suffered from a weak heart?"

"Yes, yes, I remember something like that!"

"Yes, sir. And also, if you recall, a marriage had been arranged between Lady Helen Loring, his lord-ship's daughter, and Mr. Kit Farrell, the barrister?"

"Ah, and I remember that ruddy Irishman too! Between you and him and the young lady, you hocussed me so thoroughly that . . ."

Again Benson coughed.

"A *ruse de guerre*, sir, which I am sure you will agree the peculiar circumstances made not only pardonable but essential. However, if I may explain: I regret, Mr. Masters, that his lordship passed over during the early years of the war."

"Hurrum! Sorry to hear that."

"Thank you, Mr. Masters," said Benson, softening a little. "I need add only that Sir Henry, hearing I was in temporary need of a position, was kind enough to offer me the stewardship of his household."

"He did, eh? Yes, and I can guess why! Can't you guess?"

Benson considered this, his lips pursed a little.

"It would scarcely be my place, sir, to enquire into the concatenation of motives which led to Sir Henry's decision. I might venture to think, however, that he finds my presence congenial . . ."

"I'll bet he does! By George, I'll bet he does!"

". . . and my stewardship reasonably satisfactory. It was something of a wrench to leave Severn, sir. But, had I been asked to change Severn for anywhere else, I am sure I should have chosen Cranleigh."

So deft was Benson's manner that a casual observer might not even have noticed how he rather hastily changed the subject. Throughout his conversation with Masters, he did not even glance at Virginia. But

32

his aura, so to speak, had been taking her in with ever-growing admiration and deference.

Now Benson did look at her.

"I beg your pardon, my lady," he said, in a tone he reserved only for the elect. "But I believe I have the honour to address Lady Brace?"

"Well," said the unassuming Virginia, "at least that's me."

"Thank you, my lady. Your ladyship has been pointed out to me in the village. I have a message for you.'

"For me?"

"Yes, my lady. I fancy your ladyship telephoned to Telford Old Hall from London, saying that you would be driving down with a gentleman from Scotland Yard, and that you would break your journey here?"

"That's right. I spoke to our butler."

"Lord a'mighty, miss," cried the galvanized Masters, "don't tell me you've got a butler, too?"

"I'm terribly afraid we have." Virginia flushed with a guilty look. "I—I was wondering if I could keep it from you, but I didn't see how. Anyway, Jennings has only been with us for a few months."

Quickly, to avoid Masters' sternly rebuking eye, she turned back to Benson.

"Jennings phoned here?" she asked in surprise.

"No, my lady. It was his lordship, your husband, who telephoned, though he remarked in passing that Mr. Jennings has been unfortunately taken with a raging toothache. His lordship desired me to state that he would call for you here at five o'clock. His lordship further observed that he had," here Benson coughed slightly, "heard certain things about Sir Henry Merrivale and was most desirous of making Sir Henry's acquaintance."

"Benson, that's wonderful!"

"Thank you, my lady. I—"

Here Benson paused. Shining of white hair, glossy of collar and cuff against the black coat, as speckless as though he had just been unpacked from old years, he did not in the least resemble a solemn-faced cherub. Yet, towards those of whom he approved, he had a way of showing friendliness without a muscle moving in his countenance.

"Benson," said Virginia instantly, "you were going to tell me something else, but you stopped. What is it?"

"My lady, I . . ."

"Benson! Please!"

"It is only, my lady, that I beg leave to consider this a happy day. This morning, by a singular coincidence, we made the acquaintance of the tenth Viscount."

"The tenth Viscount?" repeated Virginia, with a wrinkle between her eyebrows. "Oh! You mean Tommy?" Her warm laugh suited the house and the grounds, and she turned to Masters. "That's our son. You remember, I told you Tom and I have a son nine years old?"

"Ur!" said Masters, who had been darkly brood-

34

ing.

"But what on earth," asked Virginia, with some alarm, "was Tommy doing six miles from Telford?"

"You may reassure yourself, my lady. The tenth Viscount was merely playing red Indians. He carried an extraordinarily large bow and a sheaf of arrows, which he informed us that his grandfather had bought for him."

"Oh, yes! My father got him a full-sized bow at Selfridge's. Benson! Tommy didn't get into any mischief, did he?"

For a moment Benson's gaze wandered away. A mother more possessive than small Virginia might have felt disquiet at a certain look in the butler's guileless blue eye.

"Not at all, my lady. On the contrary, if I may say so, it was a pleasure to find a young gentleman with such a healthy interest in playing Indians and robbers and pirates in these days when the young seem so passionately addicted to reaching the moon in rockets or murdering the world with atomic bombs."

"Did Tommy get home safely?"

"Yes, my lady. Sir Henry had him sent home in the car."

"And he didn't bother anybody? Thank heavens! Then that's all right."

"Yes, my lady. The visit of the tenth Viscount was in strong contrast to a call paid by a certain Miss. E.M. Cheeseman, Labour Member of Parliament for East Whistlefield, who threatens to bring an action of law against Sir Henry. However, forgive me. I . . ."

"Just a minute!" cut in the heavy voice of Chief Inspector Masters, who could stand these amenities no longer. "Fair's fair and talk's talk, and that's all right, too. But I came here to see Sir Henry on very important business!"

"Indeed, sir?"

"Yes, indeed," retorted Masters, who had never forgiven Benson for the latter's part in the imposture at Severn Hall. "My time's valuable, I might tell you, and I'm here at the express request of the Assistant Commissioner. So just be good enough to tell me where the old boy is, or take me along to see him."

Still not a muscle moved in Benson's face.

"I regret, sir," he replied politely but firmly, "that Sir Henry is engaged. It is quite impossible for you to see him."

3

Masters looked as though he couldn't believe his ears, as in fact he couldn't.

"What's that?"

"Sir Henry, Mr. Masters, is engaged. It is now a quarter to five o'clock. Should you care to wait until six-thirty, he may perhaps be induced to spare you a few minutes before dinner. But I can promise nothing."

Masters fell back a step, and with good reason.

For this was monstrous, unheard of. It was all very well for H.M. to play the coy violet and refuse to answer the phone when he was buried in the country, and far from London. But for him to refuse to see Masters, if only to call the latter a crawling snake, had never occurred before. It reached the realm of the unthinkable. It was as easy to see H.M. as to see the Albert Memorial, and upon the aesthetically sensitive it had often the same agonizing result.

"But why can't I see him?" shouted Masters. "What's he engaged in?"

"His singing lesson, sir."

"His—his . . . ?"

"Yes, sir. For the past six months he has been training his voice." A certain terrible memory showed its reflection even in the eyes of the imperturbable Benson. "Next Tuesday he gives his first public performance before the Tuesday Evening Ladies' Church Society of Great Yewborough."

"Public—public . . . "

"A concert, sir. At the moment he is occupied with Signor Ravioli, his Italian music-master, and must on no account be disturbed."

Masters choked.

"Singing lessons!" he raved, clutching at his bowler hat with both hands. "Then that's what he's been doing for six months! But why? Why?"

"Sir Henry is a *basso*, Mr. Masters."

"I know, but—oh! You mean he *sings* like that?"

"Certainly, sir. A *basso profondo*. What else could I mean?"

"Hurrum! Never mind," said Masters, with a quick glance at Virginia. "But don't tell me," he cried wildly, "don't tell me the old basso thinks he can sing in grand opera, or something like that?"

Benson considered this, his fine head a little on one side.

"I do not apprehend such a contingency, Mr. Masters. Sir Henry is conscious of his own limitations. Even if he were not, he would be handicapped by his fondness for old English ballads of a somewhat vulgar nature."

"You don't say, now?" demanded Masters, not without sarcasm. "You don't say!"

"Yes, sir. I venture to doubt whether such items as 'O Tarry Trousers' and 'The Minstrels Sing of an

English King,' while spirited and even admirable in their own way, would be altogether suitable to the stage of the Covent Garden Opera or even to the concert platform."

"He's crackers! He's off his rocker at last! I always knew it'd happen! Miss, I've been half afraid of this all along. I hope you're not too shocked?"

"N-no," replied Virginia in a strangely tremulous voice. Her beautiful, innocent grey eyes were half-bright and half-blurred, and her breath came in gasps. "No, not shocked. I should call it f-f-fascinated. Yes, that would be a better word."

"He ought to be locked up! He . . ."

But Virginia had already turned to the butler, allowing her meek magic to work its effect.

"I do hope, Benson," she pleaded, "you're not going to forbid me to see Sir Henry as well?"

Despite himself the butler was shaken.

"I am exceedingly sorry, my lady. But Sir Henry's instructions were quite explicit."

"You see," said Virginia, "I ask only because it's almost a matter of life and death. There's been a horribly mysterious occurrence at Telford, which nobody can explain, and poor Tom is in agony. The only reason why Mr. Masters is here is because I brought him."

"A criminal case, my lady?" asked Benson, interested.

"Yes!" said Virginia.

"No!" said Masters.

Since both of them spoke together, the effect was a little contradictory. But Masters had sense enough to shut up and let the small girl continue.

"There's one thing I did notice," she pursued. "Believe me, I shouldn't dream of disturbing Sir Henry at his rehearsing, especially if he wants to render 'The Minstrels Sing of an English King' before the Tuesday Evening Ladies' Church Society. In fact, I know Tom and I will want to buy all the tickets we can."

"This is most gratifying, my lady."

"So I hope you'll allow me to ask a question. A minute ago you said my husband was coming here at five o'clock; you said he was very anxious to meet Sir Henry. Oh, Benson, I *can* understand that so well! But you implied, or at least I thought so, that there wouldn't be any trouble about seeing him."

"My lady, I . . . "

"Benson! Mr. Masters is a wonderful man and a great detective. But he'd be the first to admit—wouldn't you, Mr. Masters?—that sometimes he's a little tactless about the way he makes enquiries. Benson, please. Is the real reason why you won't let us see him—well, is it the way in which Mr. Masters phrased his request?"

This was a facer, being true.

Nothing could ever disturb the serenity of Benson's round, fresh-complexioned face. At the same time, he hedged a little.

"Not altogether, my lady."

"Benson!"

"No, my lady, I assure you. My meaning was this: that Lord Brace, like yourself if not some others, is always welcome at Cranleigh. Particularly, as I have said, considering the visit this morning of your son, the tenth Viscount. Sir Henry spent several hours with him."

It must be repeated and emphasized that the ordinarily shrewd Masters had not been himself ever since he heard he must deal with another locked room.

"Lord lummy, miss," he exclaimed in real horror, "they didn't let that old devil come anywhere near your innocent child?"

Virginia was startled. "But why on earth not?"

"Miss, you haven't heard the half of it! He gives kids cigars and encourages 'em to bet on dog-races! I know that for a fact!"

For a moment Virginia turned away, her shoulders shaking, no doubt to hide her maternal apprehension. But she turned back.

"Benson! Tommy didn't suffer any harm, did he?"

The butler shook his head.

"No, my lady. Sir Henry merely gave the tenth Viscount a quite innocuous lesson in archery."

"Archery!" said Masters. "God's truth! He's crazier than he ever was! Look here, Benson, if the old boy's all worked up about singing lessons, why does he have to mess about with a bow and arrow?"

Benson's aura shimmered with a thoughtful frown of recollection.

"I fancy, sir, it was due to a remark which the tenth Viscount made to Sir Henry."

"Oh, ah?"

"Yes, sir. For some reason, I fear quite inexplicable to me, the young gentleman's grandfather—her ladyship's father—seems to cherish a passion for all things American. He appears to have told the tenth Viscount that the greatest marksmen of all times were those red Indian heroes and white scouts of whom we read in

41

the *Leatherstocking Tales* of the late J. Fenimore Cooper."

"Yes," agreed Virginia, "that sounds like Dad. But what about it?"

"Well, my lady, Sir Henry took strong objection to this remark. He informed the tenth Viscount that the only important bowmen of whom history speaks were all English, and that the greatest of these was the half-legendary character known as Robin Hood."

"Please go on, Benson. Don't stop there!"

"There is really nothing more, my lady. Except that Sir Henry, while demonstrating the use of a forty-pound bow, told the tenth Viscount a series of thrilling tales—to which the young gentleman listened with rapt attention—about Robin Hood and the villainous Sheriff of Nottingham."

"But what's wrong with that?" cried Virginia.

"Nothing whatever, my lady. Except that, to an impressionable young mind, the stories may perhaps have been a trifle misleading."

"Misleading?"

"Yes, my lady. I myself received a distinct impression that the tales concerned less the adventures of Robin Hood than deeds of rather exaggerated derring-do which were performed, in youth, by Sir Henry Merrivale himself."

Masters was again in a state.

"I'm just warning you, miss! It's on your own head if you don't pay attention. You'd think," said the Chief Inspector, "you'd think any kid would take one look at Sir Henry's dial and then run screaming. Wouldn't you?"

"I—I really don't know. Is he as bad as that?"

"Worse."

"Oh, surely he can't be! Anyway, I haven't met him."

"But," argued Masters, "for some reason it don't work like that. I can't tell you why, but on kids he's got an effect like the what-d'ye-call-it, the Pied Piper. It's a good job he's got no grandson of his own, or we should have to get Borstal ready for the lad at twelve and Wormwood Scrubs or Dartmoor at eighteen. That's straight!"

"I think you're the one who's exaggerating, Mr. Masters. In any case, Benson, you haven't answered my question." Virginia's warm lips pouted. "You *will* let us see Sir Henry, won't you?"

Benson drew a deep breath.

"If it is a matter of your personal happiness, my lady, and—er—perhaps another instance of a mysterious disappearance under the eyes of witness or a vanishing from a locked room . . . ?"

"It is! It is! Mr. Masters, I think you suffer from high blood-pressure and you must please, please not upset yourself."

Benson nodded gravely as though in agreement.

"Will you and the Chief Inspector be good enough to follow me, my lady?"

He led them through a spacious if rather low-ceilinged hall. The sunshine through leaded-glass windows made a warm blur of mellow brown oak in a twilight redolent of age and furniture-polish.

For one of such unmentionable character and appearance, H.M. certainly had a number of impressive-looking ancestors. The portrait of a lady by Sir Peter Lely hung over the fireplace in the hall, and there was a larger Gainsborough against the right-hand wall.

Virginia, Masters could see, was growing ever more enchanted as Benson took them through room after room. Though at any moment they expected to hear the ogre's voice upraised in song, the house still remained deathly silent when Benson went down a short ground-floor passage towards a closed door at the back.

"Stop!" said Masters in a low, hoarse voice, and nodded towards the closed door. "Is that where he is now?"

"Yes, sir." Benson spoke patiently. "That is the Grey Study, opening on the Elizabethan garden. Sir Henry has caused a grand piano to be placed in there."

"You know, miss," growled Masters, suddenly embarrassed, "I'm not sure you ought to go in at all."

"Not go in?" repeated Virginia. "Why not?"

"Because—oh, lummy!—the fact is, miss, that old blighter'll probably wallop out with something a nice young lady like you oughtn't to hear. Stop a bit!" Masters turned to Benson. "Didn't you say he's got an Eye-talian music-master?"

"Yes, sir. Signor Luigi Ravioli, a famous *maestro*."

"Well, whatever else you say about Eye-talians, they're wizards when it comes to music. Can't this chap persuade him to sing something proper, if he's got to sing at all?"

Once more Benson's eye, strangely, sought a corner of the ceiling.

"It is true, sir, that Signor Ravioli has often remonstrated with Sir Henry about his choice of songs."

"The Signor Ravi—the Eye-talian's ruddy well got to persuade him! So help me, I won't let this young lady's ears be soiled by . . . "

"Mr. Masters, it's awfully nice of you," said Virginia with real sincerity, "and I do appreciate it. But, after all, I *am* a married woman."

"Eh?"

"I am, really! And you said yourself Sir Henry was a changed man. You said he was too old to be anything else."

"I thought he was," raved Masters, touched on the real sore spot. "I was fool enough to believe that!"

"You said he was collecting stamps or bits of pottery. You said there hadn't been a single noise out of him—"

Here Virginia stopped abruptly. The flourish of a piano, with its *rum-tiddle-ty-um-tum* of opening bars for a song, issued from behind the door. But this was not what made Virginia stop, her hand at her mouth. And Masters, despite all the care he had tried to take of his language in her presence, could not help what he said.

"Goddelmighty!" whispered the Chief Inspector.

"Oh, dear!" whispered Virginia, and recoiled in spite of herself.

When the *basso profondo* burst forth beyond that closed door, both Masters and Virginia had been prepared for something pretty bad. But they had not expected the worst. The horrible blast of sound was reminiscent of high explosive in old days, without even a warning whistle to precede it.

Only Benson, who had got over the worst, remained unmoved. Indeed, one who knew the butler's somewhat peculiar sense of humour would even have said he looked pleased. Putting an admonitory finger on his lips, he softly opened the door wide. Virginia saw as impressive a tableau as she had ever beheld.

A spacious square room, with plaster walls painted grey and framed pictures which she had not time to inspect, had modernized French windows opening on a large garden of entwined colours. In the midst of the garden was a good-sized fountain, at the centre of which a charming female figure in greenish bronze seemed to bathe under the fountain's soft and luminous spray.

Inside the room, between the door and the windows, stood a grand piano with its keyboard towards the door. At the piano was a small, stoutish man with such a quantity of very long, fluffy black hair that it danced all over his head with the slightest motion as he sat with his back to the door.

The singer, a large, stout, barrel-shaped gentleman in a white alpaca suit, also had his back turned to the door. His bald head glimmered in the late afternoon sun. He stood beside the piano, his ample posterior stuck out. His right hand rested negligently on the piano, and his left hand was lifted in an airy operatic gesture reminiscent of Marcel Journet.

What he sang was as follows:

"My sister's young man he's a hundred and three,
    He's the oldest young man in town!—
But he'll never go to bed
For to rest his hoary head—
    He's dead but he won't lie down!"

46

The small plump man with all the hair, clearly, was getting mad. In order to make the piano heard under the blare of that terrifying voice, he was now hitting the keys like a pugilist. But you still couldn't hear it.

"On his funeral day he was twenty miles away,
    Drinkin' doubles at the Rose and Crown,
And for booze he was the worse
So he rode up on the hearse—
    He's dead but he won't lie down!"

The small plump man with all the hair, Signor Ravioli, bounced up from the piano-stool. He shivered all over. From his expression you would have judged he was about to begin an impassioned speech lasting twenty minutes. But all he said, pinching his thumb and forefinger together as though holding an insect very tightly by the tail, was one word.

"No!"

The singer broke off and turned round.

"Hey?" he bellowed.

Again Signor Ravioli, shivering even more, pinched his thumb and forefinger together.

"*No!*" he said.

As Sir Henry Merrivale turned round, showing a broad face with shell-rimmed spectacles pulled down on his nose, the expression on the face was such that Virginia felt compelled for an instant to shut her eyes.

"Lord love a duck, what am I doin' now? Ain't the song all right?"

"No!"

"Then what's wrong, son? You tell me!"

Chief Inspector Masters, huddled hypnotized in the doorway with Virginia, drew a breath of relief.

"Thank the merciful powers, miss," he muttered under his breath, "that the singing master at least has got some sense! He'll teach the old blighter not to sing low music-hall songs like that! *He'll* tell him!"

Whereupon Signor Ravioli told him.

"It's-a your breathing," he shouted. "She's-a all wrong!"

"What's that, son?"

"Your-a breathing," yelled Signor Ravioli, beginning to make horrible panting noises like a leaky bellows. "*Corpo di Bacco*, I am disgusting with you! Wait! Wait! I show you how to seeng thees-a song!"

He bounced back to the piano. His hair flew again as he smote the keys. It must be acknowledged that Signor Ravioli had a truly fine voice, a golden tenor with a smoothness like Pilsner beer, and it filled the whole room with creamy power.

"My seester's young man he's-a kicked da bucket now,
    He's-a mourned by his old bull-pup!—"

Bang, bang went the piano.

"He's-a gone, we all regret,
    Nevermore he'll eat spaghett'—
        He's a spook but he won't shut up!"

Sir Henry Merrivale, about to make some scarifying retort, let it die on his lips. A strange expression crossed his face, and he adjusted his spectacles.

48

"I say, son!" demanded H.M., impressed in spite of himself. "Where'd you get the new verse for that song?"

"Da verse? Pah! I make-a her up joost-a now!"

"Burn me, you made it up on the spur of the moment? Son, that's not half bad at all! Could you make up some more verses?"

Signor Ravioli, instantly mollified, snapped his fingers with careless artistic pride.

"Sure-a theeng! The song, she's-a easy. Not like beautiful Italian song." Suddenly, remembering an injury, Signor Ravioli whacked his hands on the keys of the piano. "But why you not seeng beautiful Italian song like I want you to?"

"Now looky here, son!" thundered H.M., bringing his fist down on the piano-top with a crash which jarred every string inside. "You're a fine music-master. I admit that! But I am not goin' to put up with any more of this deplorable Latin temperament! I'm English; got that? I can't stand temperamental people!"

"So-a?" enquired Signor Ravioli, with sudden sinister calm. "You want-a me to make up more verses for da song, yes?"

"Yes!"

"Okay," said Signor Ravioli, folding his arms. "I not do it."

"Now wait a minute, son!" blared the stricken H.M. "Keep your shirt on, can't you? You've *got* to make up more verses! That one you just warbled, in its way, was pure genius! Think of your art!"

"H'm."

" 'He's a spook but he won't shut up.' Lord love a

duck, it's better than the original title! It's a star-gazin' beauty! If you made up some more verses—twenty or thirty, maybe—I could sing 'em all at the concert and bring down the house. I say! I might get a pretty fine effect, too, if I sang 'em with an Italian accent."

Decidedly, this was not one of Chief Inspector Masters' luckier days.

For some moments Masters had been repeatedly clearing his throat, in the vain hope of attracting H.M.'s attention. Now, succumbing to the general atmosphere of temperament, he banged his knuckles with sharp *rat-tat* on the inside of the open door.

H.M. and Signor Ravioli, roused, turned fully round at the same time. As H.M. caught sight of Masters, there crossed his face a look of such appalling malignancy that Virginia all but fled.

"Just be quiet and stop everything, sir!" instantly said Masters, holding up his hand with the dignified traffic-policeman's gesture. "Don't speak yet. Don't say one word, if you please, until you hear what I've got to tell you.

"Very well!" continued Masters. "Now I'm not here to disturb you, and I'm not here because I want to be here. No, sir! I'm here because the Assistant Commissioner, in defiance of police rules and wasting taxpayers' good money, ordered me to come here about a matter of a locked room that—hurrum!—that seems to be more locked than any one I ever heard tell of. But don't say anything yet!"

H.M., as a matter of fact, did not say anything.

He was incapable of it. Standing there with his fists on his hips, a rich purple colour coming into his face and his eyes bulging behind the spectacles, he merely breathed in a way which suggested Signor Ravioli's illustration of a few minutes ago.

"Just so," pursued Masters, at ease and smooth again. "Now this little lady here is Miss—Lady Brace, a neighbour of yours at Telford Old Hall. I understand, from information received, you've met Lady Brace's nine-year-old son, named—named. . . ."

"The tenth Viscount, sir," interposed Benson deftly.

"Named Tommy," snorted Masters, with a brief glare, and became urbane again. "From information received, this morning you made a fool of yourself as usual by teaching Mr. Tommy how to shoot bows and arrows. However!

"Two nights ago—on Wednesday, to be exact— there was a very odd happening at Telford Old Hall. At least, *you* might call it odd. Telford, her ladyship tells me, is a very historic old house. It's not quite as old as Cranleigh Court here, but it's a good bit more historic and far more interesting."

Still Sir Henry Merrivale did not say anything. But at these words a strange whistling sound escaped his lips. His purple colour deepened, and his eyes protruded still more.

"Just so!" said Masters. "Now it seems, from what Lady Brace tells me, there's a historical legend attached to a room there, called the Oak Room. Not," Masters spoke with some contempt, "That anybody cares two pins about history in these days. We've got rid of history; history's all my eye. But I've got to tell you the facts."

51

"Really, Mr. Masters . . ." Virginia began to protest. The Chief Inspector shushed her.

"Well, sir. This legend dates back to the Civil Wars, and I think it's the year 1645. If I've got it straight that was the year of the battle of—the battle of . . ."

"The battle of Naseby, sir," murmured Benson, a mine of information.

"Oh, ah! That's it. But to get back to the Oak Room! Nowadays, Lady Brace says, there's not much in that room except some musical instruments—including the funny kind of piano they had even in those times—and a solid iron safe—ah, safe for valuables!—to which Lord Brace has got the only key.

"Right you are! Next, as an heirloom in the Brace family, there's a whacking great thing that they call, in capital letters as you might say, the Cavalier's Cup.

"Stop a bit! You're going to ask straightaway whether the Cavalier's Cup is an old antique that dates back to the same time as the legend about the cavalier. The answer is no, it's not. There was some Viscount Brace in Victorian times, it seems, who'd made a sinful pile of money. Well, there wasn't any Cavalier's Cup to go with the cavalier legend, but this gentleman thought there ought to be one.

"So he just had it made, according to his own taste. Got that, sir? I take it Lord and Lady Brace, the present ones I mean, don't much like this cup. Eh, miss?"

"No. It's *awful*," murmured Virginia, shaking her head sadly.

Masters whipped a notebook out of his inside breast pocket.

52

"It's been described to me," he went on, "as being like a large goblet, made of solid gold, with a ring of big diamonds round the drinking-edge, and—ah, here we are—a pattern of other precious stones, rubies and emeralds, worked round the middle."

Virginia shuddered. Even Benson frowned slightly.

"All the same," pursued Masters, "this cup is in the family and apparently it's got to stay there. If it's got no value as a relic, its money-value—lummy! It wouldn't take a half-nippy crook to prise the jewels out of a soft setting like gold, sell 'em separately so they couldn't be traced, and even melt down the gold, too. This Cavalier's Cup is a crook's dream!

"Ordinarily, sir, the cup is kept at the bank, Messrs. Cox & Co.'s, in London. But on Wednesday night, as it happens, it was in the safe in the Oak Room at Telford. Young Lord Brace himself sat up all night in that room—or tried to, rather—to make sure nobody broke in and pinched it. So!"

Here Masters, as one who has stated his facts succinctly, replaced the notebook in his inside breast pocket.

"I've come to ask for your help, Sir Henry," he declared. "First, because it's a problem that's brand-new; I think it'll interest you." If there was faint malicious glee hidden behind his bland manner, it did not show. "Second, because as a friend I'm bound to tell you, and I'm sure Lady Brace and Benson and even Signor Spaghetti will agree, that it's doing a public service if I can keep you from driving people crazy with the ruddy awful caterwauling you call singing. There you are, sir; that's all."

There was a pause. At long last Sir Henry Merrivale found his voice.

"So that's all, hey?" he asked hoarsely.

"Easy, sir! Keep your shirt on, now!"

"It's a brand-new problem, is it? And you think it'll interest me, do you?"

"I only said . . ."

"And you've come to ask for my help, hey?"

"Maybe I didn't say it exactly . . ."

"And above all things, above all things in this green world, you think you're doin' a public service?"

"Sir Henry!"

The whole room shook as H.M., despite his bulk, did a little dance back and forth between the windows. Distinctly, Masters had not made himself popular. Signor Luigi Ravioli, who had furry black eyebrows and a fine nose made blooming by many a bottle of good Chianti, was glaring at him. H.M. passed from dangerous excitement to a sort of inhuman calm.

"Y'know, Masters," he said, "you really fascinate me. You do, honest. For sheer simon-pure nerve—for kite-flyin', unadulterated cheek—there's been nothing like it since a young feller kept a daughter of mine out all night and then spent two more hours sayin' goodnight to her while he leaned his elbow on the goddam doorbell."

"Sir Henry! There's ladies present!"

But H.M.'s wrath-blurred eye could see no lady present, or, indeed, see anything except the unspeakably vile presence of Chief Inspector Masters.

"So it's a new kind of problem, is it? What in the name of Esau is new about it? I can tell you what you want to know without another word out of you! You want to know, I suppose, how and why somebody stole the Cavalier's Cup?"

"No, no!" interposed Virginia, greatly daring. "Please, Sir Henry, that isn't it at all!"

H.M. was vaguely conscious that someone else had spoken.

"Hey?" he demanded.

"No, no! Blame me if you blame anybody, because it's all my fault. But that isn't the problem!"

"It ain't?"

"No," said Virginia. "Please Sir Henry, I want to know how and why somebody *didn't* steal the Cavalier's Cup!"

4

Half an hour later, when introductions as well as some spectacular displays of temper had been completed, four persons had also completed a very late tea beside the fountain with the green-bronze nymph in the Elizabethan garden.

These persons, taking them in order from left to right as they sat in canvas chairs or deck-chairs round the broad basin of the fountain, with a table near them, were Chief Inspector Masters, Virginia Brace, Sir Henry Merrivale, and Signor Ravioli.

H.M. had soothed himself with six cups of strong black tea without sugar or milk. Removing the napkin he had tucked into his collar, uttering an expiring sound like, "Haah," he contemplated Virginia in high approval and with almost a human look.

"Now, my dolly!" he said. "I can listen to you for just thirty minutes by my watch, because I want to help you."

"Sure-a theeng!" agreed Signor Ravioli with enthusiasm, and his nose bloomed over a white tea-cup. "I help-a you, too, you know what I mean?"

"No more than thirty minutes, mind!" warned

H.M. "I'd like to, yes. But my time's not my own. It's occupied with very important work, so important to me and maybe to the world that I've got to rehearse practically every minute of my waking day."

"Singing! Ur!" whispered Masters.

H.M. ignored him as though he did not exist.

"And I'll do it, my dolly, in spite of the heavy demands on me. 'Cause why? 'Cause I never met a gal who represented a mystery to me in quite the fetchin' way you did. It'd be dull and dreary just to find out how a crook got in and out of a locked room to steal a gold-and-jewelled cup. But it's very rummy, and fascinates the old man a bit, to wonder why a crook *didn't* steal a gold-and-jewelled cup he should have stolen. You see that?"

"Of course. And poor Tom, my husband . . . !"

"So I want you to be very careful, my dolly. When you describe this Oak Room that's supposed to have been locked up, I want you to give me an account as complete and minute as a surveyor's plan, without a detail left out. In the words of Joseph Conrad, I want you to make me see it."

"That's-a-right!" approved Signor Ravioli and gargled tea.

Though Masters had resolved to take refuge in the stateliness of silence, he was badly jarred by this.

"Look here, sir! Why should the lady do all that? There's a car at the door, and Telford's not very far away. If you want to see this room, why don't you just go over and look at it?"

There was a silence. Then H.M. bent forward towards Virginia.

"You see that snake?" he hissed.

Virginia gave a violent start and glanced hastily at the ground, honestly expecting at least a medium-sized cobra in the path round the fountain. Then she realized that her host was referring to Masters.

"Really, Sir Henry," protested Virginia, who liked the Chief Inspector in spite of everything, "he isn't at all like that. It's true I don't know him intimately, I met him only this morning, but—well, it's just that there's something wrong with him."

"Lord love a duck, did it take you all day to discover *that?*"

"No, no! I meant—for some reason, I don't believe he's quite his usual self."

"He's got no soul," said H.M., firing up. "He can't understand that nothing upsets an artist, or disturbs sensitive feelings, more than having interruptions, interruptions, the whole bloomin' day! Why, you take me! This morning, for instance, I couldn't keep my mind on rehearsals at all . . ."

"Because of my Tommy? I *am* dreadfully sorry!"

H.M., surprised, raised his almost invisible eyebrows and peered at her over his spectacles.

"The kid! Oh, my dolly! I didn't mean him. He's a fine boy, and you ought to be proud of him. No, I meant that goddam woman who was here kickin' up a rumpus, and saying she was going to bring an action at law.

"Woman?" repeated Virginia and thought back. "Do you by any chance mean Miss E.M. Cheeseman, the Labour Member of Parliament from East Whistlefield?"

"Yes. But how'd you learn about it, my dolly?"

"Benson told me." Virginia hesitated. "You—you

haven't done anything to make her bring a lawsuit against you, Sir Henry?"

H.M. was galvanized.

"It's all lies," he yelled. "I am absolutely inner-cent! Burn me, I'm as guiltless as an unborn babe." He appealed to the music-master for confirmation. "Ain't that so?"

"Absolutely!" affirmed Signor Ravioli, putting down cup and saucer in order to snap his fingers. It may have been noted that he spoke English with a slight American accent. "Anyway, what's all da fuss? A week ago, I tell you, thees sour-puss broad has-a get exactly what she deserves."

"Sh-h!" hissed H.M. "Just say yes and don't elaborate!"

"But what happened?" asked Virginia.

H.M. first peered round cautiously, as though wondering whether Miss Cheeseman might be lurking in the Elizabethan garden.

"Well—now. It was in the Majestic Theatre at Cherriton, y'see. That's a big old theatre of the sort they used to use a lot for pantomimes. I don't know whether you've ever been in the Majestic Theatre, my dolly?"

"No, but I understand what you mean."

"Uh-huh. Well," said H.M., peering round again, "a week ago there was a big political debate. La Cheeseman was speaking for the Labour Party, of course, and it just so happened," said H.M., convey-ing the idea that he was there purely by accident, "it just so happened I represented the Conservative inter-est."

"Yes?"

"The low-down chairman began proceedings, rot his liver, by sayin' he'd let her speak first, and then allow her a rebuttal after I spoke, without giving me a chance to rebut at all." H.M., firing up still more, stuck out his unmentionable face. "Was that justice?"

"Yes!" said Chief Inspector Masters.

"No!" said Signor Ravioli.

"And then?" prompted Virginia.

A look of awe stole across H.M.'s face.

"La Cheeseman," he said, "had been speaking for forty-three minutes by the clock, and she was goin' on something powerful. 'Under the glorious Labour Party, I will now show you the direction in which this great nation is going!' And, wham! She stepped backwards and dropped sixteen feet through a trap-door into the cellar."

"Good heavens! Was the poor woman hurt?"

"Not a bit, my dolly! But the Labour Press carried on awful, and one or two evil-minded people said I bribed the stage-hands to unloose every trap-door on the stage. They actually said *I* did that! *Me!* Can you imagine it?"

"I certainly can," retorted Masters. "I'll bet you anything you like that's just what you did!"

"Oh, my son! It's a wicked falsehood! Anyway, I had 'em spread mattresses all over the floor so she couldn't possibly get hurt."

"You see?" demanded Signor Ravioli triumphantly.

"So help me, Sir Henry," cried Masters, again seizing at his bowler hat, "I can't understand you! You used to have sympathy for the working man!

What have you got against the working man?"

H.M. momentarily forgot that he was not on speaking terms with Masters.

"Nothin' at all," he said. "That's the point. If these Labour M.P.'s were really working men, they'd have some sense. But most of 'em, or at least the ones I've met, seem to be half-baked intellectuals who've specialized in economics or some such dreary muck."

"Mr. Masters is quite right," said Virginia, though with trembling lips and moist eyes. "It was p-p—*blub!*—perfectly dreadful of you, and you ought to be ashamed of yourself. I imagine Miss Cheeseman must be some frightful-looking old battle-axe?"

But H.M. shook his head.

"You're wrong, my dolly. There's the pity of it. Elaine Cheeseman's not as young as you; she's forty, maybe. But she's not bad-looking at all. If she took the trouble to dress properly, and if occasionally she smiled instead of keeping a frozen, holy-zeal look as though she were goin' to the Crusades instead of only to the polling-station, she might even be a bit of a smasher."

Masters gave it up.

"It's no good talking to you, sir," he said, not without some reason on his side. "You're all prejudices and nothing else." Exasperation shook him. "But *are* you going to pay some attention to this problem about the gold-and-jewelled cup?"

"Sure I am, son." H.M. gnawed at his lip. "And there's one question in particular I'm flamin'-awful anxious to ask."

"Oh, ah? What's that?"

"Never you mind. The wench has got to tell her

story. When you do that, my dolly, I've got a reason for asking you not to keep to a settled plan. Tell me the first thing that comes into your head. Hey? Then fire away!"

Shadows were gathering in the bright-coloured Elizabethan garden, drowsy with its soft but heady flower-scents. The faint splash of the fountain, in which the smallish green-bronze nymph stood and bathed under spray, also sang more drowsily towards the hour of sunset.

Virginia meditated. H.M., Masters observed, suddenly glanced at the nymph in the fountain, and then looked very hard at Virginia herself, but he did not comment.

The girl herself did not notice this. Knees crossed, elbow on one knee and chin in her hand, she considered the past with dreaming eyes and gave a rather self-conscious small laugh.

"I suppose," she answered, "the first thing I think of is the first time I ever saw the Oak Room. That was in the spring of 1941, just a little over ten years ago, when Tom and I were married. We were married at a registry office in London and came down to Telford for our honeymoon.

"You see, up to that time I knew nothing about Tom. I never heard he was well-to-do, or had a lovely house like Telford. He wasn't even an officer in the Durhams; I thought his name was Mr. Brace.

"We drove down from London in a rattling old jalopy Tom borrowed from somebody and scrounged the petrol for. I imagined we were going to some inn. Then we turned in at the drive—it was just at sunset, as it is now—and saw Telford, with all its chimneys black against the pink sky.

"If anything, Tom's more in love with the place than I am. At the time there weren't any servants except one old caretaker who's dead now. I remember how Tom carried me across the threshold and took me round from room to room. The third—no, the second one he showed me—was the Oak Room."

Virginia paused, half crossing her heavy-lidded eyes to live in every detail of which she spoke. The fountain sang thinly.

"It isn't much to look at, except for one thing. The room is about fifteen feet square, with a rather low ceiling. And, as you'd naturally imagine, it's panelled to the ceiling in dark oak. There's only one door, and two leaded windows facing west.

"When I first saw it, it was just as it is now. There's a medium-sized fireplace with a stone hood. The floor is of worn, polished boards, with three high-backed oak chairs and a small narrow table. In one corner is a harpischord—that's the seventeenth-century kind of piano Mr. Masters was talking about—and a lute, lying on the harpsichord. There isn't anything else but that iron safe, not very large. As a rule nothing is ever kept in the safe; Tom can't even remember where he keeps the key.

"But, when I first saw it—as I say—it was sunset. Tom said, 'Look at this, my dear.' And he took me over to see the writing on the left-hand window as you look west."

Here Sir Henry Merrivale, though deeply interested and clearly reluctant to interrupt, raised his hand.

"Oi, my dolly! Hold on! What do you mean by the

63

writing on the window?"

Still Virginia did not rouse out of her dream.

"It's scratched on the glass," she replied, "with the point of a diamond from a ring. You know how diamonds can make marks, or even write words, on window-glass? Yes. Well, this window is a leaded one composed of a number of oblong panes, each pane about the size of—say a little larger than Mr. Masters' hand, if he held it up straight.

"But, oh, dear! I keep telling you how Tom and I first entered that ground-floor room, with the trees just coming into bloom outside. 'Look here, my dear,' he said, 'this is called the Oak Room or the Cavalier's Room.' Across one pane in the left-hand window, running rather sideways and upwards in tiny little handwriting, I saw just five words:

" 'God bless King Charles and—'

"That was all. It ended there. Not even a dash after the 'and,' as it must sound when I say it. The words were scrawled, all quick and hasty, because the man who scrawled them was dying.

" 'God bless King Charles and—'

"So, while Tom and I stood there by the window in the twilight, he told me the legend about the cavalier. The King Charles in question, of course, was King Charles the First, and I hardly have to tell you he was beheaded several years after the Cavalier forces lost the last decisive battle at Naseby to the Roundheads in your English Civil War.

"Naturally you'll ask whether this cavalier was one of Tom's ancestors. He wasn't. He was from Kent, and his name was Sir Byng Rawdon. But Kentish Sir Byng was in love with a certain Marian—Lady Marian, they called her, though she hadn't any right to the title—who *was* one of Tom's forbears.

"The first part of the story, at least, is authenticated historical fact. Sir Byng Rawdon was a gentleman-trooper in Prince Rupert's Horse, the famous Royalist cavalry which made the equally famous charge at Naseby against the opposing cavalry, commanded by Ireton, Cromwell's son-in-law, on the Roundhead left flank.

"I'm not going to be presumptuous enough to debate that battle. People still argue about it, according to the side on which their sympathies lie. The Cavaliers were outnumbered two to one, but, as Tom says, they would still have won if it hadn't been for— sorry! Never mind!

"It resulted in complete defeat for the Cavaliers and the end of King Charles's hopes. Afterwards, the survivors on the Royalist side—except the leaders, of course—would mostly have been free to go home in peace, provided they behaved themselves. But Sir Byng Rawdon couldn't leave the vicinity of the field. After that battle the Roundheads did something— never mind what it was—but, on top of everything else, it sent him completely crazy with grief and rage.

"At nightfall, when the Roundheads had lighted fires and were singing psalms for victory over the 'Man of Blood,' Sir Byng managed to collect a dozen men. They were wounded men on spent horses, but they were all he could find or all he could persuade.

"These lunatics decided to wait until the Roundhead camp was asleep, and then stage a suicide-raid. Their idea, before they were killed, was to do as much damage as possible with double-edged cavalry swords. It's true that sentries had been posted, but the sentries were off guard and not expecting trouble. Sir Byng and his dozen men would have had practically a clear field.

"And then, just as he was about to give the order to charge, he found he couldn't do it without warning.

"Please understand! It wasn't a squeamish age, from what I've read. And, as Tom says, most of our ideas of sportsmanship originated in Victorian times. But Sir Byng Rawdon found he couldn't, literally and physically *couldn't*, kill sleeping enemies or men just roused out of sleep without weapons.

"So, before he gave the order to charge, he shouted something in a voice that would have waked a hundred-acre graveyard. One version of what he shouted is in the history books, but there's another that's something else altogether, and that's what he really said.

"Then all thirteen of them cut loose with the great Cavalier battle-cry, 'God for King Charles,' and drove in their spurs, and galloped straight into the middle of Oliver Cromwell's whole army, and oh, Sir Henry," cried Virginia, her voice rising and becoming distinctively American, "oh, Sir Henry, Tom says there was one *hell* of a scrap!"

Virginia, suddenly embarrassed and pink in the face, sat back in her chair.

But, though Masters looked at her in pained astonishment, she need not have worried about the other two incorrigibles. Both Sir Henry Merrivale and Signor Ravioli, their eyes bulging out, were listening with rapt attention.

"Thees-a sound like Italians!" cried the latter.

"No damn-a good soldiers if you got a lot, plenty damn-a good if you got a few! What happen, signora?"

"And, I say, my dolly! What was it Sir Byng really shouted to wake 'em up? No, I see you don't want to tell us. But what happened?"

The fervency of these unconscious tributes restored Virginia's confidence. Eagerly, now, her soft voice flowed on.

"Well, I'm no authority on battles. Thirteen men couldn't be expected to last very long, especially against such troops as the Ironsides. But—I don't know. Sometimes it seems that men—yes, and even women too!—if they believe in a thing strongly enough, they get a strength or endurance that they wouldn't have believed possible."

(Was Virginia again remembering old days of her own?)

"In any case," she said, "two of those Cavaliers in the charge actually got away alive. One of them even lived to tell the tale to a ripe old age, but it wasn't Sir Byng Rawdon.

"He knew he had his death-wound. His only notion was somehow to get to Telford Old Hall and see his Lady Mirian, even if he saw her only once.

"But you can understand how difficult that was. The battle was fought in Northamptonshire, and he had to get all the way to Sussex. The other survivor hid; Sir Byng didn't. From that night he was a marked man with a price on his head. Nobody now knows how he made the journey, how many horses he used, or even how he could stay in the saddle.

"Meanwhile—now we're into the realm of the legend—Lady Marian had nearly gone crazy herself, wondering where he was and what had happened to him. On a June evening at twilight, according to the story, Marian was sitting at the harpsichord in that Oak Room. She hadn't heard anything. But all of a sudden she looked up, and there was Sir Byng Rawdon in the doorway.

"At Naseby he'd been wearing half-armour, as they all did: lobster-tail helmet, breastplate, and backplate. But he'd had to discard that, as well as his cavalry sword. In the way of arms he was wearing only a cup-hilted rapier, of a style new in England then: a long thin blade without a cutting edge, for play with the point alone.

"Still, apparently, you couldn't tell much about his clothes or his face either, what with the mud and dust and blood. So his Marian saw him standing there, swaying, with his long matted hair on his shoulders.

"She ran to him and put her arms round him. He tried to say something, but for some reason—a wound? I can't tell you—he couldn't speak. It seems she thought he was stifling and needed air. She drew him over towards the left-hand window. He tried again, but still he couldn't speak.

"On his right hand there was a heavy gold ring with a big diamond in it. Instead of opening the window, he used the diamond for a pen.

" 'God bless King Charles and—'

"What was the rest of it? Probably he meant to write 'and you,' of, 'and Marian'; something like that. But he never had the chance. Just then they both heard horsemen in half-armour and buff-coats sounded like death riding past.

"Lady Marian screamed, 'Hide! Hide! Hide!' But what happened was the sort of thing you must have seen yourselves: the—the maniacal burst of strength that can occur just before—well, the other thing.

"He knocked open the window and jumped out on the ground. His idea was to get out of Marian's sight before they killed him. They loved each other, you see, although they couldn't ever marry because she was married already.

"So he jumped out on a broad green stretch of turf, much as it is today, with an oak tree about a dozen yards from the window. But the Roundhead patrol had dismounted; they were converging round both sides of the house, and they caught him near the middle. He set his back against the oak tree, and drew the cup-hilted rapier. Old Bliss, the caretaker who died in 1946, would often point out to visitors the scene of Sir Byng Rawdon's last fight.

" 'God bless King Charles and—'

"They couldn't be blamed for coming at him six to one and in half-armour. He was dying, but he was too dangerous. He got two of them, with lightning thrusts over the gorget and through the throat, before they smashed his guard and—and—chopped him down with a backsword-cut from shoulder to breastbone.

"Lady Marian stood at the window and saw it. She couldn't run to him, she didn't dare even cry out, because her husband and her parents were at Telford, and the house might have been burnt over their heads for harbouring a fugitive Royalist.

"Mercifully, she didn't see him go down. She fell forward in a faint, though it took a good deal to make them faint in those days. The last thing she saw, according to the story, was her lover with his back against the oak tree, and the glitter of the big diamond on his darting right hand.

" 'God bless King Charles and—'

"That's all. It's a foolish old legend, and I hope I haven't taken up too much of your time with it. That's the story Tom told me, when *we* stood by the window in the twilight on the first evening of our honeymoon. And nowadays, I know, we're not supposed to be stupidly sentimental. But I couldn't help myself, I cried."

5

Reality was restored with hard common sense as Chief Inspector Masters cleared his throat.

"Touch of liver, miss," he said consolingly, and added in an embarrassed way, "Most young ladies get like that on their wedding trips. Even my wife did."

"Cor!" said H.M.

Virginia looked at Masters, and her mood changed. Her soft, warm laughter echoed delightedly in the sunset garden, above the splash of the fountain.

"Yes, I see what you mean," she admitted. "Thanks awfully for waking me up. In the old days I would stand at that window looking at the writing, and dream for hours, but now I'm so used to it that I take it for granted. Still, you do understand?"

"Understand, miss?"

"I mean, you understand how that story can have a powerful effect on people? That's why Tom's great-grandfather, just a hundred years ago in the year of the Great Exhibition, had the fake relic of the Cava-

71

lier's Cup made of gold and diamonds and rubies and emeralds."

Again Virginia smiled.

"You see, I tell people, mainly to protect myself, that the story about Sir Byng and his Marian, and the death of Sir Byng under the oak tree, goes into the realm of legend. Really it doesn't; Tom and I could make out a very good case for it as fact. Surely, Sir Henry, you must have heard the story?"

"Oh, the part about what happened at Telford?" asked H.M., massaging his big chin. "Yes, my dolly, that's a well-known story in Sussex. But I hadn't heard the battle-of-Naseby part."

"It was Tom's great-grandfather," Virginia explained, "who created the actual legend when he had them make the Cavalier's Cup. He claimed, when this relic was displayed at the Crystal Palace Exhibition, that the cup belonged to Lady Marian; and when Sir Byng returned wounded to Telford, she gave him a drink of wine out of it, and that's what gave him strength for his last fight. I don't blame Tom's great-grandfather. After all, there *ought* to be some relic."

"Whereas," enquired H.M., "there isn't any at all?"

The girl looked dubious.

"Well, there's a cup-hilted rapier which now hangs on the wall in the passage outside the door of the Oak Room. They claim that belonged to Sir Byng Rawdon, but Tom doesn't believe it."

"So?"

"The rapier there is a Clemens Hornn. But you remember, I said there was one Royalist who escaped alive from the raid on Cromwell's camp? Long afterwards he left an account and put it into writing. He swore the only cup-hilted rapier owned by Sir Byng Rawdon was a Thomas D'Aila. That's so probable as to be nearly conclusive. The greatest sword-makers of the seventeenth century, for weapons of beautiful lightness and balance, were all Italian or Spanish."

"Not-a Spanish!" cried Signor Ravioli, turning a distinct old-fashioned raspberry which made Virginia jump. "Italian! All Italian! And Italian history, she's-a hot stuff. Everybody stab everybody else, you know what I mean?"

Again Masters' throat-clearing called for order.

"This may be all very well, Sir Henry! But it doesn't help us with our problem!"

"You think not, son?"

"Lummy, sir, how can it?"

"I dunno, Masters. But you may have noticed, from the past, that nothing we hear ever seems to be at random, or just for dramatic effect. Somehow it's all a part of a plan."

"This time it's not, by George! The young lady's told you a lot of unnecessary stuff she didn't tell me this morning." Masters shook his head. "And what beats me is that a nice young lady, instead of—instead of bringing up a lot of children, as you might say, is interested in things like that and seems to know so much about swords."

H.M.'s withering glare might have caused the nymph in the fountain to shrink back.

"Masters, my son! It's her husband! Didn't you ever hear of Tom Brace?"

"In my notes, from what the A.C. told me,"

retorted the other, "I wrote down that Lord Brace is quite a sportsman. But, since you ask me—no, sir, I can't say I ever *have* heard of him."

"You wouldn't, you weasel. He's not keen on Association football, and he's never gone in for much amateur boxin', so he's no hero of the great British public. But he's got very few superiors as a swordsman, horseman, and pistol-shot." H.M. regarded Virginia with a hideously thoughtful look. "All the romantic sports, my dolly."

"Oh, yes!"

"Romance! Ur!" snorted Masters. "You give me practical reality. This Sir Ryng, he hadn't got any sense, that was what ailed *him*. What's more, Sir Henry, if you've got questions to ask about the cup that wasn't stolen . . ."

"I'm goin' to," yelled H.M. "Burn me, Masters, I'm goin' to, if you'll just stop drivellin' on about legends and gimme a chance. Now, my dolly!"

Virginia had not yet learned how sharp and discerning could be the eye of Sir Henry Merrivale. But she was learning.

"It's occurred to me that one of the questions I wanted to ask, though not by any means the important one, may be answered for me already. Masters says this cup is usually kept at a bank in London. I'd been wondering what it was doing at Telford last Wednesday night."

"It was there because . . ." began Virginia, but H.M.'s look stopped her.

"Sure, my dolly. You mentioned the Great Exhibition of 1851. I keep forgetting that this is the summer of 1951, and the year of the Festival of Britain. Also, in the museum at Cherriton, they've been holding an exhibition of relics connected with the history of Sussex. Was the Cavalier's Cup exhibited there?"

Virginia nodded.

"Yes. And the rapier as well; the rapier's quite authentic as to age. Tom told them that neither the cup nor the rapier had the slightest connection with Sir Byng Rawdon. But the curator said nothing mattered so long as it looked all right to the ignorant."

"Sort of government motto. I see."

Masters jumped to his feet.

"I won't stand this! Fair's fair, Sir Henry, but if you're going to turn everything into a use for your prejudices . . . !"

"All right," said H.M. "Then you take your blinkin' case and you shove it—you shove it all the way back to London. Instead of devoting myself to my art, which I ought to be doing, I've tried to help you. I'll probably get a sore throat from sittin' here in a damp garden, and then how can I please my public at all? But what do you do, you ungrateful wart-hog? I'll tell you! You . . ."

"Now stop a bit!" snapped Masters, wiping his heated brow and sinking back into the chair. "Will you listen to me for a second?"

"Uh-huh?"

"It may be—I don't say yes or no—but it may be," stated Masters with dignity, "that there have been what the Yanks call cracks made on both sides. But from this minute on I'll agree to forget my honest views if you'll agree to forget your prejudices. Is it a go?"

"Right!" said H.M.

"Fair enough. Then in lum's name get down to cases!"

H.M. turned back to Virginia.

"So," sneered H.M., "forgettin' all about a certain snake in a bowler hat, we'll just continue. The cup and the rapier were loaned to the exhibition at Cherriton. How is it they're not still there?"

"But haven't you heard?"

"Oh, my dolly! I've been practising like a galley-slave to get the best results out of a pretty fair singin' voice. Heard what?"

"This is Friday," answered Virginia, almost with a wail. "The exhibition wasn't supposed to end until tomorrow, Saturday."

"Well?"

"Then, as so often happens, they suddenly found they needed the space for something else. Don't ask me what. But you know how it is. They badger you and badger you to lend them something, and do it in a hurry. You break your neck to do it, then all of a sudden, at the most inconvenient time, they ring up and say they don't want it any longer, so will you please take it back in a hurry?"

"I've experienced it, my dolly. And that's what happened?"

"Yes. Tom's awfully careless, and I'm afraid I am, too. But the Cavalier's Cup did belong to his great-grandfather, and he cherishes it because of that. He'd arranged for a special messenger from the bank to go to Cherriton on Saturday morning and take the cup back to London before the bank closed at noon. Only, as it happened, the curator of the Cherriton Museum

76

phoned Telford late on Wednesday afternoon; he asked it we'd be good enough to pick up the cup immediately."

"Uh-huh?"

"Tom used some appalling language, but he climbed into the car and drove straight to Cherriton. He brought back both the cup and the rapier. Then we were stuck with the cup."

Here Virginia hesitated, frowning a little.

"I don't want to say anything against Mr. Loaf, the curator," she added. "The exhibition at the Cherriton Museum was splendid. And Jennings gave a lot of help with it, too."

"Jennings, my dolly? Who's Jennings?"

It was Masters who answered, in a somewhat menacing tone.

"Jennings is the butler at Telford," he said, his eye darkling as clearly his thoughts hovered over the absent Benson. "Butlers!" He repeated certain former words spoken by Virginia, and then, strangely, Masters began to smile. "But Jennings has been taken with a toothache, the little lady says. Yes, by George!" Masters' smile became a deep chuckle. "The poor devil's down and tortured with a raging toothache. Ha ha ha."

"What's-a matter with you?" demanded Signor Ravioli, stung. "Man get a toothache, you think she's funny as damn-a crutch, eh? You gotta no heart?"

"Certainly I've got a heart. But—butlers! Grr! Just so."

"Shut up, can't you?" requested H.M. sternly. "Now, then, my dolly! We come to the night on which this cup *wasn't* stolen."

Since the cup had not been stolen, any outsider might have wondered why an odd air of strain and constraint had crept into that group. It touched, apparently, everyone except Signor Ravioli.

"From what Masters said," pursued H.M., "your husband decided to lock the cup in the safe in this Oak Room and then sit up all night beside the safe. Lord love a duck! Do you usually take such elaborate precautions as that?"

"No, no! Never! You know what it is in the country. We never even think somebody might try to steal the pictures or the plate. But then there really have been several burglaries in the neighbourhood recently." Virginia brooded. "The real cause, I'm certain, was that we simply talked ourselves into an uneasy state of mind. Even aside from the question of the cup, we'd all been in something of a flap."

"You'd all been uneasy? Why?"

Virginia spread out her hands.

"Well! Just to take one very small point. My father, from America, has been staying with us for about ten days . . ."

"Your father? From America?"

"Please, Sir Henry! I was hoping you at least wouldn't say, 'You're not an American, are you? You don't talk a bit like the people in films!' "

"I wasn't goin' to say that, my dolly. I was only wondering whether I might have met your old man. Who is he, by the way?"

"The young lady's father," interposed Masters, "is Senator Harvey . . ."

"*Congressman* Harvey! Or Representative Harvey, if you insist on saying it at all."

"Oh, ah," agreed the unruffled Masters, taking out his notebook. "From the 23½ congressional district of Pennsylvania."

H.M., who had been taking a cigar case out of the side pocket of his white alpaca suit, stopped with the case halfway out as though he were drawing a revolver.

"Oi!" he said. "You don't mean Bill Harvey? From just outside Pittsburgh? A lawyer?"

"Yes, that's Dad! Do you know him?"

"I certainly do, my dolly. And . . ."

"Sir Henry," snapped Masters, "I should be obliged to you if you wouldn't get such a funny look on your face! From what I've heard, Mr. Harvey is the only sensible man in this affair."

"He is, Masters. That is, he's A-I, and a good friend of mine. Only . . ."

"Only what?"

"Cor! There never was such a feller for makin' Old Glory fly, and everything in Europe is pretty degenerate, and hooroar for Jeffersonian Democracy." H.M. scowled musingly. "And yet all the time . . ."

His big voice trailed away. But into Virginia's face came an expression as though at last, at long last, she had found someone who felt what she herself felt yet could not quite put into words.

"I think I understand," she said with a rush of gratitude which remained cryptic to Masters. "Anyway, it doesn't matter. You were asking why we'd all been in such a flat spin."

"You mean your husband and your old man don't get on well together?"

"No, I don't mean that at all!" cried Virginia,

indignantly and truthfully. "They get on very well. Each of them secretly admires the other, though of course they wouldn't admit it. But . . ."

"Yes, my dolly?"

"Dad *will* argue with Tom about how our Tommy ought to be brought up. Dad thinks Tommy ought to be brought up as an American, and Tom—well, Tom isn't exactly convinced of it. Then they get to shouting and pounding their fists on the table, and it's terrible!"

"I see," said H.M. sympathetically. "Can't your mother keep order between 'em?"

"My mother has been dead for so many years I'm afraid I don't even remember her. Dad's a widower and rather susceptible."

"Oh."

"Then, to add to it, on Wednesday, before Mr. Loaf at the museum phoned about the cup, Dad got a cablegram from home. It said he must return instantly for a conference about some law case.

"Fortunately," continued Virginia, "on Thursday morning there was another cable saying he needn't go back just yet. In the meantime, though, things were hectic. Dad said he had to get an immediate plane reservation. He wouldn't take a booking on the B.O.A.C. plane, because it's called *The Monarch*. He insisted on having the Pan American plane, because it's called *The President*.

"By pulling a lot of strings, Tom obtained a seat for Thursday evening. As I say, it turned out he didn't need to use it. But both Tom and I were in a state on Wednesday when Mr. Loaf phoned."

Virginia shook her head and sighed, her grey eyes

considering matters domestic.

"I can add one last thing," she said. "Speaking of Dad's being a lawyer, we've had plumbers at Telford for days and days, and that hasn't helped either."

Now Virginia was not the sort of girl to indulge in such a clear *non-sequitur.* H.M., who had again begun to take the cigar case out of his pocket, stopped and blinked at her over his spectacles.

"Sorry!" she murmured. "That must have sounded rather odd. But you see, Dad tells everybody he began life as a plumber—to such an extent that you get the notion his true joy in life would be to set up as a plumber."

"And that's absolutely untrue, my dolly?"

Virginia pursed her lips.

"Nothing Dad ever says," she replied, "is *absolutely* untrue. My grandfather, old John D., had an *idée fixe* that every young man ought to learn some trade . . ."

"And what's wrong with that, miss?" truculently asked Masters.

"Mr. Masters, there isn't anything wrong with it! Except surely there's no reason why you should learn a trade if you don't have to and don't want to? Dad loathes working with his hands, he always has, though you mustn't ever tell him so. When he was in school and college, my grandfather made him spend all his vacations learning to be a plumber. And now Dad, who's grown to be a bit like old John D., is really convinced he missed his vocation in life."

"So that's the explanation, hey?" muttered H.M. with an air of enlightenment.

"Has Dad told you about it, too?"

"Oh, my dolly! Has he told me! I couldn't quite understand it, because I knew from some friends of mine your old man had taken his M.A. degree at Princeton before he even entered law school. To hear him talk, I wondered where he'd got time for all that; he seemed to have done nothin' from early childhood except mess about in people's bathrooms."

"Is this getting us anywhere?" demanded Masters.

"Yes, yes!" insisted Virginia. "You must understand it in order to have a clear picture of what happened on Wednesday night."

Again that odd air of constraint settled on the group.

"After Tom returned from Cherriton with the Cavalier's Cup and the rapier, we were all having cocktails before dinner . . ."

"Just a minute, my dolly! Aside from the servants, who was there?"

"Only Tom, and Dad, and Tommy, and myself. I don't mean Tommy was having a cocktail, but when Dad's there, Tommy is allowed to stay up and have dinner with us."

"Uh-huh. Go on."

"Tom was worried, and mentioned the burglaries in the neighbourhood. Then Dad chipped in. My goodness! It's true he's a criminal lawyer, but I never *heard* so many stories about burglars. Dad went on to Raffles, and Arsène Lupin, and somebody called Jimmy Valentine. Of course he only did it to devil Tom . . ."

"Any special reason for devillin' your husband?"

"None at all, except that Dad hates tradition and respecting anything that's old. He says all the stately homes of England ought to be torn down and replaced with modern apartment houses with steam heat.

"Finally Tom got annoyed and said, 'Now look, sir! I'll lock up the cup in that safe in the Oak Room. The windows of that room have been fitted with the most modern fastenings; nobody can possibly get in from outside, and the door can be sealed like a fort.'

"But Dad gave a kind of horse laugh. He said, 'My boy, let me tell you that a good second-story man . . .' "

Again Masters intervened, to the immense and seething irritation of H.M.

"Miss, you're telling Sir Henry this is in a good deal more detail than you told me. What's a second-story man?"

"Corpo di Bacco!" exclaimed Signor Ravioli, addressing H.M. but pointing dramatically at Masters. "That man ees-a one ignorant cop! A second-story man, she's-a what you call in England a cat burglar! If thees room she's-a on ground floor, why you need a cat burglar?"

Virginia remained very serious.

"Dad didn't think of that," she pointed out. "He didn't really care one way or the other; that's what made me furious. He said, 'A good second-story man would just break a window quietly, pick up the little safe, and carry the whole safe away in a car.'

"Still, Dad's suggestion might have been the best one. He said, 'My boy, why don't you take the cup to your bedroom for the night? You're husky enough so that nobody could take it from you.' And he insisted. The trouble was that Tom's always been a heavy sleeper, and so am I. We both sleep heavily, that is, when we do get to sleep."

Masters made another note.

"Forgive me, miss, but what exactly do you mean by 'when you do get to sleep'?"

There was a brief pause. A baleful glare, from the eyes of both Sir Henry Merrivale and Signor Ravioli, fastened upon the unfortunate Masters like the rays of a sulphurous searchlight.

"Only a manner of speaking!" said Virginia hastily. "But you can't say life at Telford is ever dull. One thing led to another, and Dad and Tom were shouting at each other and pounding the table again. That's how Tom decided he wouldn't disturb me at all; he decided to put the cup in the safe and sit up all night in the Oak Room."

As Virginia neared the crux of her narrative, she hardly seemed to breathe and she spoke each word with care.

"At a little past eleven o'clock," she said, "Tom put the Cavalier's Cup in that safe. He locked the safe and put the key in his pocket; I saw him do it. He'd had a hard time finding the key; even Jennings didn't know where it was, but we discovered it hanging up where the key to the wine cellar should have been.

"Tom had been drinking black coffee all evening. Jennings brought him a last big cup, and he swallowed that to make sure he didn't go to sleep. He went over and made sure the windows were firmly locked—they have long steel rods that go down vertically into the window-sill from a handle at one side. Please take my word for it that those windows can't be tampered with.

"Finally Tom kissed me goodnight. When I went out, he closed and fastened the door. The door not only has a lock; it has two rather stiff-working bolts, one at the top and one at the bottom. After locking the door, he fastened both the bolts as well.

"'The rest he'll tell you himself.

"He sat down in one of those high-backed chairs, which aren't very comfortable, with the narrow little table in front of him and an ash tray on it. In spite of everything, of course, he did fall asleep.

"When he did wake up—all of a sudden—it was in that hushed, ghostly time just before sunrise, when the sky is all greyish-blue with a kind of luminousness. He didn't realize he'd been asleep. But there he was, with his arms on the table and his head on his arms. When he raised his head, he saw something straight in front of his eyes that nearly made him drop dead.

"Tom ran to the windows. But both of them were still securely locked, just as they'd been the night before. He ran to the door. But that was still locked, with both the bolts firmly in place. He even tried to look up under the hood of the chimney-piece. But a little way up there's a solid iron grating across the flue; it can't be moved and wasn't moved. And there's no such thing as a secret entrance or exit.

"Nobody got in and out of there. Nobody could have got in and out!

"And yet—the door of the little safe was standing wide open. On the table, close to where Tom's head had been lying—he could see the gold and diamonds and rubies and emeralds all touched with the first light of sunrise—on the table stood the Cavalier's

Cup."

Virginia made a slight, helpless gesture, sighed, and sat back.

"That's the problem, Sir Henry. What do you make of it?"

6

On this occasion the silence stretched out for some time, while a few more shadows stole into the garden. Masters, keeping a bland card-sharper's face, eyed the spray of the fountain as though disinterested.

"Hurrum! Yes," he said. "What do you make of it?"

H.M. looked at him very hard. Having at length taken out the cigar case, he bit off the end of one of his villainous black cigars, expectorated tobacco neatly, and lit the weed with cross-eyed concentration and a pocket lighter.

"You want to know what I think, hey?" he asked slowly.

"I'm a bit curious. Ye-es! You might say I'm a bit curious."

H.M. drew a deep lungful of smoke, took the cigar out of his mouth, and gave an answer.

"Then I'll tell you," he bellowed. "Masters, I've known you to sink to murky, muddy depths of human depravity! But, burn my britches, you've never flopped so low in the spiritual bathysphere as this! You think Tom Brace walked in his sleep, do you?

You think he opened his own safe and took out the cup? And you'll put me through the hoop tryin' to find a solution when you claim there's no solution?"

Masters sat rigid. It was as though his notebook had turned to stone.

"Now, sir, what call have you got to go and say that?"

"Because I'm the old man," retorted H.M., tapping himself on the chest. "I can read the hearts of vultures and hyenas as easily as—looky here! I'll bet you revelled in it! I'll bet you gloated like a grinnin' cannibal! Before you deny that, let's ask the gal. What about it, my dolly?"

It was not that Virginia objected to telling lies. She had as much taste and indeed natural preference for telling lies as any other normal woman. But under H.M.'s eye she could only make a noise in her throat and look at the ground.

"So!" said H.M. "No, Masters, I'm not mad. But I'm goin' to take your own knife," here he made a horribly realistic gesture with the hand that held the cigar, "and twist it in your black heart. What if there is an explanation? Suppose somebody did get in and out of that room?"

"It can't be. If the little lady's got her facts straight . . ."

"Mr. Masters, every word is true!"

". . . then it's impossible!"

"Son, how many times have you said that before? Remember the bronze lamp case?"

"Don't I, though!" snarled the Chief Inspector. "I've been thinking of nothing else. Benson! If I didn't know what happened in this case, I'd know just where to look."

"Oi! You don't think Benson had anything to do with the Cavalier's Cup?"

"He had a good deal to do with the bronze lamp, didn't he? And if I didn't know the truth here—but I do. Butlers!"

H.M. put the cigar in his mouth, but took only a short puff before he removed it. He seemed about to draw Masters' attention to something, and then changed his mind.

"Son," he said. "I'll make a very great concession. You're not a fool."

"Thanks a lot."

"Then stop behavin' like one! Don't be clean-bowled by this thing before you've even looked at it!"

"As how, for instance?"

"Well—now. Accepting the gal's account as being accurate, which we'll do until we prove otherwise, didn't it strike you that there were one or two very rummy and fetchin' points?"

The old duel was on, and Masters' guard up. His eyes moved sideways; wary, alert, he was looking for the *botte* with which he could be done down.

"That's as may be, sir. There may have been, or there may not."

"Let's assume, for the sake of argument, that this gal's husband didn't walk in his sleep. No, you don't believe that! But let's assume it. Is there any way of establishing what sort of occurrence we're dealing with?"

"In what way?"

"For example, could it have been a hoax or a joke?"

"Joke? Again?" cried Virginia.

"Like this, my dolly. Would your Dad have done something like this in order to devil your husband still more?"

But Virginia shook her head.

"No, he wouldn't," she replied, with a very accurate estimate of William T. Harvey's character. "Even if he could get in and out of locked rooms, Dad's mostly talk. He wouldn't *do* anything except for a serious purpose; he's really fond of Tom, and he'd never carry a joke so far."

"Uh-huh. That's my view, too. Is there anybody else who'd enjoy a trick like that?"

"Yes. *You* would," said Masters, running over a touch. "You'd enjoy it no end. Good job there aren't many people with your kind of mind! But I don't imagine you did it, and it'ud have to be you or somebody like you."

H.M. did not even trouble to deny this, but scowled at the cigar.

"I don't honestly think it was a hoax or a joke," he said. "Anything's possible, but still—! Masters, in that case, what's the next point for you to worry about?"

"Stop a bit, now! Since there's no criminal case, I haven't got anything to worry about! And you're not going to drag me into it, either. Lummy, though! I wonder what Lord Brace himself says? He was the one concerned, but we don't seem to hear from him at all."

Virginia sprang to her feet.

"Tom!" she said. "Darling!"

The others craned round to look in the same

direction. The young man who was walking towards her, through the entwined paths of the garden where flowers grew waist high and box-hedges breast high, did not approach from the direction of the house. Otherwise Benson, a stickler, would have insisted on announcing him formally, even in a garden.

He was a young man of middle height, strongly and wirily built without being heavy, and his look expressed good-nature together with that same sort of intelligence and interest in life which made him a masculine counterpart of Virginia herself.

His thick fair hair contrasted in colour with Virginia's brown hair. He wore an old tweed coat, patched with leather at the elbows, an open-necked shirt, and a pair of grey-flannel trousers. Ordinarily Tom Brace's lean face and blue eyes glowed with health and vitality. Now, despite his happy grin when he saw Virginia, his whole appearance was dogged with strain and harassment.

Virginia's eyes remained no longer sleepy.

"Dar-ling!" she repeated, and ran swiftly to meet him.

"Angel-face!" said the young man in a fine ringing voice.

Catching her under the arms, he swept her off her feet and held her up in the air to look at her fondly.

"Tom! Put me down! Please. You know I don't like . . ."

Though Tom and Virginia must have been all of twelve or fifteen yards away from the group by the fountain, it cannot be doubted that both of them, in that romantic garden where trees had been allowed to grow wild, imagined themselves to be entirely alone.

There ensued the following romantic conversation:

"Love me, Jinny?"

"Oh, Tom!—Put me down. Please. That's better—you know I do!"

"Then why the reproachful look? What's wrong?"

"You told Benson you'd be here at five o'clock, and it must be half-past six now!"

"Sorry, old girl. Meant to be here, but couldn't make it. I was occupied with a blasted woman."

"*Tom!*"

"No, no, not what you're thinking. Angel-face," said the ninth Viscount, still fondly and happily, "why have you got to have such a low mind?"

"Darling, haven't you got a lower mind than I have?"

"Yes, but that's neither here nor there."

"Tom, this woman you were . . ."

"Sh-h! Don't use the word you were going to use! In any case, I wasn't doing it and you ought to know that. Woman wasn't a bad looker, though; got to admit it."

"Oh?"

"Jinny, stop!"

"She made a pass at you, I suppose?"

"No, she wasn't there to make a pass at anybody. Wanted to see Jennings."

"Jennings? Why? Tom, if there's anything comical, please don't stop yourself from laughing! You've been so horribly depressed that I'm scared, and it'll do you good!"

"There's nothing funny, old girl. Last week there was a big political meeting at the Majestic Theatre in Cherriton; Jennings was there, or so she says, and she wants him as a witness. The blasted woman is collecting evidence that, she says, will send Sir Henry Merrivale to jail. Claims he shoved her through a trap-door in the stage."

"Tom!"

"Fact, Jinny. I've got her card somewhere in my pocket. Her name's Cheeseman. Elaine Cheeseman. Lives near East Whistlefield, but just now she's stopping at that temperance hotel in Great Yewborough. You know, The Blue Nose."

"But Tom! You didn't let her . . .?"

"No, of course not! Told her Jennings is a studious character—Sussex man, all wrapped up in local history and archaeology, and not concerned with politics. What's more, Jennings has a devil of a toothache. I won't have any member of my household disturbed or bothered when he feels like that."

"You kicked her out?"

"Figuratively, yes. But there was rather a row, and it took some time. Damn woman called me a member of the effete aristocracy—effete, eh?—and also a bloated capitalist. That last is the only thing that's funny."

"Listen, Tom! I've been telling them . . ."

Rapidly, as though they were alone on some fond, isolated island, Virginia sketched out what she had been telling the others, and then drew him forward to introduce him to the group beside the fountain. Whatever H.M. or Signor Ravioli may have felt about the news brought by Tom Brace, they did not comment on it when he was presented to them. Seen at close range, the young man was genuinely haggard.

Masters, who had determined on his line of attack,

remained catlike and bland.

"Evening sir!" he said heartily. "No, don't thank me! Yes, as you say, I'm a busy man, but only too glad to be here on my own responsibility and investigate this matter for you. *If*, of course, there's anything to investigate, Er—forgive me, Lord Brace, but you're not looking exactly up to the mark. Sleep well last night?"

Tom gave him a quick look.

"Well, no," he admitted, opening and shutting sinewy hands. "To tell you the truth, Chief Inspector, I haven't slept for forty-eight hours."

Masters clucked his tongue.

"Tut, sir! Got to get our sleep. Eh? Just so. Still, there are lots of good doctors in London."

"Doctors!" exclaimed Tom, and passed a hand over his forehead. "Look here! Never been to a doctor in my life, except when I was a child!"

"Oh, no call to be alarmed. I didn't necessarily mean a brain specialist."

"You didn't necessarily mean—" Tom paused, and swallowed.

"Not a bit of it! The fact is, in my own family—" Now it was Masters who stopped, but abruptly and frowning, as if a little embarrassed. "Still, it's nothing!" he added cheerfully. "Best not mention it at all."

"No, wait. You seem a friendly sort, Chief Inspector, if you don't mind telling me, I should rather like to hear about it."

"Well, sir," said Masters, lowering his voice. "It was an aunt of mine. Lived at Hackney Wick eighteen, twenty years ago. Walked in her sleep."

Not even the look of horror on Virginia's face, nothing whatever, could stop Masters when he honestly believed he was right. For a moment Tom, a very quick-witted and alert young man who nevertheless had not slept since Wednesday night, clearly was impressed by the guile of Soapy Hump.

"It wasn't serious, was it?"

"Ah!" said Masters wisely. "Odd you should mention that. No, but a lucky thing it wasn't serious! She woke up one night, and found herself standing in the gutter on the roof, ready to jump over. Then there was another night, when she and my uncle were asleep. Nobody knows how the carving-knife got into that room—"

Again he broke off, but this time for a different reason. Tom Brace had been looking at him more closely.

"Chief Inspector Masters!" said Tom. "Got it! Ever since Jinny phoned the Assistant Commissioner this morning, and he recommended going to—yes! Been trying to think where I'd heard that name."

Here Tom turned to H.M.

"Sir Henry, it's only in England that I could live six miles from you and yet never associate your name with the great detective I've read so much about. Only spotted *you* this afternoon. Isn't Chief Inspector Masters the bloke who's always trying to do you in the eye?"

"Got it, son. Lowest weasel on earth."

"You may think I'm trying to swing the lead, Lord Brace!" warned Masters in an ominous voice. "But I'm not. Why should I? Let me ask you something: doesn't all this worry you a bit?"

Tom's grin faded. "Yes! Naturally it does!" he burst out.

"Ah! Well, as I was saying! My uncle was sleeping so that you could see that jugular vein in his neck, and this carving-knife . . ."

"Masters! *Oi!*"

"Easy, Sir Henry!"

"You and your goddam aunts at Hackney Wick!" said H.M. "Now looky here! I said I'd give half an hour to this thing, and it's been over an hour already! Do you realize what I've got to do this evening?"

"I was hoping you'd go over to Telford and . . ."

"When I've got to practise sea chanties every night? Don't gibber, Masters!" He glanced at Tom. "Now, son. You sit down there. I'll give it ten minutes more, but that's all."

"Right," agreed Tom quietly.

Tom considered Masters. Though a nerve twitched inside his cheek, there was in his eyes that glint of amused devilment which had been seen so many times on a polo field or in a *salle d'armes*. Tom Brace was an individualist who deplorably lacked the team-spirit, but captains endured him because he could always ride wild and win for them. In the *salle d'armes* he was an unorthodox swordsman with a trick of developing startling attacks from forgotten eighteenth-century books in the library.

Now, as he studied Masters, anybody could have seen he was thinking of reprisals. But for the moment he flung the thought aside.

"Y'see, son," continued H.M., "I was asking your wife . . ."

"Yes. Jinny told me. Well, ask *me*. Here, angel-

96

face, I'll sit down in your chair, and you sit in my lap. But none of your tricks, mind!"

Virginia, after a quick glance at the others, looked unbelievably innocent.

"Tom, I really can't imagine what you mean."

"No? But it beats me," brooded Tom, voicing a deep philosophy of life, "why women always think it's so funny when—right you are, my girl! Not another word. Sit down."

That was done, though not until Virginia had delivered a mild-voiced but impassioned little speech in which she promised to poison Masters at the first available opportunity. Her husband shushed her. His troubled gaze never left H.M.

"Look, sir. If you want to ask me whether somebody tampered with those two tight-fitting bolts on the door, in any way fooled about with the windows, or got down the chimney, or perhaps was hidden in the Oak Room—you can save your breath. It won't do! Thought of all that myself."

"I wasn't thinkin' of it. But do you remember the moment you woke up?"

"Wow! You can say I do, yes."

"Uh-huh. Now the door of the safe was standing open. Was the key to the safe in the lock?"

"No. I found it where I'd put it—in the right-hand pocket of my coat."

"Then, while you were asleep, it would have been easy to slip the key out of your pocket and slip it back in again?"

"Yes. Quite. Or, for that matter, the key'd been knocking about for weeks or months. Simple matter for anybody to get a duplicate cut."

"So! Meanin' what, exactly?"

"Hang it, what if I was drugged?"

H.M.'s cigar had gone out. Instead of relighting it, he threw it away and surveyed Tom with an air of refreshed interest. But it was Masters who spoke.

"So you've thought of that, Lord Brace!"

"You mean," snapped H.M., who was annoyed, "you mean *you've* thought of it, Masters?"

Across the Chief Inspector's stuffed-owl countenance flickered a faint smile. To change the duelling metaphor, it became apparent that Masters was not showing all the cards in his hand.

"We-el!" he said. "We hear the gentleman drunk a big cup of black coffee before he—hurrum!—sat down to guard the cup. Always a possibility, even if it's not likely. Ha ha ha."

"Tell me, son. When you woke up, did you feel drugged?"

Long pause.

"I don't know," Tom answered simply. "Before you look like that, either of you, wait! Ever had the experience of falling asleep in an uncomfortable chair and waking up suddenly, several hours before you should? Even if you haven't been drugged or haven't had a drop to drink, you feel cramped, fuzzy-headed, all out of sorts. Don't you?"

"Fair enough," grunted H.M.

"Unless it's knockout drops, according to Jinny here, you don't necessarily wake up with a thick head. And unless somebody gives you a blood test immediately, how can you tell?"

"It's a fact," said H.M., "that a medium-stiff dose of chloral hydrate would have had just that effect—

Masters, shut up—but there was one really important question I'd got in mind . . ."

"Yes," nodded Tom, "and I think I can tell you what it is."

"You can, hey?"

"At least I can try. From what Jinny says, you don't believe this business with the Cavalier's Cup was a joke or a hoax. Right you are! Now, let's say a thief somehow gets into the room. He takes the cup out of the safe, examines it—and then doesn't steal it."

"Yes, sir?" prompted Masters, in a way reminiscent of a poised cat.

"So you'll want to know whether the cup really *was* made of gold and genuine jewels. Whether, in short, it was the Cavalier's Cup at all?"

7

This was the point at which H.M. and Masters, despite their mutual distrust and loathing, exchanged surreptitious glances.

Tom Brace did not notice. Absentmindedly stroking the back of Virginia's neck while she bent forward in as much fascination as her husband, Tom was throwing out the words as though to convince himself he had not danced in a nightmare.

"It's the Cavalier's Cup," he declared. "It was, and is, the one and original cup my great-grandfather had made. If our Scotland Yard boy-friend knows anything about jewels, as he probably does, he can test that for himself."

Again H.M. and Masters flung mental daggers at each other.

"It's like this," Tom explained, with a forward thrust of his head. "I wouldn't sell so much as a tin plate or a song sheet that belonged to any member of my family. They'd have to take Telford away from me, as they may do, before I'd do that.

"It's stubborn, and cherishing the past? Well, there it is. But," Tom smiled, sheepishly yet engagingly, "you can't be expected to take my word for it. I'm very far from being a millionaire, in spite of Miss Cheeseman or anybody else. That cup, intrinsically, is worth a lot of money . . ."

H.M. raised a hand. "Is the cup insured, by the way?"

"Yes, but not for anything like its real value nowadays."

"And I daresay, sir," observed Masters, with considerable sarcasm, "even the amount of the insurance has never been changed?"

"Quite right. It hasn't." Tom smiled good-humouredly, but there was a quiet devil in his eyes which silently added, "And if you don't like that, my friend . . . ?"

This challenge, however, faded in an instant.

"If Sir Henry's the man I know he is," said Tom, "he'll have thought, 'Oho! Brace sold the jewels and gold of the original cup; he got a duplicate made, with clever imitation stones and gold plate, and this was shown at the Cherriton Museum. But a knowing criminal, who slipped in and out of that room without disturbing the door or the windows . . .' "

"How could anybody do that?" shouted Masters.

"Sweet Fanny Adams!" said Tom. "If I could guess that, we needn't have troubled you. But here's the thought: 'This criminal gets a close look at the cup for the first time, sees it's a fake, and contemptuously leaves it behind on the table in front of Brace.'

101

Possible?"

"It did just cross my mind," growled H.M., rather guiltily.

"No, sir. That's the real Cavalier's Cup, so the explanation won't do. Any other explanation?"

"You tell it," said Masters.

"Right. 'Hum!' thinks Sir Henry. 'The phantom burglar, who's got a way of melting in and out of a locked room, wants to nick the Cavalier's Cup so they won't suspect a theft at all. *He* gets a duplicate made, changes the cups, and disappears.' "

"Stop talking about people disappearing!" said Masters.

"Glad to, Chief Inspector. That explanation won't wash either."

"Why won't it, darling?" asked the rapt Virginia, trying hard to sound dense so as to make her husband appear more brilliant.

"Because he'd have been a prize idiot to behave as he did. His game would have been to stick the duplicate cup in the safe, lock the safe again, drop the key back in my pocket, take the real cup, and dis—and leave. If he'd done that, I might not have noticed any substitution at all.

"But no!" said Tom, drawing a line in the air. "By that theory, he calls attention to the fact that there's been jiggery-pokery. He leaves the safe open, puts down the fake cup in front of me, asks for investigation. If it won't even work as a theory, it won't work as a fact; we've still got the real Cavalier's Cup."

H.M., about to speak but thinking better of it, ruffled his big square-tipped fingers at his temples.

You could almost hear the crash as Tom destroyed one possibility after another.

"Looky here, son!" said H.M. "How did you come to have so many bright ideas about this?"

"That's easy," Virginia answered for him. "It's because both Tom and I *adore* detective stories. Isn't that so, Tom?"

"Right!" agreed her husband, now absentmindedly drawing a line along Virginia's backbone in a way which made her wriggle. "But they've got to be proper detective stories. They've got to present a tricky, highly sophisticated problem which you're given fair opportunity to solve."

"And," amplified Virginia, "no saying they're psychological studies when the author can't write for beans."

"Correct!" her husband agreed again. "Couldn't care less when you're supposed to get all excited as to whether the innocent man will be hanged or the innocent heroine will be seduced. Heroine ought to be seduced; what's she there for? The thing is the mystery. It's not worth reading if the mystery is simple or easy or no mystery at all."

"Now wait a minute, both of you!" blared Sir Henry Merrivale. Truth must be told: the old maestro had grown a trifle rattled. "Masters, are you listenin' to this?"

"No!"

"Shut up. Masters, that cup ought to have been stolen! There's no point to this case unless the cup's been stolen. Why wasn't it stolen?"

"Never mind why it wasn't stolen," retorted the

Chief Inspector. "How could anybody have got in to steal the cup that wasn't—hurrum! Getting too mixed for me; stop it!"

Whereupon H.M., with a sniff, assumed a lordly and austere air.

"Well, it's your responsibility, Masters. I can't devote any more time to a case that's as simple and easy as this one. You solve it! Burn me, it's gettin' towards dinner-time, and this evening I've got to practise sea chanties." Once more he appealed to his music-master. "Haven't I?"

But Signor Ravioli, who had been shivering all over, refused to back him up. Very carefully, as though sighting through them, he pinched his thumb and forefinger together in the air.

"*N-n-n-o!*" he said with passion. "Wan t'ousand times I tell you: you practise too damn-a much! Lose-a da voice; not a peep-peep; then thees-a concert she's-a sweet Fanny Adams, too."

"Oh, lord love a duck! You think I might lose my voice?"

Signor Ravioli bounced to his feet and took the floor.

"Fine young lady! Fine young gentleman! Ignorant cop think thees young gentleman she's-a crazy as bedbug. Why you not help? Why you not think-a da song, se-a da clue? Eh?"

"Clue? What clue?"

"He's dead but he won't lie down!"

"Who is?"

"Thees-a spook!" said Signor Ravioli, enraged by such apparent denseness. "Rattle da chain! Move-a da cup! Make . . ."

"Son, are you seriously tryin' to tell me that the ghost of Sir Byng Rawdon unlocked the safe and took out the cup?"

Masters' sarcastic chuckle echoed so derisively that Tom Brace closed his eyes and could be heard counting to ten.

"*I'll* accept the explanation," offered Masters. "If Lord Brace didn't walk in his sleep, as I told his wife, then the ghost must have moved the cup because it's the only thing left. Don't put me in the wrong! I don't say Lord Brace is insane."

"That's very kind of you, Mr. Masters," breathed Virginia.

"I don't say that at all, miss! All I say is that he's a little abnormal . . ."

"Abnormal, eh?"

"Easy, my lord! And, after all, what's so serious about losing a night's sleep? I'm a reasonable man; you'll agree to that. I'm perfectly willing to investigate anything under the proper conditions."

Tom snapped his fingers and leaned forward so abruptly that he almost spilled Virginia off his lap.

"Chief Inspector, do you mean that? You won't go back on your word?"

"Eh? Mean what?"

"That you're perfectly willing to investigate something under the proper conditions?"

"Oh, ah! Of course!"

"Right!" said Tom. "Then spend tonight in the Oak Room, with the door and windows locked on the inside, and guard the cup yourself. I challenge you!"

Distinctly, now, the whole atmosphere had changed.

Signor Ravioli, his mouth a round O, slowly feathered back into his chair. Four pairs of eyes, all alight with the same sudden inspiration, were fixed upon Chief Inspector Masters. That tormented worthy, staring back at them incredulously, felt as we all sometimes feel in dreams. Had he been standing up, he would have retreated before the pressure of the eyes.

"Now why should I do a fool thing like that?" he demanded, in an incredulous voice which called for sanity.

"I don't know," retorted Tom. "But you said you'd investigate it under the proper conditions. Very well! Do what I did, and see whether the same thing happens again."

"It can't happen again! You're asking me to lose a whole night's sleep just because . . ."

"After all," said Tom, "what's so serious about losing a night's sleep?"

"But give me one sensible reason for doing that! Lummy! 'Tisn't as though—" Masters stopped, his hand at his chin, as a new idea occurred to him. "Lord Brace!" he said. "Of course you've—ha ha! — you've already had that cup sent back to the bank in London? It's not still in the safe at Telford?"

"Yes, it is," admitted Tom. "Hang it all! I was worried! Forgot the blasted cup completely. Messenger from the bank's coming down tomorrow morning, Saturday, just as he'd intended. But the cup's still there."

Sir Henry Merrivale, who was eyeing Masters in a fashion singularly lacking in any intimation of secret glee, shook his head in a doubtful and ominous way.

"Y'know, Masters, this puts a very different complexion on things."

"How does it, Sir Henry? Just tell me how!"

"Oh, my son! When the Assistant Commissioner specially ordered you to come down here . . ."

"Specially ordered him to come down here?" interrupted Tom. "I thought he was here out of the pure goodness of his heart."

"Well—now. Masters is rather a slippery customer."

"That's all very well!" raved the Chief Inspector. "But I'll turn your own guns on you, Sir Henry! *You* don't seriously think the ghost of Sir Byng what's-his-name will take the cup out of the safe again?"

Signor Ravioli's gesture was worthy of a scene in *La Traviata*.

"Don't-a you laugh," he cried, "at what you don't-a understand. Every good castle in-a Italy, I tell you, she's-a full of spooks! She's-a so full of spooks these-a spooks scare each other. Thees man, he's-a been stab, poison, any good way to die, he *not* come back? Pah? Got-a no enterprise, no good to anybody."

"You keep out of this, Signor Spaghetti! Sir Henry! Do you seriously believe that?"

"Maybe not, son."

"And you don't think the Cavalier's Cup will get up and walk out of the safe by itself?"

"I dunno, Masters. But I'll tell you this. Since you've been sent here to investigate a stolen cup . . ."

"The cup wasn't stolen!"

"All right, if you're goin' to quibble about it! Lemme finish what I had to say. If that cup gets up and walks out of the house into some crook's pocket, when a police-officer has been sent here to guard it, then what the Assistant Commissioner will do to you just won't bear thinking about. And you know it."

Virginia, her dimples and her sleepy alluring smile again in evidence, slid off Tom's lap and stood up.

"Then that's settled, Mr. Masters?" she asked gently.

"No, miss, it's *not* settled! I'll do no such tomfool thing! I wasn't sent here to guard the cup, and I'm sure you'll be good enough to tell the old devil that yourself."

"But, Mr. Masters," pleaded Virginia, "surely somebody asked you to go to Telford and look into the matter? You haven't even been to Telford."

This was the last straw.

"No, miss, I haven't. And do you know why I haven't been to Telford? Because you and Sir Henry, between you, have done nothing for hours but go on about rubbishy legends and low music-hall songs. Now, miss, don't be upset! I don't want to hurt you! But this is ridiculous."

"Put it this way, Mr. Masters. You'll have to have dinner somewhere, won't you?"

"I can get a bite to eat at a pub on the way back!"

"Mr. Masters, we shouldn't *dream* of letting you go to the pub! You must have dinner with us. That's not all. You said this morning how tremendously you enjoyed the flicks, and I told you about the private film-projector we have at Telford. Do please let me keep a promise I made! Before you go to the Oak Room to guard the cup, Tom and I would be awfully happy to show you the Marx Brothers in *A Night at the Opera*."

The bulk of Sir Henry Merrivale suddenly stirred with ghoulish interest.

"*A Night at the Opera?*" repeated H.M.—who is not a film-goer despite, or perhaps because of, his passion for the stage. "Oi! My dolly! Is that a film about singing?"

Virginia looked taken aback.

"Ye-es, I—I suppose you could say that."

Now it was Virginia and Tom who exchanged glances. Tom's eyes flashed with that glint, this time of purely happy devilment, which gave him the look of one viewing some Promised Land. But Virginia, who as a rule did not believe in any limits on anything whatever, was nevertheless a fair-minded girl.

"No, Tom!" she begged, and clasped her small hands. "I can guess what you're going to suggest. But please don't. Sir Henry must practise sea chanties. Truly he must! Besides, if he saw the Marx Brothers it might—it might give him ideas I tremble to think about."

"I know just what you mean, miss," snapped Masters. "And blowed if I'm going to be put in the wrong, having all these people look at me as if I'd been in the wrong, and even feel myself as if I might be in the wrong! Is that justice?"

"Yes!" said Tom.

"Sure," agreed H.M.

"*Si!*" proclaimed Signor Ravioli.

Virginia made a deprecating gesture towards them.

"You see, Mr. Masters," she continued, "you wouldn't really lose your sleep. We can get permission from your Assistant Commissioner so that tomorrow, when the cup goes back to the bank, you can sleep all day at Telford if you like. And I'm sure there's one other favour you haven't the heart to deny us."

"Oh, ah, miss?"

"Truly there is! My father will be awfully disappointed if he doesn't get a chance to meet you. As a criminal lawyer he's rather well known, and, as you must have guessed, he reads a tremendous number of detective stories. I'm afraid he doesn't like England much, or says he doesn't, though he's very polite about it except in private. But the one thing that does interest him is Scotland Yard. He'll be frantic if he misses a real Chief Inspector. Dad doesn't get back from London until late this evening, and if you rush away now . . ."

Masters saw his chance.

"Ah!" he said gruffly. "If there was a chance of meeting your father, now, I might be persuaded to do what you want."

"You might?"

"Yes, indeed, miss! Your father's a sensible man. If he was here, I tell you straight, I could definitely promise to do this nonsensical stunt. But he's not here, and there's no likelihood of him being here. So there you are. I'm sorry."

From some distance away there was a discreet cough.

They were all so preoccupied that nobody had heard the seraphic approach of Benson, deferentially leading a newcomer. Benson coughed again, and paused before formally announcing: "The Right Honourable William T. Harvey!"

8

"Tut, no!" observed the newcomer, stopping short
and turning to Benson while both of them were still a
good ten long paces from the group by the fountain.
"You've got it all wrong. Not 'the Right Honourable,'
if you don't mind. That's *English*."

Benson hesitated.

"I am extremely sorry, sir. Did you wish me to
announce you in some other language?"

"No, I expressed myself badly," said the newcomer.
"The term 'Right Honourable' is English usage. It's
not necessary to give me any prefix, but if you must
do it, in America we just say 'the Honourable.' "

Masters, even in sick realization of how the high
gods had snookered him again, felt a little surprise
when he saw Mr. William T. Harvey.

Already he had formed a mental image of what
Virginia's father must be like. Mr. Harvey would be
tall and burly, with silver-grey hair, spectacles, and an
impressive or even stately bearing. But he wasn't.

True, the newcomer had a strong and rather explosive personality, which he was always trying to sub-

112

due. He had a powerful voice, long trained in every trick of the speaker's platform—"Let me hear your consonants!"—to which voice, after the difficulty of dropping each word clearly into the farthest back row, the use of a microphone was childishly easy.

But he was neither tall nor burly, despite a deep chest. Though he could not have been less than fifty, there was no hint of grey in William T. Harvey's dark-brown hair, and his waistline had not increased a quarter of an inch in thirty years.

He had a merry, stubborn, actorish kind of face, mobile and ugly, but lighted by a pair of vivid greenish eyes, and a habit of gesturing when he spoke. His clothes were so conservative as to go beyond even the English notion of conservatism in dress.

Completely oblivious to his host or to the others, again engrossed in preaching something, he detained Benson and spoke with lifted forefinger.

"I don't know anything about England, remember! But I think you call your Cabinet Ministers 'the Right Honourable.' It's the same at home. But we also apply to it members of the Senate and the House."

"You refer to the White House, sir? Where the President lives?"

"No, no! The President doesn't live in the House. Nobody lives in the House."

"Sir?"

Masters, gritting his teeth and determined to do his best, rose to his feet. In his notebook, which could not lie, he had carefully written: "Senator Wm. T.

113

Harvey. Republican. Don't mention Democratic Party."

So Masters went forward, with what ghastly semblance of affability he could muster.

"Evening, Mr. Harvey!" he said. "My name is Masters, Chief Inspector Masters. I'm a police-officer, sir. Sent from Scotland Yard at the request of your daughter."

Forgetting Benson, Mr. Harvey was instantly engrossed in something else.

Seen at closer range. Mr. Harvey showed more signs of his real age. In the past, clearly, he had been no stranger to the booze or the women. But his vitality crackled like electricity in that quiet garden. His green eyes kindled with pleasure, his smile had charm.

"Very glad to meet you, Mr. Masters," he said, cordially gripping the other's hand. "Scotland Yard, eh?"

"That's right, Mr. Harvey. Very pleased to make your acquaintance, too."

"I've heard a lot about your great institution, Chief Inspector."

"And I've heard a lot about your great political party, Mr. Harvey. There's a presidential next year, eh? Just so. Let's hope the Republicans get in this time."

It was exactly as though Masters, while greeting the newcomer warmly with his right hand, had lifted a water-pistol in his left hand and squirted Mr. Harvey in the eye.

But Virginia's father, after long toughening in legal

114

and political battles, was immune to almost any shock. The green eyes in his expressive face took on only the slightest suggestion of wariness, as though he wondered whether to laugh lightly. Then, as he glanced past Masters, he saw Sir Henry Merrivale.

"Hold her, Newt!" he said. "I think I begin to see everything. Whatever I may think of this country, I'm not in the habit of meeting gratuitous insult."

"What's that, sir?"

"Just tell me." Mr. Harvey nodded towards H.M., and his voice acquired richness and volume. "Did that old buzzard there tell you to say I was a Republican?"

Masters' esteem for the Honourable William T. Harvey rocketed even higher.

"Buzzard? How right—yes, Mr. Harvey, he did. Lummy! I haven't said anything wrong, have I?"

"No, it's not your fault. I ought to have known it! Mr. Masters," said the other, again shaking hands heartily, "you're a man after my own heart! So is Benson here. Please don't go away, Benson."

Benson was sincerely gratified.

"Very good, sir."

Completely ignoring his daughter, his son-in-law, Signor Ravioli, and especially Sir Henry Merrivale, Mr. Harvey, summoning the whole force of his personality, proceeded to air certain grievances before a sympathetic audience.

"The point is, I didn't intend to come back from London until late tonight. But I got a phone call. That's why I returned. Not only did I return, but I took a taxi straight to the house of a certain man concerning whose ancestry, morals, and general behaviour I shall say not one word, save only the trifling fact that he ought to spend the rest of his life in jail."

"Mr. Harvey, shake hands!"

"Glad to, Chief Inspector. There you are. Now listen. Mr. Masters," said Congressman Harvey impressively, "I have a grandson!"

Virginia uttered a slight moan. Tom Brace closed his eyes. As husband and wife looked at each other, it was plain that both had at least a partial foreknowledge of what was coming.

By tradition, young parents are believed to be somewhat prejudiced about their offspring. But this is not always so. For fondness bordering on fatuity, for a supreme conviction that nobody on earth ever had grandchildren before, the prize example is usually grandpa.

"He's a fine boy, Chief Inspector. If *I* were responsible for bringing him up—however. Even in the short time I've been here, I'm happy to tell you I've got in a lot of good spade-work. Are you following me?"

"Hurrum! In jail, eh?"

"Every morning, when I come down to breakfast, I put Tommy through a sort of catechism. 'Tommy,' I ask him, 'what's the greatest nation on the face of the earth?' And he answers—with no prompting from me, either!—he answers, 'The United States of America, Gramp!' "

"In jail. By George!"

"Then I say, 'Barring religious matters, Tommy, name the greatest man who ever lived.' And all his fine young nature shines in his eyes when he throws back his head and answers, 'Thomas Jefferson, Gramp!' "

Congressman Harvey was a real spellbinder. Though he had no great height and no bulk, he had voice and he had presence.

"You're right, Mr. Harvey. In jail!"

"Thomas Jefferson? In jail? What are you talking about? Listen, Chief Inspector. I'm not saying a word against my son-in-law. For an Englishman, he might be a whole lot worse. But has he got any gumption? No! If he had, would he let me get away with this? No! When I ask, 'Barring religious matters, name the greatest man who ever lived,' then the kid should say, 'My Dad!' Tom Brace should have beaten me to the punch!"

Tom uttered a strangled noise. Virginia had retreated to his lap, but once more she was all but spilled off when Tom rose to his feet.

"Look, sir! Don't be an ass!"

Mr. Harvey at last noticed him. He turned round. In his unobtrusive and well-cut grey suit, with a plain dark-blue tie, it is a sober fact that he now seemed about seven feet high.

"Were you addressing me, my boy?" he asked, in a kindly tone.

"Yes. I couldn't teach Tommy to say anything like that! It would embarrass the boy too much. But, by the Lord Harry! Not half as much as it would embarrass me."

"Embarrass you, would it?" enquired Congressman Harvey, with pouring scorn.

"Yes!"

"Oh, dear!" said Virginia, with her hands at her ears. "Here we go again."

But William T. Harvey had too much on his mind to pursue this. Having now acknowledged the presence of the others, he at last acknowledged the presence of someone else.

"Chief Inspector," he said, "I'm sorry to see there's an old friend of mine here. I hate to come to his house and raise a rumpus. But the matter's too serious for me to do anything else. Good evening, Henry."

Throughout the foregoing exchanges, H.M. had been sitting with his big bald head lowered, drawing slow and deep breaths as though to banish the monstrous injustices which invariably surrounded *him*. Now he rolled up his head with a malignant look, but he spoke mildly enough.

" 'Lo, Bill."

"How are you, Henry? But what the hell," exploded Congressman Harvey, "did you mean by it?"

"Mean by what? For the love of Esau gimme a chance to . . ."

"Now don't give me any of that! Did you, or did you not, meet my grandson this morning?"

"Looky here, Bill! I was having my singing lesson, and . . ."

"Did you, or did you not, meet my grandson this morning? Answer yes or no!"

"Yes! Signor Ravioli was showing me . . ."

"Good! We've established that. Now tell His Honour and the ju—I mean, what did you mean by teaching him that?"

"Burn me, son, try to make some sense. I'm a

118

barrister too. What did I mean by teaching him what?"

"Teaching him," shouted Mr. Harvey, "to shoot people in the seat of the pants with a bow and arrow?"

A distinctly guilty look flashed across the bottle-nose of Signor Ravioli. Virginia's half-parted lips opened still more.

"And don't swear you didn't," pursued Mr. Harvey, "because I've talked to Tommy. Every day when I have to be in London, I still don't forget to phone him. You've hypnotized the poor kid. He actually thinks it's fine to do a reprehensible and antisocial act like that! Did you, or did you not, teach Tommy to shoot people in the seat of the pants with a bow and arrow?"

Virginia's mind being what it was, leaped to one conclusion.

"Oh, good heavens!" she exclaimed. "Miss Cheeseman! Miss Cheeseman, the Labour Member of Parliament from East Whistlefield! Sir Henry! You didn't tell Tommy to shoot Miss Cheeseman in the seat of the—of the skirt?"

Conscious of his innocence in this respect, H.M. permitted himself a look of martyrdom which would have done credit to St. Sebastian.

"Oh, my dolly! No! Burn me," he added, with a flash of vexed disappointment, "I never thought of it. But how could I? The woman was gone before Tommy got here!"

"I can make nothing," said Congressman Harvey, "of the obstructive and antisocial tactics of this wit-

119

ness. Let's have some sensible person for a change. Where's Benson?"

The butler took a hesitant step forward.

"You spoke, sir?"

"Benson, kindly tell us in your own words exactly what happened. Did you see this deed done?"

"Yes, sir. I must confess at once, sir, that a certain individual was indeed struck rather sharply at the base of the spine with a clothyard shaft. But the person in question, sir, was not Miss Cheeseman. It was our gardener."

"Your gardener?"

"Yes, sir. A taciturn and somewhat dour individual named Colin MacHolster."

"Persecuting the Scotch again," said Congressman Harvey, with a broad and fierce gesture. "What else can you expect from a degenerate Empire-worshipper who quotes Kipling in every other word? Benson, where did this occur?"

"The scene of the cr—the incident, sir, took place here in the garden."

"Thank you. What did you see and hear?"

"I fear, sir, that I heard only two very brief sentences uttered in a very loud voice by Colin MacHolster himself. Being inside the house and at an upstairs window, I was too far away. If I might venture to express an opinion, sir . . ."

"Thank you, Benson, but we don't want your opinions. Just tell us what you saw."

"Very good, sir. From the window, sir, I perceived Sir Henry, with a large strung bow in his hand and a quiver of arrows on his back, crawling on his hands

120

and knees along one of the paths which you observe here. It was just *there*, sir," Benson nodded, "where the hedge is waist-high, and Sir Henry appeared to be taking cover behind it."

"Yes, go on!"

"He was followed by Signor Ravioli, also crawling on all fours . . ."

"Wait. Who's Signor Ravioli?"

"That's-a me!" said the gentleman in question, tapping himself on the chest. *"Il maestro.* Teach-a to seeng Sir Henry." He got up and ducked a little bow, his hair flying. *"Fortunatissimo, signore."*

"Fortunatissimo, signore, Sta bene?" replied Mr. Harvey in an absentminded way. Then, for some reason, he flushed angrily and corrected himself. "I mean: howdy-do, my friend? How's every little thing? Never mind!"

Mr. Harvey's eyes, green and glittering and alive, hovered over Signor Ravioli as though trying to place some elusive memory. But he was too genuinely infuriated by H.M.'s conduct, and he flung away whatever notion may have been in his mind as he raised his eyebrows at Benson.

"Yes, sir," said that worthy. "Following Sir Henry and Signor Ravioli, sir, was the tenth Viscount."

"Not the tenth Viscount!" snapped Mr. Harvey. "His name is Tommy! It ought to have been Thomas Jefferson! What were they doing?"

"From their demeanour, sir, I could only deduce that they were tracking or trailing someone after the fashion of red Indians."

"Not 'red' Indians, if you don't mind. Just Indians. There aren't any other kind."

Benson coughed.

"Though I should not venture to take issue with you, sir, yet I feel compelled to point out that a universal application of the term you mention might cause some protest, for instance, in Calcutta or Bombay."

"Yes, you've got a point there. But American Indians are the only Indians that count. Were they tracking Colin MacHolster?"

"I believe so, sir. At this moment Colin MacHolster stood some six or seven yards beyond the hedge, his back turned. He had just bent forward to scrutinize the root of some flower or plant, and presented a dorsal elevation of considerable magnitude."

"And that was when . . . ?"

"Not immediately, sir. Since the three gentlemen were obliged to keep silent, there ensued a pantomime which I could interpret only as a somewhat acrimonious dispute as to which of them should loose the clothyard shaft. This dispute was finally resolved by eliminations with the spinning of various coins. By the baffled look on the faces of Sir Henry and Signor Ravioli, it became plain that the choice had fallen to the young gentleman.

"I may remark, sir, that the tenth Viscount could not be expected to draw the string of a forty-pound bow to his ear. Had this been so, the dorsal elevation of Angus MacHolster must have suffered irreparable damage. Even as it was, however, the young gentleman, with a strength and skill remarkable in one of nine years old, sped the shaft straight and true to its target."

"He's my grandson!" said Congressman Harvey, with instant pride. But, correcting himself, he flapped his arms, stamped on the ground, and addressed Benson and Masters.

"You know Henry! You must know him. Just tell me: what makes the old buzzard tear around like that? It's not a rhetorical question; I really want to know."

"Dad," interposed Virginia quietly.

"You keep out of this, Jinny!"

"But, Dad, it was you who bought Tommy the bow."

"Yes, but I didn't tell him to shoot anybody in the seat of the pants!"

"And I suppose, Dad, that you never did anything completely and perfectly silly just because you wanted to?"

Congressman Harvey's fair-mindedness became manifest.

"As a boy, even as a young man," he conceded, "I've done a lot of things of which my mature judgment disapproves. But I don't do it now. And that evil-minded ghoul there, who's old enough to be *my* father, still rampages around like Henry the Eighth." Again he appealed to Benson and Masters. "I shouldn't mind so much if somebody would just tell me why?"

This time Benson coughed behind his hand.

"I fancy, sir, that Sir Henry may partly have been influenced by his choice of a song."

"Song? What's a song got to do with it?"

"The tenth Viscount, sir, appeared at a French window of the Grey Study, the bow in his hand, when Sir Henry had just concluded a fairly long rehearsal of one particular number."

"Well?"

"I am happy to inform you, sir," said the glowing Benson, "that Sir Henry's taste in music is not entirely confined to musical numbers of a vulgar or even questionable nature. True, they fall only into two other categories. These may be designated as the extremely sentimental, such as 'Annie Laurie' or 'When Irish Eyes Are Smiling,' or, on the other hand, drinking songs and marching songs of spirited and rousing character."

"Sorry, but I still don't get you!"

"Sir Henry, Mr. Harvey, had been rehearsing an item called 'The Song of the Bow,' or perhaps, 'The Bow was made in England.' "

"Wait a minute!" said Virginia's father.

The eyes in his stubborn, actorish face seemed to drift far away with concealed joy. Instinctively he fell into the attitude most natural to him, and which suited him best: the attitude of the swashbuckler. For an instant, to Masters' astonishment, there roared out a brief snatch of song.

" 'Of yew wood, of true wood,
    The wood of English bows!' "

"Forget that tripe!" said Congressman Harvey, recovering himself. "I can't imagine where I picked it up. It's out of a book. Books!"

If even H.M.'s unmentionable face looked surprised, Virginia and her husband appeared stupefied. Mr. Harvey saw it instantly.

"I say nothing against books as such, you understand! I say merely that the patriotic American, in this streamlined age of progress and the near-millennium, hasn't time to do much more than keep well-informed of current events. Why, Jinny, today there are educational opportunities unknown to my generation and even to yours. With the perfected technique of movies, with the nearly perfected technique of glorious television, I mean . . ."

"You mean, son," interrupted H.M., "that you'll reach the millennium when they can just look at pictures and not have to use their brains at all?"

Mr. Harvey put his fists on his hips.

"Your weakness for smart cracks, Henry, is as great as your weakness for the outworn and effete principles of monarchy. A king! Why in the name of sense," cried Mr. Harvey, as though all grievances boiled down to this, "have you got to have a *king?*"

"Y'see, son . . ."

"No, don't answer that. There is no answer, and it's not what I was going to say. Where are you, Chief Inspector?"

"Here, sir! Just behind you."

"Well, get this. I once heard that old buzzard make a speech in the United States. Far be it from me to pronounce any judgment which I could call unfair. You understand that?"

"Just so, Mr. Harvey."

"There wasn't a cough or a rustle in the audience,

in spite of the fact the he violated every speaker's principle; his address was in the worst taste; he told anecdotes which ought to have made every true lady blush. But that wasn't the worst of it. He actually had the nerve to quote no less than two sentences in Latin. *In Latin!*"

It became obvious that the enormity of this offense had not quite penetrated to any of his listeners, who looked at each other.

"What's-a da mat'?" asked Signor Ravioli truculently.

"What's the matter?" repeated Congressman Harvey, taken aback.

"Sure theeng! Latin, she's-a only what Romans speak before getting-a sense to speak-a Italian. What's-a da mat'?"

"To quote Latin is snobbish; it's in bad taste; it shows you're trying to high-hat the only person on earth who matters—the average man, the little man, the common man!

"Does the average man, the little man, the common man, know anything about Latin? No! Does he care anything about it? No! I'm happy to say that Latin is dying out even in our moss-grown and reactionary colleges. Latin ought to be prohibited! Any man who would even know Latin, *tempus edax rerum, tuque, invidiosa Vetustas, omnia destruitis,* ought to be shot!

"Why, ladies and gen—that is, Chief Inspector— what is the idea before which we should all humbly bow down? I may say without fear of successful contradiction that it is this same average man, the

126

little man, the common man! This is so and shall forever last, immutable and immortal, wherever the torch of civilization casts its far-flung rays!"

At this point Congressman Harvey was automatically on the point of adding, "I thank you," when there penetrated to his mind certain words which he had heard, or thought he had heard, a moment ago.

"Jinny," he demanded, "what did you say just then?"

9

Matters had reached such a pitch that every person except H.M. was now standing up, and several were bristling. In contrast to this was Virginia's look of flower-like innocence, which, in such a garden, might have inspired a quotation from *Maud*.

"Say anything, Dad?" she murmured.

"Answer yes or no. Did you, or did you not, say, 'To hell with the average man'?"

"Dad! I'm your daughter. Can you imagine me saying anything like that?"

"I hope you wouldn't, Jinny. I sincerely hope not. But I'm afraid that's just what you might say. It's not your fault, though. It's this infernal and degenerate British influence. That's what's changed you from the fine young American girl I used to know!"

"Now half a tick, there!" said Tom Brace, striding forward. "Just what do you mean by infernal and degenerate British influence?"

"What I say! Furthermore, young man . . ."

"Dad! Tom! Please!" begged Virginia, getting between them. "A real Scotland Yard detective is going to solve our problem by spending tonight in the

Oak Room. Sometimes I can't understand either of you! I simply don't see why you can't discuss matters as two sane and steady-going American and English people should, instead of stamping and tearing your hair like a couple of temperamental Ital . . ." Virginia broke off, horrified. "Signor Ravioli! I *am* so sorry!"

But Signor Ravioli was not in the least offended.

"What's-a da mat'?" he enquired, beaming happily. "I tell-a you something, mees. Before you try to understand other people, why you not try to understand yourselves?"

"Understand ourselves?"

"Sure theeng! You think Italians, French, Spanish only people what blow-a da top, go nuts? English, Americans, they never do? Pah, I am revolting! Sir Henry, hee's-a carry on like six Italians."

Tom Brace and William T. Harvey looked at each other.

"Tom," observed the latter, "maybe Signor Ravioli's got a point there, too."

"Look, sir! I didn't mean to . . ."

"At the same time," thundered Congressman Harvey, waving his hand in the air, "I still say there's something insidious and undermining in the very air of this country. You couldn't find anywhere in the world a more level-headed man than *I* am, for instance. And yet I felt it, I felt that influence not half an hour ago when I got off the train at Great Yewborough. Otherwise I shouldn't even have thought of speaking to the lady!"

"Speaking to . . ." Virginia, putting her head on one side, studied him a little more closely. "Dad," she added very softly. "Are you getting tangled up with another girl-friend?"

"Virginia!"

"Oh, dear, I know what it means when you start calling me 'Virginia!' "

"Girl-friend!" said Congressman Harvey, a picture of offended outrage. "Really, Virginia, I should think you would have more respect for your poor old father than to talk like that!"

"But . . ."

"I'll put the incident up to any fair-minded person here! Where's the Chief Inspector? Where's Benson?"

Two voices glumly assured him that their owners had not yet run away.

"I was simply walking from the station," pursued Mr. Harvey, "to that garage where you can hire a taxi. And I was going past one of those joints where they don't serve liquor. In this country I think you call 'em temperance hotels. This place is named . . ."

"The Blue Nose!" said Tom, with a thoughtful look.

"No, no, my boy. The Blue Lamp. I was walking past the The Blue Lamp, thinking about murdering that old ghoul who's got such a funny look on his pan at this moment, when out of the hotel walked a daughter of the gods, a dream, a vision; and I'm not kidding either! A statuesque blonde, with warm-blooded cheeks and rosy lips, who walked in beauty like the night."

"Just one moment, Dad," breathed Virginia, whose eyes were no longer sleepy but almost round. "Sir Henry?"

"Yes, my dolly? Believe me, I'm not missin' a

130

single word of this."

"Sir Henry," said Virginia, "I'm thinking of a person. I won't say who it is, except that her last name begins with the letters 'C-h.' 'C-h!' Sir Henry, is she a statuesque blonde with warm-blooded cheeks and rosy lips? Is she?"

"Uh-huh," said H.M.

"Oh, dear!"

"What are you two gassing about?" asked the puzzled and conscience-shaken Mr. Harvey. "What's all this 'C-h' business, anyway?"

"It doesn't matter, Dad. Go on."

From the beginning Virginia should have realized that her father, like Chief Inspector Master and her own husband, was in an upset state of mind and could not be called quite himself in a matter of degree. Though unquestionably William T. Harvey, he was, so to speak, a heightened and more glittering version of himself.

And Mr. Harvey, though perplexed, was encouraged and perhaps even flattered by the extraordinary pressure of attention which had fastened on him. Had he expressed it in a speech, he would have said that the fate of a nation was riding that night.

"I don't know what came over me!" said Mr. Harvey, "Jinny, I swear I don't. But I couldn't help myself. I said, 'Madam, I trust you will forgive this word from an ill-mannered but well-intentioned stranger. Madam, I have been looking for you all my life!'

"She stopped and gave a funny kind of gasp. She said, not very loudly, 'Looking for me?' And I said— if my son-in-law laughs, as I can see he's beginning to laugh now, I'll break his neck—I said, 'The face that launched a thousand ships, and burnt the topless towers of Ilium!'

"Hell's *fire!* The woman must have seen I was sincere, and for a second there I could have sworn she liked it. But no! All Englishwomen are cold! Everybody knows that. She froze up like a clam. She said, 'You must forgive me, sir, if I am not interested in poetry. I am interested only in things of the intellect.' "

Here Congressman Harvey uttered a groan like a man in the last extremity on the rack.

"I should have left it at that," he said. "I ought to have known better. I should have raised my hat" —in point of fact, he was wearing no hat— "and walked away. But no! I said . . ."

"Yes, Dad?" prompted Virginia. "What did you say?"

"No, that's enough! For the first time in years and years I was really serious. But I was asleep at short, and a hot grounder got past me. Forget it!"

"Please, Dad. For me. What did you say? You said . . .?"

Mr. Harvey could not control himself.

" 'Madam,' I said, 'the hell with your intellect! You're the most beautiful thing I ever saw! ' "

"And what happened?"

"Jinny, what do you imagine happened? With a cold Englishwoman? Not that she wasn't justified, because my manners were abominable. She gave another gasp, worse than the first, and simply marched straight away from me. When she turned around to look back . . . "

"Oh? She turned round to look back?"

"Yes, twice!" groaned Mr. Harvey, and beat his fists against his temples. "Probably wanted to snub me again. If I'd been in America—but wasn't! I honestly was serious, and now I've cooked my goose to a cinder."

"Listen, Dad. There's something I ought to tell you."

"No, Jinny. I forbid it. If you have any respect for the feelings of your poor old father, not a word more. I don't know why I degraded myself by telling this. I should be grateful"—real dignity surrounded him now— "if all of you would refrain from mentioning the matter henceforward."

There was a bursting kind of silence, everyone held mute by this request, while Mr. Harvey stood, lost in brooding.

But with Signor Ravioli, who seethed and bubbled under a suggestion he wished to make, it was a near thing. The music-master was kept silent only by a long, steady glare from Sir Henry Merrivale.

"In that case, Bill," said H.M., with a heavy and gusty sigh, "we'll respect your wishes. Still and all, if you were honest-Injun serious, it seems a pity you didn't learn the gal's name. If she's staying at The Blue Lamp, we could easily find out for you."

"You bet!" burst out Signor Ravioli. "Thees-a sour-pus broad, she's-a want to chuck Sir Henry in da can!"

"For the love of Esau, sh-h!"

"But now we feex, eh?"

"Are you goin' to shut up, or aren't you?"

Fortunately, William T. Harvey was too bound up in an agony of self-reproach to follow this. Besides, he was again frowning at Signor Ravioli with the air of one troubled by memory.

"Excuse me, but haven't I seen you somewhere before? I always boast, like many people, that I never forget a face." Congressman Harvey laughed a little. "But it wasn't in England. I've got an idea it was somewhere in or near Pittsburgh."

"Could-a be," instantly conceded Signor Ravioli. "Sure theeng! I work in Pittsburgh. Twenty, twenty-five year ago. Learn-a da Engleesh there."

This was news to Sir Henry Merrivale.

"You taught music in Pittsburgh, son?"

"Not joost a that," said *il maestro*, carefully defining his terms. "Play da piano in-a music department Joseph Horne's. Fire' from Joseph Horne's, go to Kaufman's. Fire' from Kaufman's, go to Kaufman & Baer's. Fire' from Kaufman & Baer's . . ."

"But, burn me, why? You're a first-class teacher, and you've got a voice that would put you on the stage if you wanted to sing."

"You betch-a two dollar! All these-a department stores admit it."

"Then why did they sack you?"

"Say I seeng too damn-a many Italian songs. Say customer want-a hear something else besides-a 'Santa Lucia,' 'O Sole Mio.' Pah! Fire' from Kaufman & Baer's sling-a da hash at Joe's. Who care?"

"I don't recall ever having been in the music department of any store," replied Mr. Harvey. "Seems to me it's connected with my law practice. You weren't a client of mine, were you? No, I see you weren't. Never mind! I was only trying to take my mind off the cold divinity who's passed forever from my life."

"Now don't go pourin' sackcloth and ashes on your head, Bill! I'll take your mind off it fast enough. By the way, how's the plumbing business?"

"The what?"

"You missed your real vocation in life by not sticking to plumbing, didn't you?"

"Oh, that?" Mr. Harvey tried to speak lightly, but it was with a certain strain and an air of gloom. "There wasn't much to that; forget it. I'm afraid I wasn't very much good as a plumber."

H.M., who had again taken out his cigar case, stopped and looked at him curiously.

"Lord love a duck! Y'know, son, your preoccupation with—h'm. Well! At least you've got a whole lot of skill at constructin' defences for criminals and hoicking 'em out of clink before they even get there. What's *your* opinion about the problem of the Cavalier's Cup?"

"Henry, to tell you the truth . . ."

"For instance, did you hear what your daughter said a minute ago? Masters has promised to spend tonight in the Oak Room at Telford and find out whether a ghost did the dirty work, or else how in Satan's name somebody got in and out of another locked room."

"Yes, so I gathered."

Chief Inspector Masters, who had put away his notebook, grew more red in the face and squared himself like a swimmer ready for buffeting water.

"If you'll excuse me, Sir Henry, I don't recall promising anything of the kind!"

"*What?*" exclaimed Tom Brace.

"Mr. Masters, you awful fibber!" whispered Virginia. "You gave a definite promise. Didn't he, Tom?"

"He did, angel-face. He said your father was a sensible man; and if your father were only here, he'd do it like a shot. And your father is here. He said that before witnesses! He can't back out now."

It is possible that Masters' opinion of William T. Harvey's level-headedness had received a slight setback by the recital of what had taken place before a temperance hotel in the High Street at Great Yewborough.

The lady in question could only be Miss Elaine M. Cheeseman, Labour M.P. for East Whistlefield. One thing Masters admitted to himself. Congressman Harvey did not know it, but he had a technique which would knock Englishwomen silly, and though Mr. Harvey himself would never have used so crude a term, made them pushovers.

But—level-headedness? Lummy!

"Jinny, I've said it before," fretted her father. "I wish you and Tom would keep out of that Oak Room. Why do you and Tom want to fool around in the Oak Room? And how can it serve any good purpose for the Chief Inspector even to go in there, let alone spend a night there?"

"Ah!" said Masters, and in an instant his old opinion of Virginia's father was fully restored. "Exactly what I've been telling them myself. Took the words straight out of my mouth! That's your own view too, Mr. Harvey?"

"I can't help thinking it. I was all against this idea of going to Scotland Yard."

"And in your opinion, sir, it was Lord Brace himself who merely—hurrum? Eh?"

"Right you are!" snapped Tom. "Say it! I'm ten times madder than a March hare. Sign a paper to that effect, if you like. But, just in case there's a chance I'm not scatty, you're blasted well going to keep your promise and see whether the ghost walks again."

"What ghost?" demanded Congressman Harvey.

"Dad, I really don't know," confessed Virginia. "They do say Telford is haunted but nobody claims to have seen the ghost of Sir Byng Rawdon since the eighteenth century. I can't think how the subject of ghosts got into this conversation at all."

"Just so, miss. And I've said, sir," explained Masters, touching Mr. Harvey on the shoulder, "I don't believe Lord Brace is off his rocker, only a bit peculiar like an aunt of mine. No call for *you* to be upset about it, Senator Harvey."

"No, no, no!" encouraged Signor Ravioli. "He be fine, eh, when-a he meet theese dame Elaine Cheeseman?"

"Cheeseman?" repeated Mr. Harvey, and several persons jumped. "Is this more of the mysterious 'C-h' gag, whatever it is? Elaine! That's a pretty name. I've always liked it. But Cheeseman!" added Mr. Harvey, much amused. "What sort of comic English name is that?"

Now it was H.M. who fired up, pointing an unlighted cigar at his guest.

"As for the wench," he said, "you call her whatever you like. But if you know what's good for you, son, don't you utter one word about the name. Cheeseman

137

is a good old Sussex name. So's Cherriton." H.M. cast up his eyes musingly. "So's Harvey, by the way."

A distinctly different turn had come into the whole atmosphere. William T. Harvey stiffened, his upper lip drawn back from his fine teeth.

"Meaning what?" he demanded.

"Nothin', son. I just said Harvey was a good old Sussex name."

"It's despicable Republican propaganda," yelled Congressman Harvey. "My forbears were all Scottish and Irish, every single one of 'em. There's not a drop of English blood in my veins! Not one drop!"

"All right, son, all right." H.M. spoke with a sort of querulous mildness. "Lord love a duck, don't go on like a whiffled motorist swearin' there's not a drop of alcohol in his body. I'm not saying anything against your ancestors."

"Ancestors?" said Mr. Harvey, stiffening. "I'd have you know something else, Henry. No American citizen, if he's a really patriotic American citizen, has anybody related to him who came to our great country before the year 1900. If he has, he's no true American and he'd better hide it p.d.q.! Ancestors? I've got no ancestors!"

Though Virginia did not comment, her expression had grown so unbecomingly drunken that her father felt compelled to notice it.

"And if you're thinking of Colonel Harvey of Virginia, in the Revolutionary War, that was all a fiction dreamed up by your grandmother!"

"Dad, why was I named Virginia?"

"Because your mother and I liked the name, that's all. Lots of girls are called Virginia."

"Dad. There *was* a Revolutionary War?"

"Childish sarcasm, Jinny, does not in the least become you. But there's one thing you'd better remember. Practically nobody of English stock fought on the American side in the Revolution, and I can give you chapter and verse. Aside from the Scots and the Irish, nearly all the important men were either Germans or Poles."

"Scots and Irish, yes. Also quite a few Welsh. But, Dad, for heaven's sake! You've got to draw the line somewhere, and I will not accept a fine old Czechoslovakian family named Washington. What's happened to *you*? If you're talking about outsiders who helped the American colonists, you always said the most important ones were French."

It was as though someone had done unto William T. Harvey what the tenth Viscount did unto Colin MacHolster.

"French?" he yelped. *"French?"*

"Yes! You said so!"

"A frivolous, immoral people who do nothing but dance and drink wine and—and other things? French?"

"The teaching of French ought to be prohibited too, I suppose?"

"Tais-toi, ma petite! Ferma ca! Yes, it ought!"

"La barbe, papa!" Deplorably, Virginia added in the same language, "Take the chewing gum out of your ears!"

" 'How sharper than a serpent's tooth!' " said Mr. Harvey, who, if he had really attained the venerable age and dignity he believed he ought to have attained, would have worn an aspect not unlike King Lear.

"This is what comes of young people reading books! What do *you* say, Chief Inspector?"

"Couldn't agree with you more, sir! So help me, I never said I'd spend a night in that Oak Room . . . "

"Yes, you said that. I heard you when Benson was bringing me . . . " Mr. Harvey, appalled, stopped short, but it was too late.

"Aha!" shouted Tom. Deliberately he picked up a garden chair and flourished it above his head. "That's got you, Chief Inspector!"

"Tom," said Mr. Harvey, with desperate reasonableness, "I'll swear I've read almost every locked-room story ever written. So, to do you justice, have you. Will you tell me how . . . "

"And how many times must I repeat," said Tom, "that I haven't got any idea?" Clearly bewildered, apprehensive as dusk began to gather, he dropped the chair with a clatter. "The windows, maybe?"

"My boy, skip the windows! Listen. They're not sash-windows."

"Hang it all, I've seen 'em! I live there!"

"But listen! Each window opens out like a little door. On the right hand side there's a steel rod through the frame. When you turn the handle inside—and it's hard to turn—the steel rod goes down through the sill on each window. There's nobody alive who could monkey with that contraption and still leave it fastened on the inside.

"As for the door," pursued Mr. Harvey, gathering eloquence, "we've all heard of a lot of trick ways to bolt doors from the inside by somebody who's standing outside. But there are two bolts. *Two!* One at the top, one at the bottom. The door fits so tightly in the

140

frame that it scrapes the floor when it swings. In addition to the fact that both bolts are as stiff to work as the handles on the windows, you can't get at 'em. They . . . "

Tom held up his hand, in a gesture so imperative that even his father-in-law paused.

"Chief Inspector!" said Tom.

"So help me, Lord Brace," exploded Masters, "I'm bound to tell you . . . "

"Are you, or are you not, going to keep your promise? Answer yes or no!"

"Very well, my lord," replied Masters, after a pause. "If it will make you feel any happier, I'll do it. But nothing's going to happen there! Nothing can happen!"

That was what Masters thought.

And now, with regard to the wild events of that black Friday night at Telford Old Hall, we need only a brief glimpse or two before the time when, at half-past three on the following morning, and in the bedroom of Sir Henry Merrivale at Cranleigh Court, the telephone rang.

10

A bird or an aircraft, hovering over sleeping Sussex towards midnight, might have reported all well. But the peaceful look of the countryside was deceptive.

Against a three-quarter moon, in a pale summer sky as soft as the velvet a swordsman wore, the tall chimneys of Telford Old Hall stood up in silhouette. The facade of the Hall, long and rather high-built, of black timbers and plasterwork once white, had a Georgian north wing whose incongruity lay softened and smoothed by the moonlight to as reasonable a symmetry with the older part as was the Queen Anne south wing.

At ten minutes to twelve, then, in all Telford there burned only one light. This was in a room on the ground floor, at the rear, facing west. The glow from two windows with leaded panes fell palely on grass and, a little distance away, on a venerable oak tree. Inside that room, sitting in an uncomfortable chair and doing his best to stay awake, was Chief Inspector Masters.

Behind Telford Old Hall lay only lawn and trees. But, at the side of the south wing, there was a large garden. Unlike the untrammelled Elizabethan style of the garden at Cranleigh Court, this was a Dutch garden laid out in that severe geometrical design introduced to England by a detestable sour-puss named William of Orange.

And in the garden something stirred.

A tall, rather thin man with an uneasy whitish face rose suddenly from behind a bank of tulips now drained of colour. If anybody had seen him—which nobody did—that observer would have said the man had been crouching there, wondering whether or not he dared creep into the house.

Now, in his sober dark clothes, he stood up and listened. We have not actually met this man before, but he had a long, not unpleasing face, intelligent, middle-aged, though in unguarded moments his expression might have seemed a little tricky.

He could hear not a sound. A fragrance of grass and flowers was made dreamy with dew; there might have been perhaps an occasional night-rustle, but no noise to be counted as such.

The tall man hesitated. His eyes moved towards his right, towards the long front lawns of Telford which at the line of the main road were enclosed by a very high fence of iron railings. There he saw something. Though it was far away, a firefly torch and moving slowly, it made the night-watcher hastily crouch down again for cover.

143

He need not have done so.

The faint glow came only from the bicycle-lamp of Police-constable Frederick John Horsham, who was cycling majestically along the road leading from Cherriton through Great Yewborough, past Cranleigh Court, and thence to the policeman's destination at Golywog.

The stately bearing of P.C. Horsham, even when riding a bike alone on a deserted road at ten minutes to midnight, would have made the gait of metropolitan police-officers on their rounds seem careless and even frivolous by comparison.

P.C. Horsham's back was as straight as that of a sentry outside one of the royal palaces. Such was his dignity that he did not merely seem to ride a bicycle, he was like an emperor being carried in a litter. He did not even move, as in official language, he "proceeded" another mile and a half to the High Street of Great Yewborough.

However, it would have been a mistake to think P.C. Horsham anything but a human being. He had been on duty all day, and needed sleep. Nevertheless, he was proceeding towards the home of his niece, Annie—the wife of Bert Stevens, one of the two plumbers now employed on a long job at Telford Old Hall—because Annie expected her first child before morning.

P.C. Horsham did not expect to return that night, and he was resigned to this.

The High Street also lay deserted and silent. But, curiously enough, two windows showed faint light in a bedroom up on the first floor of a temperance hotel called The Blue Lamp.

As P.C. Horsham proceeded through the High Street with the slow majesty of a great galleon, he glanced upwards. He was not surprised to see, against the faint light from one window, the outline of a female figure which appeared to be looking up at the moon.

He was not surprised, however, only because his friends swore that nothing on earth could ever surprise him, much less detract a shade from his unshakable poise. Never, in his experience, had any guest at The Blue Lamp kept lights burning as late as twelve. On the other hand, guests at The Blue Lamp were not notorious for giving trouble to the police.

So he pedalled on. But a closer inspection of what P.C. Horsham saw only in vague outline would considerably have astonished any friend of Miss Elaine M. Cheeseman.

That night, after a splendidly austere and uneatable dinner, Elaine Cheeseman had gone up to her small chaste room. There she made a number of notes, assembled from testimony in the village. Miss Cheeseman had suffered a real humiliation, though no physical injury, when she fell through a trap-door in the stage of the Majestic Theatre; it is impossible not to sympathize with her, or share some of her anger at a certain old reprobate.

After finishing her notes, she had seen that it was fully an hour before her bedtime at ten o'clock. So she began to read a new book called *Our Duty to the State*, published under one of those Latin pen-names such as "Senatus Populusque Romanus," or the like.

But *Our Duty to the State* had strangely failed to command attention. Putting it aside, Elaine had fallen to musing. It must not be thought that this very pretty woman, with her heavy golden hair and fine figure, had no use whatever for the softer emotions of. life. Though she was not exactly engaged to be married, there had been for some years a sort of tacit understanding with Professor Hereward Wake, who occupied the chair in economics at Highgate University.

It would have been too sentimental to have carried about a framed photograph of Professor Wake. But Elaine Cheeseman had in her handbag a good snap shot of him. Sitting there meditating, she took the snapshot from the handbag and considered it. Professor Wake was not at all unhandsome; certainly his countenance was in great contrast (say) to the homely dial of Congressman Harvey. Yet Elaine did not seem to find great consolation in the picture.

Since we cannot know the inner thoughts of *any* person in this chronicle, except those of Chief Inspector Masters, the subject of her meditations must be left undescribed. But she looked restless, troubled. So long did she reflect that she gave a start when her blue eyes registered the time after looking for minutes on the travelling-clock.

Even then she did not seem inclined to turn in. Voicing what in another would have been called a deep sigh, she wandered over to a window and stood there breathing the scents of a summer night. And her eye was caught by the moon over Sussex.

Cree-ee-ee sounded a clicking noise from the street,

apparently as harsh as the noise of a torture-rack turned in one's conscience.

"Oh!" said Elaine, and gave another start.

But the sound was less than a whisper, not one thousandth-part so loud as it appeared in the hush. It was the soft chain-murmur of bicycle-pedals, as a large and impressive policeman—another reminder of law and conscience—loomed past beneath shadowy old house-fronts.

Police-constable Frederick John Horsham, in his turn, had scarcely noticed Elaine. On he proceeded, well over another three miles, until there began to rear up on the right of the road the boundary wall of Cranleigh Court.

Much has been said of P.C. Horsham's progress, goodly and great. Therefore it is startling to record that, as he passed the gates of this historic mansion, it was as though he had received a violent shove in the middle of the back.

His right foot slipped on the pedal, his bulk wavered, and he almost pitched headlong over the handle-bars into the ditch. Saving himself by a miracle, he dismounted and looked towards Cranleigh Court.

The red-brick front of the house was in complete darkness. Yet, though it was quite some distance to the front, let alone the back, he was not mistaken and could not have been mistaken.

"Sixteen men on a dead man's chest,
  Yo-ho-ho and a bottle of rum!
Drink and the devil had done for the rest . . . "

And once more, as though with inhuman savagery and bloodlust, blasted that appalling deification of grog.

P.C. Horsham frowned. About the owner of Cranleigh Court, in recent months, there had been circulating curious rumours. Unquestionably the noise was a nuisance. But it could not legally be called a public nuisance, since nobody except the policeman could now hear it. P.C. Horsham, though even his nerves shied, managed to smile tolerantly.

"Only Sir Henry," he said aloud to the night air. "Nobody else does it. So that's all right."

And mounting his bike, this worthy member of the Sussex County Constabulary pedalled away with the ghastly blare still following him.

It did not cease until nearly one o'clock. But in the ensuing calm, these rolling slopes seemed to sink in even more blessed quiet. Far away, miles too far to be heard, the clocks at Cherriton dropped the ring of the hours into a hollow light, fading amid air-vibrations which were answered by a deep-toned church clock at Great Yewborough.

The moon had set; the air, with an uneasy shiver, was black tinged with a breath or tremor of grey which brought coldness and a slower pulse-beat; in short, it was half-past three in the morning, stealing towards dawn, shen . . .

Br-ring, br-ring. Br-ring, br-ring. Br-ring, br-ring.

The clamour of the telephone, in that dark bedroom at Cranleigh Court, cut across a whistling snore. For perhaps twenty seconds the phone screamed, as though it could not bear to be imprisoned in four walls, while nothing happened.

Then you might have heard a creaking from an ancient four-poster bedstead, a few vile words, and the rattle of a bedside tablelamp on its base as someone groped for a switch in the dark.

The light went on. It disclosed an infuriated Sir Henry Merrivale, clad in pyjamas with vertical stripes of purple and gold. Reaching out and putting on his spectacles so as more effectively to glare at the phone, he let it scream for several seconds more before answering.

Then, whatever he had intended to say, it was stopped in his throat by the soft but frantic voice of Virginia Brace.

"Sir Henry! I'm sorry to disturb you, but dreadful things have been happening here! Could you please come over to Telford as soon as possible?"

H.M.'s expression changed, though his ogre's look remained incredulous.

"Easy, my dolly! You're not goin' to tell me somebody's been murdered?"

"Murdered? No! But . . . "

"Seriously hurt, then?"

"I—I don't know. Not *seriously*, perhaps. But . . . "

"Lord love a duck, did you wake me up at this hour of the morning just to tell me that?"

"But you don't understand! It began just after dinner, when Mr. Masters said he saw a forger in the tulips. Only it wasn't, it was Jennings, or Mr. Masters said it was, and then he disappeared."

The sweetest-tempered of us, awakened at half-past

three in the morning, might not be in a state very receptive to information like this.

"Hold on, my dolly! Will you try to tell me what you're talking about?"

"After dinner! Tom, and Dad, and Mr. Masters went for a stroll in the Dutch garden on the south side of Telford. They were smoking cigars. All of a sudden Mr. Masters gave a shout and chased down one of the paths, but didn't find anybody. When he came back . . ."

"Uh-huh? Don't stop there!"

"They asked him what was wrong. There was a moon, you know. He said he'd seen a famous forger, a man who can imitate anyone's signature and engrave Bank-of-England notes just like the original. Mr. Masters said this forger was in the Dutch garden, looking at him through some tulips.

"Sir Henry, I'm afraid Tom wasn't awfully nice about it. Tom said, 'Chief Inspector, are you sure you haven't inherited any trait from your aunt?' But Dad said, 'What did this crook look like?' Mr. Masters began, 'Name, Prentice Thorne. Age, 48. Height, six feet one-half inch—' And so on through a lot of Bertillon measurements, or whatever they call them now.

"It meant that this Prentice Thorne, with about four aliases, is a tall, thin man with dark hair and brown eyes, a high forehead and a long nose, and a little scar under the right side of the jaw. Tom made a peculiar noise and said, 'But that's a description of Jennings! You haven't seen him tonight, because he's still confined to his room with a bad toothache. This

150

man can't be Jennings, our butler!' Then Mr. Masters said, 'Butlers!' and went off the deep end."

H.M., instead of being merely furious, was now serious. There is a great difference. Propping his back against the headboard of the bed, he spoke in a quieter tone.

"When it comes to professional crooks, my dolly, you can trust Masters. If he says the Dean of Canterbury is Red Joe, the Poisoner, which may not be so far-fetched at that, I'll take his word. That's his job, and he knows it from A to Z."

"Good heavens, do you think I'm not serious?"

"I know you are, my dolly. Go on from there."

"So they had a terrible argument, and finally they all went up to Jennings' bedroom. But Jennings wasn't there. He's disappeared and hasn't come back again. At least, we can't find him."

"So!" muttered H.M., as though this news came not altogether as a surprise.

"Sir Henry! Were you expecting that?"

"Well—now. As I told Masters, there were a few rummy and fetchin' points in what I heard this afternoon and evening. All of a sudden, and quite without warning, this Jennings was taken with a toothache. Not only a toothache, but one that made him keep to his room. When did this toothache strike him? Just after he heard over the phone that you were comin' down to Telford with a copper from Scotland Yard."

"I—it did occur to me long afterwards," observed Virginia in a small voice.

"What's more, your husband drank a big cup of

black coffee before he sat down to keep watch on the Cavalier's Cup on Wednesday night. But he went to sleep. Who served him the coffee? You said yourself it was Jennings. So, my dolly, if you'll be serious . . ."

Virginia's rapid speech had made her breathless. There was a pause while she recovered.

"Not serious?" she cried for the second time. "You still don't understand! That's why I rang up. Sir Henry, *it's happened again!*"

H.M. opened his mouth, but closed it without speech. He did not pretend to misunderstand.

"The Cavalier's Cup!" explained Virginia. "From eleven o'clock on Mr. Masters was in the Oak Room with the door and the windows all locked on the inside. The cup was locked in the safe, as it was before. But *he* went to sleep. Somebody got in, took the cup out and put it in front of Mr. Masters just where it had stood in front of Tom. But the door and the windows were still fastened on the inside!"

Another silence.

H.M.'s gaze strayed across the room. Beyond the circle of light shed by the bedside lamp, the room was dark except that both open windows were now brushed with faint grey. No birds stirred as yet. It was cold. But there was moisture on the forehead of Sir Henry Merrivale.

"Cor!" he said, clearing his throat. "In a way, my dolly, that's bad . . . "

"Bad?" said Virginia. "No! It's p-perfectly wonderful! Don't you see? It proves beyond any doubt that Tom isn't crazy. He didn't walk in his sleep, and

152

somebody else got in there!"

"Uh-huh." H.M. sounded thoughtful. "Yes, I s'pose it does."

"But I must have some help. I simply can't handle these three wild men, Tom and Dad and now Mr. Masters. Each one is as bad as the other, except that perhaps Mr. Masters is worst. And we must find out how someone got in and out of the Oak Room. Mr. Masters . . ."

"Oi! Where *is* Masters, anyway? Why isn't he talking to me?"

"He can't talk to you, Sir Henry. He's in bed."

"In bed?" bellowed H.M. "What's the lazy blighter doin' in bed at this time?"

"You mustn't talk like that, please. The poor man was hurt. He was hit over the head and knocked unconscious, and he's got a terrible bump on the back of his head."

"Masters was?" demanded H.M., beginning to tremble. "Well, well! You don't say? Clouted over the turnip, was he? But you said he was asleep."

"Yes, he was. At least, according to his story, he was asleep, but something woke him up. He heard somebody in the room behind him, he says. Before he had time to turn round, he was hit on the head with a blackjack, which he calls a life-preserver."

Now Virginia sounded desperate.

"Only," she went on, "we couldn't find any life-preserver. The only things which might have been used as weapons were that seventeenth-century lute I mentioned, and—do you recall, I told you about a cup-hilted rapier? It's supposed to have belonged to

Sir Byng Rawdon, and it hangs on the wall *outside* the door of the Oak Room. Remember?"

"Sure!"

"Well," said Virginia, "it was there. Lying at Mr. Masters' feet, in that impossibly locked room, was the cup-hilted rapier."

11

"Now looky here!" said H.M., getting a firmer grip on the phone. "Use your old man's precept of yes-or-no simplicity, can't you? Masters was keeping watch on the Cavalier's Cup, hey? And somebody clouted him on the turnip, right! When did this happen?"

"I don't know."

"You don't know?"

"No. Not exactly. At eleven o'clock ..."

"Wait. You said you were goin' to show Masters some film or other. Did you show him the film?"

"No," answered Virginia. "There was such a long argument about Jennings that we didn't have time." Virginia hesitated, her voice seeming to cloud with more trouble. "And it'll be quite all right if you come over here, Sir Henry. Dad doesn't want to cut your throat any longer. He did want to do that for a while, but he doesn't now."

"Why in the name of Esau should he want to cut my throat?"

"It's my fault. I don't tell tales on people, truly I don't! But it slipped out. I—I told him about Miss

Cheeseman, and why she wants to have you put in jail."

"Oh, my dolly! He'd have had to learn sooner or later!" Despite this reassurance, H.M.'s face began to swell. "But does Bill Harvey think I ought to be stuck in the clink, too?"

"No, he doesn't. At least that's something."

"Aha!"

"He says Miss Cheeseman mustn't do anything that might make her look ridiculous in public. He says that's what will happen if she prosecutes you for dropping her through a trap-door in the stage. But that's what made Dad so furious. Dad says you're a crafty old son of a—I won't repeat the word, but he says you planned your vengeance that way." Again Virginia hesitated, almost wailing. "Won't you back me up, Sir Henry? I'm rather worried about Dad. That awful woman!"

"Elaine Cheeseman?"

"Yes."

H.M. held the phone away from him and studied it before bellowing into the mouthpiece again.

"What's the matter with you, my dolly? Ain't you an up-to-date daughter?"

"I hope so, yes."

"Don't you want your Dad to be brought up in the right way, and have educational opportunities of that kind?"

"Of course I do!" Virginia replied warmly. "It always pleases me when Dad succeeds in his—in his educational endeavours. But this time it's a little different."

"Why?"

"First of all, I'm not awfully keen on statuesque blondes. More important, I've always known that one day he might become serious. Last night, when he wasn't arguing with Tom or explaining the difference between the Democrats and the Republicans to Mr. Masters, he did nothing but go about muttering, 'O lily maid of Astolat! With love's light wings did I o'erperch these walls.' "

"Cor! That was sort of scramblin' Tennyson and Shakespeare, wasn't it?"

"Yes, but that isn't the important thing. In public, as a rule, Dad always says the true American has no time for poetry. He says that anybody who would even know any poetry, aside from patriotic recitations, ought to be shot. And this dreadful woman . . ."

"Burn me, I can't see what you've got against Elaine Cheeseman!"

Virginia sounded rather awed.

"Sir Henry," she asked, "haven't men got *any* sense of consistency or logic whatever? Do you remember what you called Miss Cheeseman? Or what you did to her?"

"Looky here. It'd do that gal all the good in the world if a tornado like your old man got loose amid the alien corn. And I'm a forgiving Christian soul, my dolly. Curse it all, I told you the real villain at that political meeting was the low-minded chairman, a feller named Professor Hereward Wake. Now stop goin' on about your father and Elaine Cheeseman! What happened to Masters? Let's hear the story!"

"There isn't one. We all 'installed' him in the Oak Room at eleven o'clock . . . "

"Did Masters drink any coffee?"

"No, nothing at all. Nothing, that is, except what the rest of us had, too. Just before he went to the room, Tom poured out a whisky-and-soda for all of us as a nightcap. Mr. Masters had already looked over the Oak Room, when we first arrived at Telford, and oh, he didn't like it a bit!

"He'd look at the door-fastenings, and the window-fastenings, and the fireplace, and the walls. Each time he looked at something, he would breathe more loudly and say, 'Now, now!' Although nobody else had spoken a word. He'd examined the golden cup, too, and he admitted it really was made of gold and jewels.

"Still, when we installed him officially, he locked the cup in the safe, put the key in his trousers pocket, and for about the hundredth time he swore nothing could happen. Tom said, 'Well, don't let the ghost of Sir Byng Rawdon find you've gone to sleep,' and I thought Mr. Masters' blood pressure would kill him. When we went out, we heard him bolting the door."

Over the telephone line, from Telford far away in the dark hour, came an even more frantic breath.

"And poor Tom," added Virginia, "still couldn't sleep."

It could have been proved as the measure of her state of mind that Virginia, who seldom complained or protested about anything, did so now.

"When a man can't sleep," she said, "he won't let anybody else sleep either. If he doesn't go off to dreamland the moment his head hits the pillow, he gets frightfully annoyed and won't stay in bed. Tom got up and began pacing the floor and smoking

cigarettes. Then he said something that really terri-
fied me, because I'd never heard it before . . . "

Her voice trailed away.

"What is it, my dolly?" prompted H.M. "Why are
you hesitatin'?"

"I've got to tell you," gulped Virginia. "Tom said,
'Jinny, a hundred years ago people did say the Braces
were mad. That's no joke.' I hated to hear that,
because he is so nice.

"Then he said, 'But I won't disturb you, you go to
sleep. I'll go down to the library and read.' Wouldn't
disturb me! I ask you! Of course, by that time I
couldn't have slept either.

"In any case, Tom went downstairs in his dressing-
gown. The library is in the south wing, overlooking
the Dutch garden, and not very close to the Oak
Room. Tom turned on only one little light, by an
easy-chair in the library . . . "

"Just a moment, my dolly . What time was this?"

"About one o'clock in the morning, I think. Up to
that time every light in the house had been out,
except the one in the Oak Room where Mr. Masters
was keeping watch."

"Uh-huh. Did your husband look in on Masters?"

"No. He never dreamed of doing that. Tom picked
up a book and sat down to read. All of a sudden he
realized it was a detective story, and *it* was about a
locked room. He says he threw the book across the
library, and lit another cigarette. It was—oh, I should
think about three-quarters of an hour ago—we all
heard two crashes."

"Two?"

"Perhaps," decided Virginia, "they weren't quite as

loud as crashes. But they sounded as loud as that. I was wide awake, and I knew what they were: a heavy chair and the table had been upset in the Oak Room. There was also a kind of thump or clatter I couldn't quite identify.

"In two or three more minutes we were all at the door of the Oak Room, and it was still locked. Tom kept hammering on it, and shouting to Mr. Masters inside, but there was no answer. Tom said, 'We've got to break down the door.' Dad said, 'For God's sake what's the sense of that, except they always do it in the stories?' They argued about it for a while. Presently Dad said, 'Hold everything!' He ran outside and looked in through one of the windows."

"And Masters was lyin' on the floor, I s'pose? With a cup-hilted rapier beside him?"

"Yes!"

"Table and chair upset; door of the safe open; gold cup fallen on the floor, too. Hey?"

"Sir Henry, that's it. Dad called to Mr. Masters through the window. Mr. Masters must be very tough. In a few seconds he groaned and stirred; it wasn't long before he came to himself, at least partly. He managed to stagger over and open the door for all of us. When Tom asked him what had happened, and who did it—I mean the bump on the back of his head—we got rather the wrong impression."

"How do you mean?"

"We thought *you* had done it."

"*Hey?*"

"Because," said Virginia, "Mr. Masters kept shaking his fist and saying what he wanted to do to you, all foggily and not in his right mind. You already know his story: that he fell asleep, but there was a footstep or some noise which woke him. As he started to get up, he saw the golden cup on the table in front of him. Something hit him on the back of the head; the chair, the table, and the cup went over with him when he fell. That's all."

"But there was nothin' to whack him on the onion, according to you, except maybe the cup-hilt of that that rapier?"

"That, and the seventeenth-century lute. The lute usually lies on top of the harpsichord. We found it lying on the hearth in front of the fireplace."

"The fireplace?"

"Yes. But nobody could possibly have got down that chimney! And this can't go on. Won't you please, please come over to Telford and show us how it could have been done?"

Her appeal would have melted anyone's heart. H.M., with what very small remnants of hair remained to him sticking up in tufts over his ears, looked slowly round the bedroom as though for inspiration.

Anyone well acquainted with him would have said that the Old Maestro was not absolutely stumped and baffled; that a number of things he had seen, heard, or remembered were taking shape in his mind to form half a pattern. Unfortunately, it was only half a pattern and not a complete one. But it would never do to admit that Sir Henry Merrivale was not altogether master at every time of any situation.

Therefore he drew himself up.

"My dolly, do you know what time it is?"

"I—I'm afraid not. Do you?"

"Never mind what time it is, if you're goin' to be gibberin' accurate as all that. But I've got to have sleep! You know what happened last night? To me, I mean? Lord love a duck, that slave-drivin' music-master of mine kept me up until one o'clock—I'm not jokin', one o'clock!—before he'd let me stop practising."

"I'm sorry if Signor Ravioli is as bad as that."

"Oh, my wench! He's a thousand times worse. I get out of his clutches with every nerve in my body screaming for sleep, and straightaway you wake me up. . . . Now I didn't say I wasn't goin' to help you, did I? Don't talk like that! But I'll be over and see you tomorrow morning. Not so much about the problem, that's easy, I'll be there to give your son another lesson in archery, maybe. In the meantime, my head's spinnin' round from lack of sleep, and I'll die if I don't get it. G'bye."

And H.M., who had never been more wide awake in his life, carefully replaced the phone. Sitting back against the headboard of the bed, folding thick arms under the purple-and-gold striped pyjamas, he gnawed at his under-lip.

Though the inner thought-processes of Sir Henry Merrivale are those of a crafty old devil, his outer emotions may be called simple and even primitive. He himself had been roused before dawn and his sleep ruined. Therefore the obvious and indeed inevitable course was to rouse somebody else and ruin *his* sleep.

As H.M.'s eye strayed again towards the telephone, you might have guessed that under ordinary circumstances his first choice would have been Chief Inspector Masters. However, H.M. craned round so that his gaze encountered the box of a house-telephone fastened to the wall near the head of his bed.

"Haa!" said the owner of Cranleigh Court.

With concentration, groaning as he manoeuvred his corporation, he put his finger on one of the enamelled buttons of the house-phone. He continued to jab at it until a voice, wailing yet in accents of high tragedy, popped out of the small receiver.

"It's-a Luigi Ravioli," cried the voice. "What-a you want?"

"Son, you ought to be ashamed of yourself! There's the worst kind of dirty work goin' on at Telford. Listen!"

H.M. began to tell him the story, but was interrupted halfway through.

"*Corpo di Bacco!*" screamed Signor Ravioli. "You know what time it is? You wake-a me up joost-a to tell me thees?"

"Shut up! Listen!"

Despite the music-master's protests, he paid close attention to H.M.'s recital. The grey of the windows grew slowly lighter. From the barnyard, distantly, a thin but homely and heartening sound strengthened against the hush of dawn.

"Ha!" said Signor Ravioli, with relief. "We be all right now. You hear it?"

"Hear what?"

"Da rooster, she's-a crow. No more spooks; gotta go back. Punch-a clock in da graveyard."

"For the last time, Caruso, will you forget spooks? What kind of romantic story would it be if Sir Byng Rawdon walloped Masters over the turnip with a cup-hilted rapier?"

163

"What else he use, then? Eh?"

"I was just wonderin' what anybody used, son. If you clouted somebody with the cup-hilt of a rapier, holding the sword by the blade, I don't think it'd be heavy enough to knock out a big feller like Masters. What bothers me is this blinking lute. The little gal says the lute is usually kept on top of the piano. But somebody put it on the hearth. Burn me, why? And—I say!"

"It's-a Luigi Ravioli listening!"

"I've read a lot about people playing lutes." H.M. spoke with an air of truculent apology. "But, if I had to define what kind of musical gadget it is, I'm not dead certain I could. Do you blow it, or what?"

Signor Ravioli's voice poured with scorn.

"Blow her? Pah! She's-a strings. A lute, she's-a something like what you call guitar. Use-a her for play 'O Sole Mio?' Yes; all right! Use-a her for bop ignorant flatfoot on bean? No! Bust her to pieces."

H.M. pondered.

"Just between ourselves, son," he confided, "I can't resist this thing. Somebody moved the lute. Why? It wasn't moved the first time our criminal messed with that cup. Y'know, I wonder if there was any other . . ."

"Hey! Sir Henry! You sleeping on-a phone?"

"No. I was just sittin' and thinkin'. Later today, you and I are goin' to Telford for some detective work."

Signor Ravioli cheered up. "I be Dr. Watson, yes?"

"Yes, that's a part of the idea. Only—now follow me, son!—we don't *say* we're there for detective work, in case I get flummoxed. We say we're there,

164

maybe, to give the boy another lesson in archery."

Signor Ravioli became definitely enthusiastic. "Shoot somebody in-a pants, eh?"

"No! No more shootin' anybody in the pants with a bow and arrow! Congressman Harvey wouldn't do a thing like that, and neither must we."

"Okay. *Scusa*."

"In the meantime," continued H.M., fingering his throat and making dangerous experimental noises, "I've got an idea I'm going to be in very good voice today. You just hop into your clothes, son. I'll ring Benson and Mrs. Flaherty, and they'll see to breakfast. We'll go down straightaway and begin practisin' some songs."

"No!"

"I'm not going to hurry you, son! You can have time for a shave and a bath first."

"No! No! No!"

"Furthermore, talkin' about spooks, you promised me thirty new verses for 'He's dead but he won't lie down.' I hope you've got most of 'em ready. And you might see whether you've got the score of that other Gracie Fields' song; the one about the aspidistra. Don't argue, son! G'bye."

It was going to be a fine, warm day.

Pale, clear sunshine had begun to tinge the landscape as Police-constable Frederick John Horsham, seated majestically on his bicycle, proceeded along the main road from the village of Golywog back to his home at Cherriton.

To his niece Annie and her husband, Bert Stevens, there had been born an eight-pound son. All was well.

On his left, now, began to rear up the boundary

165

wall of Cranleigh Court. P.C. Horsham cast a tolerant glance towards it. As he was passing the gates, however, his right foot slipped on the pedal; his bulk wavered, and he almost pitched headlong over the handle-bars into the ditch.

For the voice he heard was not the voice of Sir Henry Merrivale. It was a fine singing-voice, a strong and creamy tenor. Rising beyond the lawn and the oak trees, rising from what appeared to be the back of Cranleigh Court and above the tinkle of a piano, its joyousness soared like a lark to the morning sky.

"'Thees-a ghost what stand-a guard met a cop from
    Scotland Yard,
  Keeping watch on da golden cup;
When da cop has gone and snored,
He's-a sock 'im with his sword!—
  He's a spook but he won't shut up!'"

12

Five feet seven inches tall, severely and neatly if not very becomingly dressed, the fair-haired beauty in the brown hat drew herself up.

"I am Miss Elaine M. Cheeseman," she said to the small, dark-haired, fresh-complexioned maid who opened the front door of Telford Old Hall. "I was here yesterday, if you recall. Will you ask Lord Brace whether he would be kind enough to spare me five minutes' conversation?"

The maid, Polly Williams, regarded her inscrutably.

"Sorry, miss. Mr. Jennings ain't here," replied Polly, and began to close the door.

"One moment. The fact is . . . "

Elaine Cheeseman's expression, trained to habitual severity despite the fulness of her lips and rather wide nostrils, became somewhat uncertain and even embarassed.

"I did not wish to see the butler. Yesterday," explained Elaine, with a slight flicker of a smile, "I—

er—spoke to Lord Brace in a manner which, though it does not in the least alter the facts concerned, may have been hasty and perhaps even rude."

"Yes, miss," said the maid, without interrogation or contradiction.

"I imagine, too, that Lord Brace must be fairly well acquainted with the—er—inhabitants of this district?"

Still Polly Williams regarded her without favour. Doubtless Miss Cheeseman had forgotten it, but she had said a few words to Polly herself. Though the words had been well meant and were entirely sympathetic, they had not been received in the best spirit. Elaine had intimated that the maid was a wage-slave, abused and shockingly held down by Lord Brace. Since it was Polly's dearest secret wish to be abused and shockingly held down by Tom Brace, and Tom had never availed himself of the many opportunities thrown in his way, these words savoured of insult.

So the maid still contemplated this visitor inscrutably.

"Let me make my position clear," continued Elaine, in a higher voice. "Suppose I were desirous of learning the name of someone—a man, let us say—with whom I am unacquainted."

The merest shading of inflection was sufficient to betray her. Polly stared back. Coo, this saucy piece was a human being! Despite herself the maid was interested.

"A man? 'Oo?"

"My dear girl, how can I know?" laughed Elaine. "I spoke only from idle curiosity."

168

"What's 'e like, miss?"

"He is about my height, but carries himself extremely well. He has dark-brown hair, rather—rather extraordinary eyes, and is acquainted with Christopher Marlowe's *Doctor Faustus.*"

"Is he a gentleman?"

Ordinarily, a question like this would have been exactly as though any questioner deliberately placed a chip on his shoulder and dared Elaine Cheeseman to knock it off. But she answered without thinking.

"Oh, yes. I should describe him as an English gentleman of the best type. But please, my good girl! May I speak to Lord Brace?"

"Yer can't speak to him. Lord Brace is having breakfast with his wife and his wife's old man from the States."

"Breakfast?" repeated Elaine.

The warm, soothing sun was directly overhead. A glance at Elaine's utility wrist watch told her that it lacked only twenty minutes to noon. Breakfast at this hour would perhaps have been another subject for a lecture. But to all other things could be added a ceaseless noise which for minutes had been sapping at Elaine's composure.

Bang. Bang. Bang. Bang.

The gracious architectural jumble of Telford Old Hall danced and re-echoed to noises suggesting that half a dozen intoxicated men were whaling away with hammers at a mile of lead pipes. There were only two plumbers, and neither of them was intoxicated. But the firm-minded Elaine faltered and lowered her eyes.

"Come in, miss," said Polly, unexpectedly thawing.

"That's it. In the little room there on yer right."

"Thank you."

"They was all up until nearly morning, miss. Coo, such goings-on last night! A man come here to disturb them this morning—a man from the bank in London, it was—wanted a cup or something, but I sent 'im away with a flea in his ear. Can't promise nothing, miss. Still, I'll find out if Lord Brace can see yer."

Bang. Bang. Bang. Bang.

The gracious architectural jumble of Telford Old Hall danced and re-echoed to noises suggesting that half a dozen intoxicated men were whaling away with hammers at a mile of lead pipes. There were only two plumbers, and neither of them was intoxicated. But the firm-minded Elaine faltered and lowered her eyes.

"Come in, miss," said Polly, unexpectedly thawing. "That's it. In the little room there on yer right."

"Thank you."

"They was all up until nearly morning, miss. Coo, such goings-on last night! A man come here to disturb them this morning—a man from the bank in London, it was—wanted a cup or something, but I sent 'im away with a flea in his ear. Can't promise nothing, miss. Still, I'll find out if Lord Brace can see yer."

Bang. Bang. Bang. Bang.

True, Polly had relented. But she meant to let the lofty-looking, saucy piece cool her heels for a time before she carried the news to her employer. Polly retired somewhere to smoke a cigarette in peace, the absent Jennings being a martinet who would not permit this, and in retiring, Polly passed the door of the dining-room at the rear of the house.

In this dining-room, a noble apartment twinkling with old silver, Congressman William T. Harvey stood at the head of a long refectory table, his forefinger raised in the air as he declaimed.

" . . . and I am saying nothing whatever of a controversial nature. I say merely that this fellow Masters is all right; he's a sensible man. Tonight, Jinny, *I* am going to sit up in the Oak Room."

Virginia and Tom, who had finished breakfast, were lounging back at the table so far as the tall Jacobean chairs permitted.

"Dad," urged Virginia, "do sit down and drink your coffee. Do *you* want to get hit over the head, too?"

"Nonsense, Jinny! Nobody's going to hit me over the head."

"Couldn't agree with you more!" Tom Brace declared fervently. Though he had just passed another sleepless night, his lean face was alight with health and happiness. "You'll walk in your sleep, that's all. Just as I did. And good old Masters. You'll walk in your sleep, and bat yourself over the head with something."

Congressman Harvey raised both fists to heaven.

"Tom, my boy, are you going to start that kidding all over again? Calling the Chief Inspector crazy?"

"I'm not kidding," replied Tom, "and I don't say he's crazy. Not a bit. Only a little abnormal."

"My boy, it's not funny! Where's the Chief Inspector now?"

171

"Still in bed," hastily interposed Virginia, in the desperate hope of keeping peace. "And we mustn't disturb him. Let the poor man sleep."

"Yes, by George!" said Tom. "Got to get our sleep, haven't we? Just so. Then, when he wakes up, we'll ring a doctor in London. I said a doctor, mind; I don't necessarily mean a brain specialist."

"I tell you, my boy, it's not funny!"

Tom's expression changed.

"It never was funny," he said. "Even when I thought I might have done it myself."

But he could not remain serious for more than a second or two at a time, and the glint of devilment returned to his eyes.

"Look, sir, did I ever tell you about an aunt of mine? Lived at Turnham Green. She . . . "

Bang. Bang. Bang. Bang.

"Jesus God!" yelled Congressman Harvey, clamping his hands over his ears. "This place is worse than the House of Representatives. Plumbers all over the place! A butler who's a celebrated crook—not that I believe a word of that, of course . . . "

"Don't you?" asked Tom. "I do. Every word of it, by George! Jennings isn't actually an archaeological student and a damn good butler who loves every tradition in Sussex. Oh, no! He's secretly an uncle of the Chief Inspector. Masters says he's done time in the States; so I suppose, Gramp, he was a client of yours, too."

"No, he wasn't. It's the same old mistake," said Congressman Harvey, addressing himself passionately to a silver sugar-bowl, "that people in this country are

172

always making about America. They don't realize the size of the United States. You say you're from Pennsylvania, and they instantly ask whether you're not acquainted with somebody who lives in . . ."

"Turnham Green," said Tom, "where my aunt used to live. Masters' uncle was born at Colney Hatch."

"The hell with Turnham Green! The hell with Colney Hatch! Will you talk sense for a change?"

Virginia rapped on the table with a knife.

"It doesn't in the least matter in front of me or the vicar or even the servants," she said gently. "But won't you both please try to control your language in front of Tommy? He's just at the impressionable age, and he picks up everything he hears."

"Tommy?" Mr. Harvey brightened, and grew rapt with a look of fond fatuity. "Where is he this morning?"

"He's out playing with the bow and arrows. Polly said she gave him his breakfast at eight o'clock, and—no, Dad! No, honestly!"

"What do you mean, no?"

"I can tell what you're thinking." Virginia was apologetic. "But he isn't going to shoot anybody in the seat of the pants! I promise, and he promised. He came into our room this morning. Tom had to string the bow for him . . ."

"*I'll* show him how to use it," declared Tom, much interested. "Stringing that bow wants a trick of the wrist and a bit of strength. It's not the heaviest, a full sixty-pounder, but it's got a lot of drive. Hang it all, Gramp, don't worry!"

173

"As a matter of fact," retorted Mr. Harvey, "I am not in the least worried. That boy has good manners, and speaks good Eng—American. What more does he need? I think I say, without the slightest taint of prejudice, he is among the finest . . ."

Bang. Bang. Bang. Bang.

The row to which they all listened, however, was not made by plumbers. Down the passage outside the dining-room door came what sounded like the troop of Roundhead cavalry which once had pursued Sir Byng Rawdon. It seemed impossible for such a racket to be produced by one nine-year-old boy, and a small one at that. But such was the case.

The tenth Viscount, in a healthy state of dirt and disorder, burst into the dining-room like a whirlwind. But, catching sight of adults who were always mysterious and inexplicable, he became quiet, casual, innocent.

Carrying a strung bow twice as tall as himself, and with a quiver of six brightly feathered arrows on a strap over the shoulder of his muddy suit, he looked as though he had come there sedately by chance.

Tommy had fair hair like his father, grey eyes like his mother, and was proud of the bow. He found it much better than another present Gramp had bought him: a toy pistol firing a light wooden missile with a rubber suction-cup at the end. Though this could also be used to shoot somebody in the pants, as he had yesterday explained to a stout and sympathetic listener, the rubber suction-cup would not stick on any but a flat surface; besides, it lacked the weight and manliness of a bow. So Tommy threw back his shoul-

174

ders.

The adults, in their turn, all tried to look very detached and grown-up, as they thought they should.

"Good morning, Tommy," they chorused.

"Hullo, Mom. Hullo, Pop. Hullo, Gramp."

"Well, well!" said Mr. Harvey. Beaming, he picked up the coffee-cup whose contents he had not yet tasted. "Sorry I'm a late riser. But your Gramp had to stay up late last night, studying a case about a murder."

The tenth Viscount, though immediately fascinated, let his gaze stray to the table on which—at least, until recently—there had been food. A thoughtful look came over his face. You would have said that he was remembering something.

"And it strikes me," Congressman Harvey went on heartily, "we haven't yet had our question-and-answer game for this morning. We—" Mr. Harvey paused. "What is it, old man? What's on your mind? Speak up! You can tell your old Gramp."

The tenth Viscount could and did. His voice, though small, rang clearly through the room. He said, "Burn me, Gramp, but ain't *I* goin' to get a bite to eat in this ruddy house?"

There was a terrible silence.

It is to be feared that Tom and Virginia, despite all their good intentions, were not the most severe and righteous of parents. Virginia, hastily putting napkin over her mouth to hide her expression, lowered her head. Tom turned around abruptly and looked out of the line of open windows, with roses outside, beyond which lay grass and trees.

Only Grandfather, his coffee-cup at his lips, stood rooted there as though the coffee has been scalding hot instead of lukewarm. But his powerful greenish eyes sought a tactician's approach.

"Tommy," he said suddenly, like one who darts at an advantage before it is too late, "I'm your old Gramp. I wouldn't tell you anything that wasn't true, would I? You know that, don't you?"

"Yes, Gramp."

"That's the boy! That's the way I like to hear you talk. Tommy, what's the greatest nation on the face of the earth?"

"The British Empire, Gramp!"

Virginia lowered her head still further. Tom, without turning round, began to whistle a tuneless tune. But Congressman Harvey, well-schooled in tactics, merely smiled.

"Well, Tommy, that's a matter of opinion," he said tolerantly. "You're quite entitled to your opinion, of course. But I must warn you about a matter of definition. Nowadays, old man, we speak of the Commonwealth of Nations. We never, never speak of the British Empire."

Tom Brace spun round.

"We do, do we? And why shouldn't he call it the British Empire?"

"You let me handle this, my boy!"

"Look," said Tom. "Hate to introduce a serious note. But it was known as the British Empire to the men who made it and fought for it. It was known as the British Empire to that boy's forbears, who loved it and died for it. Some of us will call it the British

176

Empire until the Socialists have finished giving it away. Then we can't call it anything at all."

"Gramp," observed Virginia dreamily, "give the gentleman a cigar."

"You two," yelled Congressman Harvey, "aren't fit parents to bring up any child. What do you want to do? Destroy the boy's sense of democratic principle?"

"No!" said Tom.

"Yes!" said Virginia.

The tenth Viscount, with the foot of the tall bow planted on the floor in a swashbuckling gesture not unreminiscent of his grandfather, listened round-eyed. William T. Harvey, putting his cup on the saucer with a slow, decisive, down-with-the-Republicans clink, squared himself for battle.

"Tommy, you can't have forgotten everything you worked out for yourself, without any help from me. No, of course you can't! Barring religious matters, Tommy, name the greatest man who ever lived!"

"My Pop!" said the tenth Viscount.

Mr. Harvey cast a quick glance at his son-in-law. Tom's open-mouthed astonishment—though Tom did not seem violently ill-pleased—made it clear that he could not have managed this piece of dirty work. Congressman Harvey uttered a false-hearted laugh.

"Yes, Tommy, that's a very good answer. If someone asks you that question, you stick up for your family. Perhaps I should have phrased it differently. Barring religious subjects, the whole broad range of human history lies before you, with its great achievements, its burning aspirations, its lofty flights into the empyrean. Aside from your Dad, Tommy, who was the next greatest man who ever lived?"

The fine young soul of the tenth Viscount shone in his eyes.

"That's easy, Gramp. Uncle Henry Merrivale!"

13

Congressman Harvey addressed the world in general and his senior companions in particular.

"Can you beat that? I'll give you three guesses as to the name of the old ghoul who bribed Tommy to say that, but you can save two of the guesses for future reference. Bribery! Corruption!"

"Bet he didn't, though," muttered Tom, who had been regarding his son narrowly. "Gramp, look at Tommy's face."

The tenth Viscount shied back. In the irrational adult world, such words usually meant trouble. One flick of a glance, however, told Congressman Harvey the truth. However excitable the boy might unfortunately be, there was no guile in him. If the devil had inspired Tommy with the answers to those first two questions in the catechism, the third answer had been strictly his own idea.

"But it's true, Gramp, ain't it?"

"*Isn't* it, Tommy!"

"Isn't it, Gramp, ain't it?" Now the words poured out, while the tenth Viscount danced. "Uncle Henry was the greatest Indian-fighter there ever was. He knew Sitting Bull and Geronimo and Tammany and everybody. Coo, he was super!"

"Dad!" cried Virginia warningly.

"Once, when he was in Sitting Bull's camp with *his* grandson, Sitting Bull was going to burn them both at the stake, unless Uncle Henry proved he was a better bowman than anybody. So he put an apple on his grandson's head—and the grandson wasn't a bit scared, either—and Uncle Henry stood back three times the distance of a cricket-pitch, and shot the apple in two pieces off his grandson's head."

"I'll kill him! I'll kill him! The damn liar thinks he's William Tell!"

"Dad!"

"It's all right, Jinny. Tommy, never you mind. But your Uncle Henry certainly does get round. Didn't he tell you how he sat down with George Washington and discussed the strategy of the Revolutionary War?"

"No, Gramp, he didn't say anything about George Washington. But he knew Robin Hood and Richard the Lionheart and John Chandos and Henry of Navarre. He was named for Henry of Navarre. Once, when he and Henry of Navarre were . . ."

"Tommy," interposed Virginia softly, "Gramp is only making those funny faces to amuse you, and he doesn't really mean to throw the coffee-cup out of the window. You *would* like something to eat, wouldn't you?"

All heroics fell away.

"Golly, Mom, yes! I'm hungry!"

"Very well. You go to the kitchen and tell Polly I said to get you something."

"Do I have to wash my hands and face, Mom?"

"Yes!" said grandpa.

"No!" said Tom. "Do you good. Cut along, old chap."

"There is just one thing, Tommy," stammered Congressman Harvey, and recovered his poise by laughing. "Ha ha ha!" he said, like a ghastly echo of Chief Inspector Masters some twenty-hours ago. "You might leave the bow and arrows with me. No, I'm not taking them from you. Your old Gramp wouldn't do a thing like that, and you know it. But, just in case you wanted to shoot a paleface in the pants—I mean . . . Thank you."

"Lord love a duck, Gramp, you can have 'em while I get some grub."

The tenth Viscount moved sedately to the door. Then a whole Roundhead cavalry-regiment galloped and crashed towards the kitchen.

"Now, then!" said Congressman Harvey, absent-mindedly slinging the quiver of arrows over his left shoulder, and shaking the bow with strong dramatic emphasis in his right hand. "I don't want you to think, either of you, that I am deficient in what you would mistakenly call a sense of humour. All I wish to say to you is . . ."

Bang. Bang. Bang. Bang.

"Target for Tonight," said Mr. Harvey, gibbering. "When the all-clear has blown, I shall still endeavour to drive home a few essential truths. I say nothing of the pernicious and deadly influence of all this. How can I teach the boy anything if you two won't set a better example? Still, I waive that. But—*lying!* Deliberate, outrageous, bare-faced lying by that old

181

ghoul, designed to corrupt a fine young American citizen and enmesh his sympathies in the outworn principles of monarchy . . ."

Virginia jumped to her feet.

"When I was a child, Dad, I suppose you never told me any whoppers?"

"I most certainly did not."

"Dad, are you sure? Especially when you'd had a few dr—when you were in a story-telling mood?"

"I told you stories, yes. But I was always careful to inform you that they were made up."

"Oh, Dad! For years you told a series of continued stories about the same group of people. And if in your heart you're really so terribly set against monarchies, why is it that in the stories you were always the king of the country?"

"Virginia! I wasn't!"

"Maybe you honestly believe that. You just don't remember, and I do. The stories had English or French backgrounds, but mostly English. Of course, I didn't think of them as being that. No child does. Just as a child thinks everything is happening in the present. I always imagined it all went on in our home town, or at least somewhere I could find if I walked a little way. You were the king, and you lived at a place called Frothingham Castle. Tom! Haven't I *often* told you about it?"

"You have, angel-face," assented Tom, with a vigorous nod and a look of faraway excitement. "Reminds me of the stories *I* used to hear."

"For years," said Virginia, "Frothingham Castle was so real that even now I can't see a gazetteer without half wanting to look it up. The characters in the stories, going in and out of the castle all the time, were Athos, Cleopatra, Cyrano de Begerac, Sherlock Holmes, and William Jennings Bryan. I rather got the idea, though you never said so, that they all wanted to marry Cleopatra. They were all great heroes, every one of them, but Athos and Sherlock Holmes were the only ones who stood a chance."

Then Virginia, after the strain of the past week, herself went off the deep end.

"And you don't know anything about England, do you?" she cried.

"I trust, Virginia, that I keep myself reasonably well informed of current events."

"Current events!" Nothing could have exceeded the small girl's withering contempt. "Your passion was the English Civil War. Have you forgotten how they wouldn't sell you that beautifully bound copy of somebody's eye-witness account of the battle of Marston Moor, wouldn't sell it at any price, so you pinched it out of the British Museum?"

"Virginia! You're going too far!"

"You did! You did! You could never show it to anybody except in secret, but all you wanted was to gloat over it. And Mr. Ellerby said it wasn't possible to steal a book out of the British Museum, and bet you that you couldn't do it. So you devised a horribly elaborate Arséne Lupin plot, and you . . ."

"For the love of Mike," exclaimed her father, genuinely dumbfounded, "are you trying to say I wanted to steal the Cavalier's Cup?"

Dead silence.

It was as though an evil force had struck through into the warm dining-room. Also, through Telford,

183

there now reigned an unearthly silence because the plumbers had stopped work on the shaved second of noon.

"Steal the Cavalier's Cup?" repeated Virginia.

But she looked at her father, and she knew this wouldn't do. So Virginia, after that fashion which is always mysterious to males, reacted as women will.

"Maybe I shouldn't have said that." Suddenly tears welled into her limpid eyes. "Maybe, as everyone is always telling me, I'm not f-fit to be a w-wife and m-mother. I expect I'm not."

Her father and her husband looked at her aghast.

"Here, old girl!" Tom protested in consternation. "Stop it! What's the matter? Why the water-works?"

Virginia shook her head so violently that the brown hair flew and swung.

"Go away!" she said with passion. "Both of you can go completely mad, but *I* never must. Drink some more coffee! I hope it chokes you!"

And, before either of them could utter a word, she ran out of the room. The door slammed after her. Tom, on his feet, stared at the door's uncompromising blankness.

"Well?" enquired Congressman Harvey, with sinister calmness. "I hope you're satisfied with what you've done?"

"What *I've* done?"

"Certainly. Filling my daughter's head with a lot of tomfoolery about Cavalier legends and swords!"

"Now what's the matter with swords?" demanded a three-time international fencing champion.

"Swords!" derisively flung back Congressman Harvey, settling the quiver of arrows more firmly on his shoulder and brandishing the bow. "Just tell me, if you can, how anybody can make use of a sword nowadays?"

"I use swords as they ought to be used, by God! I don't grab 'em by the blade and crack a Scotland Yard man over the head with the hilt."

"Are you saying I did?"

"I'm not saying anything, thanks. I only . . ."

"Quite frankly," said Congressman Harvey, "I'd like to get you on the witness-stand. In any important criminal case, such as crowning a Chief Inspector from Scotland Yard, we must always ask ourselves the question: *cui bono?* Who did stand to profit by this vicious and antisocial act? Well, my boy, you did. It proves, or seems to prove, you didn't walk in your sleep on Wednesday night."

"Look! Do you intimate that *I* . . ."

"Like yourself, I intimate nothing. The guilty flee when no man pursueth. But, having brought up Virginia to be a fine American girl, I won't have her principles undermined by sympathy with the Royalist side in anything whatever."

Tom dug his fists into the pockets of his ancient sports-coat. His tie was partly skewered under the collar of a frayed blue shirt. He strode towards the windows facing west, and whipped round again.

"Look, Gramp. Forget nursery rhymes or jingles or matters of that sort. Forgetting 'em, what were the first verses you ever taught Jinny to recite?"

"Verses?"

"Yes. Don't say you never heard of verses. What were they?"

" 'By the rude bridge that arched the flood . . .' "

185

"Won't do! Maintain that, and I'll bring in what you'd call the key-witness. No! I'll give you the first part, and I challenge you to give the chorus. Come on, Gramp!"

Then out rolled Tom's voice.

"Kentish Sir Byng stood for his King,
Bidding the crop-headed Parliament swing!—"

It was as though Telford Old Hall stirred in its dreams, stirred with joy at its heart, and half roused to listen.

"And, pressing a troop unable to stoop,
And see the rogues flourish and honest folk droop,
Marched them along, fifty score strong . . ."

One more line rolled out, but Congressman Harvey could stand it no longer.

"Stop that!" he ordered. "In my presence, young man, you'll not attack those stern and republican virtues which everywhere stood guard against monarchial tyranny. But, if you must recite that twaddle, at least recite it properly. Hit the right syllables, and hit them hard!"

And William T. Harvey could not restrain himself. He not only loved the lines; he lived them. His fine voice smote the chorus with a fervency and power which seemed to draw from the old house its smile of ghostly applause.

"God for King Charles! Pym and his carles

To the devil that prompts 'em their treasonous
parles!
Cavaliers, up! Lips from the cup!
Foot to the stirrup, nor bite take nor sup . . ."

Abruptly Mr. Harvey stopped in midflight.

His gaze had been resting on the dining-room door.
Now comprehension flickered in his eyes. The dining-
room door stood open. In the aperture, her hand on
the latch, was Miss Elaine Cheeseman.

In theatrical parlance, Mr. Harvey dried. He stood
frozen, the quiver of arrows over his shoulder and the
good long-bow held high. Elaine Cheeseman, her lips
half-parted, her golden hair aglow under what Virginia would have called an unfortunate hat, gave a
gasp and likewise remained frozen.

The Oak Room, which also faced west, was not far
away. If this were fancy and not fact, if it were done
on the stage or in the equally noble form of a radio
play—disregarding such dreary media as films or
television—there would have drifted to their ears the
throaty tinkle of a harpsichord playing "Here's a
Health unto His Majesty."

True, the cup-clinking beauty of "Here's a Health
unto His Majesty," as Mr. Harvey could have but
wouldn't have told you, is associated with King Charles the First only in popular tradition. Research
cannot trace the song back beyond the year 1670, ten
years following the restoration of Charles the Second.
But it would have suited such a romantic moment of
meeting: aching and dreamy, amid the scent of old-
world roses.

Unfortunately, nothing like this happened.

Elaine, after that gasp, instantly pretended she hadn't seen him and ignored him to stare at Tom Brace. Congressman Harvey, doing the same thing, looked with gloomy Byronic grandeur at the coffee-urn.

"I—I must ask your pardon, Lord Brace," said Elaine, her voice going through several levels but with her chin uptilted. "However! Your maid, having admitted me, left me for more than twenty minutes in a kind of anteroom and seems to have disappeared. My time is of value, Lord Brace. I—I ventured here, and heard someone shouting."

"Er—yes," replied Tom. "Come in!" he added. "Have some breakfast!"

Tom was trying to recover from the shock. Seeing Miss Cheeseman there, after the row yesterday, was as though all the fabulous inhabitants of Frothingham Castle had marched in and surrounded him.

"Breakfast?" said Elaine.

Raising her delicate arched eyebrows, dark against the creamy skin and contrasting with the fair hair, Elaine glanced not too pointedly at her wrist watch.

"No, thank you." She spoke crisply. "I came here, Lord Brace, to—I came here, Lord Brace, to . . ." she repeated, and stopped.

"Jennings!" said Tom.

The image of the absent Jennings, tall and thin, with his scholar's forehead and long if somewhat tricky nose under polished dark hair, haunted Telford far more palpably than did Sir Byng Rawdon.

"No hard feelings," said Tom, with a glint of joy. "But Jennings can't do you any good. Yes, that's straight! The police think he's a crook. If you hoick him out to testify against H.M., and say H.M. bribed anybody to unloose trap-doors, they'll stick him in prison faster than you want to stick H.M. there."

Elaine's countenance became pink.

"Lord Brace, if you *please!*" Tall for a woman, but supple and soft of body, she tightened her fingers round a severe black handbag, and fought for breath. "I had almost decided, against the prompting of my better judgment, not to press any charges for— for . . ."

"Damn!" said Tom, interrupting her by snapping his fingers. "Forgetting myself. I must present somebody to you. Gramp, Virginia told you a few things about this lady. Mr. Harvey, my father-in-law; Miss Elaine Cheeseman."

"Father-in-law?" cried Miss Cheeseman.

"I'm not married!" said Mr. Harvey to the coffee-urn.

"Really." Elaine spoke flatly. "In any case, I have a taxi waiting outside, and taxis cost money. It is Saturday, and my duty lies in London. In a short time I must call at the railway station in Great Yewborough to meet my *fiancé*, Professor Hereward Wake."

"*What's that?*" exclaimed Congressman Harvey.

"Really, sir. I . . ."

"You're not engaged to be married!"

"And why not?"

Mr. Harvey, very much conscious of her presence, began to stalk towards her. He did this with such intensity of jaw and gleam of eye, sweeping opposition before him, that Elaine backed and bumped against the open door in distinct if strangely pleasurable alarm.

"You're not engaged to be married! You can't be engaged to be married!"

"That isn't exactly complimentary to me, is it?"

"On the contrary, madam! Under the spell of her beauty, did any man ever stop to think whether Helen of Troy was married? Could he stop to think? Dared he stop to think, when the armèd might of Greece was drawn across the wine-dark sea?"

"Oh. Well, you didn't explain. You said . . ."

"Bah! You can't be engaged to be married? To this fellow Charles Kingsley?"

"Hereward Wake!"

" 'For a laggard in love and a dastard in war was to wed the fair Ellen of Young Lochinvar!' "

Elaine began to tremble.

"How dare you! Professor Wake has a perfectly splendid war record," she retorted quite truthfully. Then she said, perhaps not quite so truthfully, "Nobody except a beastly, unpatriotic Tory or an even more beastly, unpatriotic moderate-Labourite could call him—what did you call him?"

"Madam, your assumption is entirely erroneous! I didn't call the son of a—I didn't call him a—I called him a dastard!"

"Sir, I beg of you to keep your distance."

"Madam, I haven't touched you!"

"No, but you might. In addition to which, I am not absolutely certain I have ever learned the precise definition of the word dastard."

A wicked smile touched Mr. Harvey's lips and eyes, causing Elaine to press further back against the door.

"You have never learned the precise definition of

190

the word dastard? Then I suggest, madam," said Congressman Harvey, with a swashbuckling gesture of the bow towards his pop-eyed son-in-law, "that this dining-room is far too crowded."

"Ee!" said Elaine. The stately woman was at a loss.

"Not very far from here, madam, in a shady nook overlooking a Dutch garden, there is a library. In that library we shall find a dictionary. Let us go there, madam; let us open the dictionary, investigating it carefully, and find the precise definition of that for which we are both searching. Will you accompany me?"

"Certainly not! I have never heard of anything so utterly ridiculous! Besides, I—I have a taxi waiting."

"Madam, to hell with the taxi."

"You *dare* say that? When in this country we have so many social injustices and oppressions crying aloud to be set right?"

"In that respect, madam, I am with you four ways from the ace. I may say that the greatest of all men's dreams, the political glory in which I have the honour to share a humble part, in short, the Democratic Party of the United States of America . . ."

"But you're not an American, are you? You don't talk a bit like the people in films!"

Congressman Harvey shut his eyes and stamped on the floor, but recovered himself.

"I can only repeat, Elaine, that I agree with your remarks about a proper and more equalized distribution of money. To hell with the money! Shall I go out and buy the taxi to get rid of it?"

"No! No! I believe you would!"

"Then will you accompany me to the library?"

"Certainly not. I should never dream of it. It wouldn't take a long time, would it?"

"Aha! Properly to study a dictionary, considering each column and exploring every avenue, is in fact apt to take quite a long time; but it can lead, I assure you, to the most agreeable and improving results. Will you accompany me?"

"All right."

The door closed after them.

For some time after they had gone, Tom Brace stood motionless by the table, an awed look on his face, still staring at the door.

The sunshine was beginning to pour in at the leaded windows, making a blaze amid polished silver, and reflecting in the polished old wall-panels as in a small gloomy mirror. Tom took a handkerchief out of his pocket, mopped his forehead, and replaced the handkerchief.

Over the massive sideboard hung a portrait: a good, late seventeenth-century reproduction of that fine portrait of King Charles the Second which you will see in the National Portrait Gallery.

The so-called Merry Monarch, who actually had so little to make him merry, sits looking partly sideways with that expression, half-quizzical, all razorish intelligence, which shows how clearly he saw that the world has little to give us; but that there are at least two sources of consolation, and only one of these comes out of a bottle.

Tom looked up at the portrait of Charles the Second and back at the closed door. He shook his head. For a minute or two, which can be a very long time if you measure it, he stood reflecting. To any observer it would have been clear that his own difficulties and perplexities were crowding back on him.

"Jennings!" Tom said aloud to the portrait. "Where in blazes is Jennings? The whole house is upset without a butler! We haven't got a but . . ."

Once more, softly, the door opened, and Tom heard a discreet cough which he had heard the night before.

It was not Jennings. Nevertheless, there in the doorway with his white hair like threads of spun glass, as though he had been at Telford all his life, was Benson from Cranleigh Court.

"Sir Henry Merrivale," he announced, "and Signor Luigi Ravioli!"

14

H.M., in his white alpaca suit, concluded a brief but thrilling account of how he won the Grand Prix motor-car race in 1903.

". . . even now, y'see, I can't drive a car without busting something. In the way of records, that's to say."

"Yes. See what you mean," agreed Tom, the muscles tightening down his jaws to keep his face rigid. "You'd agree with that, Signor Ravioli?"

In one hand the music-master, impressive with his mass of hair and Chianti-ripened nose, clutched a sinister-looking black slouch hat which he refused to surrender. In his other hand he carried a leather cylinder, with a handle, which contained rolled music-sheets. Signor Ravioli nodded emphatically.

"Sure theeng! Bust-a da stern off Horsham, da cop. Drive with-a da handbrake on; can't-a understand why car-a jump like pogo-stick and burn-a out brake lining. Bring-a Benson to drive-a car."

H.M. pointed a malevolent finger.

"But that ain't all, son! Don't run away with any notion I came here about a criminal case!"

"No?" said Tom, looking worried.

"No!" said H.M., piling up reason after reason so that nobody would suspect his intent. "You haven't got a butler, have you? And I've got more of a butler than I need. So, until you snaffle Jennings or maybe the police snaffle him first, I thought Benson might be able to help."

Benson, in the background, moved uneasily. This proposition that he should serve as deputy butler in someone else's house more than embarrassed him; it really shocked him. Tom's quick eye saw this.

"Very grateful to you, H.M. Appreciate your thoughtfulness. But, after this morning, I don't think we need trouble Benson."

H.M. boiled and simmered with a grievance.

"The real reason for comin' here," he burst out, "was to give that son of yours a lesson in archery. But lord love a duck! Bill Harvey's got the bow and arrows, and he's frozen to 'em. When we saw him luring the Cheeseman wench into the library, whistlin' to her like a spider to a fly . . ."

Signor Ravioli touched his bunched fingers to his mouth, smacked his lips resoundingly, and wafted a kiss to heaven.

"We feex, eh?" he said in ecstasy.

"You met Miss Cheeseman?"

This question did not come from Tom Brace. It was asked by Virginia. Her tears dried, a strange expression on her face, Virginia entered with her graceful swift step, peeped like a small girl into the passage, and then softly closed the door.

"You and Miss Cheeseman, the most horribly deadly enemies," she cried, "met at our house? Wasn't it embarrassing? What did you say to each other?"

"Ha ha," said Signor Ravioli.

"I'm not the gal's enemy, burn it!" thundered H.M. "We may have our little differences, that's all. And, anyway, we didn't meet her. I doubt whether she'd have seen me if I'd been standing smack in her path. She was looking at your old man, and they were waftin' on golden clouds of something-or-other into the haven of the library."

"Oh, *dear!*" said Virginia. "Again! All Dad's talk to her in this very room, about Young Lochinvar and Charles Kingsley . . ."

"Look, my pet," interposed Tom, "how do you know what Gramp said in this room?"

"I listened outside the door, of course." Virginia opened her eyes with a woman's simplicity and directness. "It wasn't anything new."

"But, Jinny, I don't understand! The Elaine Cheeseman who called here was a very different woman from the Elaine Cheeseman I flung out of the house yesterday!"

"*I* understand it, darling," Virginia assured him. She hesitated. "There's one strange thing. I can't imagine just what I expected when I saw her. Sir Henry said she was attractive, of course. But, if you'll excuse my saying so, men usually have the most awfully peculiar ideas of what constitutes attractiveness in a woman. And . . ."

"And?" prompted Tom, as his wife bit at her under-lip.

"Well! She isn't bad at all. Except for one thing, she would meet with anyone's approval. Though I hate to put it quite so crudely, Dad did seem to be getting to first base."

"First-a base?" exclaimed Signor Ravioli in horror. "You want-a to insult-a your Pop? He's-a tear around-a bases going straight-a for home plate!"

Virginia did not stop to correct this vulgarism.

"Yes, that's what I mean." She seemed worried. "We shouldn't want . . ."

Looking round, Virginia saw an uneasy Benson now trapped by the closed door. Though Benson was seldom out of his element, his present position made him feel so. But Virginia correctly read in him the flawless symbol of respectability.

"Benson."

"Yes, my lady?"

"I'm not certain exactly how to express this, and I shouldn't want to convey a wrong impression of what is perfectly all right. But could you—could you . . ."

"Looky here!" bellowed Sir Henry Merrivale, a big hand sweeping through these cobwebs of diplomatic finesse. "What the little gal means, Benson, is this. You nip along to the library, hang about outside, and ring the firebell if Congressman Harvey begins chasin' that wench all over the furniture."

"Very good, sir."

"Why the devil do you want to spoil everything?"

197

demanded Tom, really annoyed. "This is my house, and I have some say about what goes on here. Besides, he won't have to chase her; he'll get no resistance at all. And you, Jinny! You, of all people!"

Virginia's fair complexion, which showed colour more easily then Elaine's, became pink, and she stamped her foot. There is a difference between what we may enjoy ourselves and what we think should be done by members of another generation.

"Tom, I don't mind!" she retorted truthfully. "But at a few minutes past noon!" she added. "And in this house, where everything is so unromantic! How many times must I tell you I don't really object to the woman? She wouldn't be bad at all, if only someone would do something about her clothes!"

"That's-a all right," Signor Ravioli soothed her. "Your-a Pop take'em off."

"Tom!"

"No, angel-face, I'm hanged if I interfere! Benson!"

"Yes, my lord?"

"Go along to the library, if you like, but remain outside the door. Whatever happens, inside the library or out of it, you are not to interfere."

"Under no circumstances, my lord?"

"Under no circumstances."

"Very good, my lord."

Benson, his poise restored by this happy turn of events and himself almost reconciled to his present role, departed in a shimmer of benevolence. Virginia, resigning herself, nevertheless fired one last shot.

"Tom, you don't understand Miss Cheeseman. Neither does Sir Henry; neither does Signor Ravioli. When I saw the lady, she wasn't just as Sir Henry describes her; she looked as though she didn't know whether to yield without a struggle, or to burst out laughing in Dad's face."

"Well? What about it?"

"That's the insidious subtlety of Dad's approach. Some women simply can't resist a technique which makes them swoon and makes them laugh at the same time."

"I may be dense, gobbler, but I don't see . . ."

"Darling! Professor Hereward Wake," said Virginia, "must have arrived at Great Yewborough by this time. I've heard of her *fiancé*. He's the sternest and most exalted kind of Aneurin Bevan follower. Suppose he traces her here by that taxi, and turns up when . . ."

"Anyway!" Virginia interrupted herself. "We have too much on our minds to be concerned about Dad and this Labour woman. It's wonderful to have Tom cleared; that's the main thing. But Mr. Masters *is* lying asleep upstairs with a fearful bump on his head, and we *are* still faced with a perfectly maddening mystery."

"I say, my dolly." H.M., glowering, hesitated to approach such trival matters as a mystery. "You had the Cavalier's Cup sent back to the bank this morning?"

"No, we didn't. Nobody was up. Polly—that's one of the maids—didn't understand. When the messenger from the bank arrived, she became all hoity-toity

199

and kicked him out of the house. Now Dad swears he's going to spend tonight in the Oak Room."

"Oh, my eye!" breathed H.M.

"Let's face it," said Virginia.

Despite herself, since she had no longer to worry about Tom, Virginia in all her troubles could not refrain from a partial smile. Yet the small girl spoke with concise good sense.

"Let's face it. The thing does have an element of—well, of what some people would call the ridiculous. But does that make the problem any less difficult? If somebody had been murdered or seriously hurt, as Sir Henry asked me, we should be chewing our fingernails and trembling at shadows. Even though that hasn't happened, does it help us?

"Put it in terms of the not-too-serious, if you like. Who got into that locked room? And how was it done? And why should the cup have been moved again? We're up against the essential detective problems of who, how, and why. Simply because there was no murder or near-murder, does that make the mystery one bit less baffling?"

"*Corpo di Bacco!*" muttered Signor Ravioli, firmly clutching his sinister black-felt hat in one hand while he juggled the music-roll with the other. "That's-a right. She's-a got what Congressman Harvey call a point."

H.M. glowered and said nothing.

"And what about the other things, which didn't occur on the night Tom spent in the Oak Room?" asked Virginia. "They might have been done simply for hocus-pocus, yet somehow I can't believe it. Why

200

should the lute have been taken from the harpsichord and put down on the hearth? Why should there be a long scratch on the inside of a bolted door?"

"What's that?" demanded Sir Henry Merrivale.

He spoke in such a sharp, suddenly alert tone, his little eyes fixed, that the nerves of all the others jumped in response.

"A scratch on the inside of the door?" said H.M. "When you spoke on the phone, you didn't say a word about that."

"No, I never thought of it. Is it important?"

"Oh, my dolly! It is important!"

"But how?" asked Tom, looking from his wife back to H.M. "It's only a scratch about seven inches long; looks as thought it might have been made with the flange of the key which opens the safe. Curse it, listen! That scratch is across the middle of the door. It isn't anywhere near the two bolts, or even near the lock. It couldn't possibly have been the result, in any wild way you can imagine, of tampering with a securely fastened door."

"H'mph," grunted H.M. He stared into space. "If I happened to be interested in mysteries, though—*if* I happened to be interested, which I ain't—it might call for a bit of a detective conference."

"Ha!" said Signor Ravioli, and burst into dramatic behaviour.

Stalking away for some ten paces towards the other end of the table, Signor Ravioli stood with his back turned. Deliberately he fitted on the black hat, giving a twist to its wide soft brim as he pulled it down. The effect, as he suddenly swung round to confront them, was sinister to the verge of unnerving.

"What's the idea of the tile?" yelled H.M. "Lord love a duck, haven't you got any better manners than to stick on your hat in the house?"

"I'm-a Dr. Watson," said Signor Ravioli, leering and smiting himself on the chest.

"I'm-a Dr. Watson!" he repeated with passion, though in fact he bore a closer resemblance to one of the less reliable Sicilian banditti. "Where's-a your soul? Now you amaze me!"

"Hey?"

"Amaze me! Get-a magnifying glass! You got-a magnifying glass?"

Despite himself H.M. was struck with this.

"No, but I expect I could get one."

"Okay. Look at da floor!" Suddenly Signor Ravioli dropped like a man shot, began tensely to examine the handsomely carved leg of the Jacobean table with the music-roll doing service as a lens, and bounced to his feet again. "You say, 'Ha! Thees-a crime,' you say, 'She's-a commit by a left-handed ghost.' I say, *'Corpo di Bacco!* How you know?' Then you tell me, and I am amazing! You know what I mean?"

"Absolutely!" said Tom, restraining with violent effort some expression which passed over his face. "I understand what the signore means, H.M. And it's time you lived up to your great reputation. Look, you're at Telford now, and it's only a few steps to the Oak Room."

"No! Fry me to blazes if I do it!"

Virginia stretched out her hands. "Sir Henry! Please!"

Wrath, doubt, indecision, all struggled behind the façade of H.M.'s unspeakable countenance.

"I'm an artist, son; I've got an artist's temperament. Didn't you know, for instance, that last autumn I took up painting? Well, I did!" He glared at Virginia. "You were in the Grey Study at Cranleigh, my dolly. You must have seen some of my paintings on the wall there."

"I—I seem to remember some pictures hanging on the wall," repeated Virginia, thinking back. "They were pictures of girls; or, rather, of the same girl. Nudes. Forgive me, but what has that to do . . . ?"

" 'Cause I'm an artist! In every way! I can't be bothered with criminal cases. But there *is* one question," said H.M., with almost bursting dignity, "you could answer me here and now, without beatin' about the bush and dodging away from a plain issue. Is there a piano in this house? Preferably a grand piano?"

Tom stared at him.

"You know damn well there isn't, H.M. Last night, in private, you took me aside and asked me that. I said we weren't a musical family, and the only thing even like a piano is the harpischord in the Oak . . ."

Here Tom paused. He repeated, "In the Oak . . ." and stopped again. Even his ears, in intense awareness and aliveness, seemed to rise towards the line of his closely cropped fair hair. After a look at the leather roll of music-sheets carefully carried by Signor Ravioli, Tom exchanged significant glances with Virginia.

It was Virginia, metaphorically speaking, who rushed forward.

"Sir Henry! We know perfectly well how long and hard you must practise. Next week you're going to entertain the Tuesday Evening Ladies' Church Society by singing 'Barnacle Bill the Sailor,' and we shouldn't *think* of spoiling it. Do please forget the Cavalier's Cup and the locked room. But—would you and Signor Ravioli care to go to the Oak Room so that you could practise?"

"Well—now."

"Then it's settled," said Virginia. She had begun to draw a breath of relief when a fresh possibility struck her. "But you'll remember, won't you, that Mr. Masters is asleep upstairs?"

"Now what do you think of that? Yes, burn me! Masters *is* asleep upstairs!"

"So you won't sing too loudly, will you?"

"Oh, my dolly! That crawlin' snake, who oughtn't to be disturbed under any circumstances, is dead to the world in perfect peace and serenity . . ."

It was at this juncture that H.M., though he is even more immune to shocks than Congressman Harvey, could not help breaking off.

At Telford Old Hall, small and narrow passages wind in a maze past its many rooms, large or otherwise, to a spacious main hall at the front. But the distance from front to back is not very great in a straight line.

Thus none of the four persons in the dining-room could see Chief Inspector Masters, freshly shaven, neatly clad again, his skull having almost ceased to open and shut with pain, standing at the top of a lofty oak staircase leading from the floor above to the main hall below.

They could not know that Masters, amid a vast clutter of objects left at the top of the stairs by Messrs. Bert Stevens and Alfred Grosvenor, plumbers of Great Yewborough, had raised his foot to descend when there came to him the inspiration which put him ahead of Sir Henry Merrivale.

But all those in the dining-room heard, clearly if from a little distance away, the shout of Masters' voice.

"Gawdlummycharley, *I've got it!* My wife's brother's got a radio repair shop; I know how it was done!"

Two other voices, equally wild but more hoarse, struck at him like cannon shots.

" 'Ere! Guv'nor! Mind yer eye!"

"Mind the tools!"

"Mind the soldering-lamp! Mind the . . ."

"Gord!"

The last exclamation went nearly unheard. It was drowned in a series of crashes, such an avalanche of clatter-bang-crashes as even Telford had not known in its long history. It would have been impossible to decide how many objects, mostly metal but one of them a human body, flew from one staircase-tread to another before clattering with one blended uproar all over the floor.

Presently the ripples of disharmony shivered away. One of the hoarse voices spoke quietly, even casually.

" 'Ave a fag, Bert?"

"You and yer ruddy fags! Look at the poor bloke, Alf!"

"Serve 'im right for kicking me petrol soldering-lamp. That lamp's busted, shouldn't be surprised. 'E'll pay for it, too! 'Oo is 'e?"

"Dunno, Alf. But . . ."

"Garn! Full of 'umankindness, you are, 'cos you've got a new baby at your 'ouse. I ain't! I'm a free British workman! Wot's the matter with 'im? Why don't 'e get up?"

" 'E can't get up! Landed on 'is onion, the poor bleeder did. 'E's knocked cold."

15

"Tell me, Doctor . . ."

"Yes, Lord Brace?"

"To be quite frank, Dr. Ashdown, that's the second knock on the head Mr. Masters has had since last night."

"You don't surprise me. Does he walk in his sleep, by any chance?"

" 'Fraid he does, Dr. Ashdown. But are you sure it's not serious?"

"As I told you when I was here earlier this afternoon, Lord Brace, I didn't think there was concussion. Now, after my second examination, I'm positive. I've given him a sedative. Let him go on sleeping upstairs; give him a light meal late tonight—he won't talk much, but never mind that—and tomorrow morning he'll be as right as rain."

The westering sun, fiery liquid gold low behind a dark screen of oaks and beeches and elms in the park, painted to mellow colours the interior of the dining-room where Tom and Virginia Brace—alone except for the lean, elderly, thoughtful-looking Dr. Ashdown, his medicine-case in hand—sat by the refectory table at their tea.

It was after the turn of half-past four, getting on towards five.

"That's very good news, Dr. Ashdown!" said Virginia, her words ending almost on a sob. "You're sure you won't change your mind and have a cup of tea?"

"No thanks, Lady Brace. I shall have to get back for evening surgery."

"Well, it *is* good news; you can't think how good. Especially with the plumbers gone, and everything quieter now."

"*Whree!*" screamed a voice. It was young, only nine years old, yet it had the high and penetrating power of a note from a penny whistle. "*Whree! Whree! Whree!*"

On the lawn outside the windows, which were built only waist-high above it, a small figure whirled past in silhouette against the black-entangled sunset. Though its legs were tiny, they made the turf shake. The figure, describing several eccentric circles, whisked away and disappeared behind a clump of bushes.

Virginia's slender hand was shaking as she put down her teacup.

"That's our son, Dr. Ashdown," she smiled. "At the moment he's being a flying squad car from Scotland Yard, and that noise is the siren, but he's been awfully good all afternoon."

"Very good," agreed Tom, pulling at his under-lip.

"You see," Virginia hastened on, "a friend of ours

has been in the Oak Room. He's been practising singing for about four hours. I'm not sure whether you heard any . . . ?"

"Ah!" said Dr. Ashdown, and seemed to meditate with his teeth almost at the edge of his bowler hat. "Singing, was it? But I'm new to this district, Lady Brace."

"Devilish good singing, if you ask me," said Tom, instantly on the defensive and speaking warmly. "Tommy sat in the Oak Room and listened to it spellbound. He'd be there yet, except that you can't keep a kid's attention on anything for too long. Besides, our friend wasn't singing all the time."

"Tom. I feel certain Dr. Ashdown isn't interested in *everything*."

"Half the time," Tom pointed out doggedly, disregarding the signal, "our friend was detecting. You could always tell when both of 'em were detecting. Signor Ravioli would put on his bandit's hat to show he was Dr. Watson. When they'd finished yelling at each other and resumed the singing lesson, he'd take it off again."

"Tom. Please! If you do feel you must be going, Dr. Ashdown?"

"And don't tell me," said Tom, his voice growing louder on a wire of nerves, "that row with the plumbers was all my fault. It didn't begin today. It began as far back as the first of the week, didn't it?"

"More tea, darling? And you haven't had a single cake. Have a cake?"

"Confound it, Jinny, it's no music-hall joke about plumbers leaving their equipment behind and having to go back for it. If they'd had any other job of work on hand except this one, very well! I shouldn't have insisted they kept all the tools here when they stopped work for the day; but I did, and it was worth the unholy schemozzle it caused. It's no good making faces at me, old girl. They've finished for good now; and as you say, it's much quieter."

"Whree! Whree! Whree!" The banshee howl shrieked past the windows and again faded into the distance.

"Then good day, Lady Brace; and good day to you, Lord Brace," said Dr. Ashdown, looking as though he might have commented but tactfully refrained. Turning towards the door, he swung back again. "Er—I noticed the very fine garden at the south side of the house. May I ask what room overlooks the garden?"

This time Virginia all but dropped and smashed the large but delicate eggshell tea-cup.

"That's the library. My father is still in there with—that is, he's looking something up in a dictionary. Why, Doctor?"

"Nothing at all. But while I was attending to the patient upstairs, I thought I heard a shout—a cry, or something of the sort—from that direction, at least. But there were other noises, and I could not be sure."

"A cry? From the library? In a woman's voice?"

"Take it easy, old girl!"

"A woman's voice? Great Scott, no! No, Lady Brace, I should say it was undoubtedly a man's. However, I was probably mistaken."

The edge of a wintry chuckle blew up behind the doctor's tombstone teeth and was immediately checked. Since they could not guess that Dr. Ashdown was enjoying himself, his lean and saturnine countenance seemed an accusation.

"Oh, and by the way," Dr. Ashdown added, as once more he started towards the door. "What shall I say to the taxi-driver? And the lady who is waiting in the limousine?"

Husband and wife, who had simultaneously stretched out a hand for the same slice of chocolate cake, and then simultaneously drawn back again as each realized the other's intention, now raised startled faces.

"Lady?" said Tom. "In a limousine?"

"And the taxi-driver. The taxi-driver, at least when I arrived," explained Dr. Ashdown, "seemed to be growing a trifle impatient. He told me he had been waiting since twenty minutes to noon. As for the lady, she told me her name is Mrs. Hornby Buller-Kirk."

"Mrs. Hornby Buller-Kirk," breathed Virginia. "Tom, that name is familiar!"

"You're damn well right it is," said her husband. "She's the president of the Tuesday Evening Ladies' Church Society."

"So I was informed." Dr. Ashdown frowned. "It seems that someone—a name like Benson, I think—phoned her last night and said that you and Lady Brace wished to buy a lot of tickets for some concert at Great Yewborough. A maid named Polly asked her to wait, and she has been waiting in the limousine."

"But we can't see anybody now!" cried Virginia, and wrung her hands. "I'm terribly sorry. I didn't know."

"Didn't know? Forgive me," said Dr. Ashdown, correcting himself as a more human voice jumped out of his throat. "But surely, Lady Brace, I gave you the message when I myself arrived?"

"Yes! Yes, you did. I remember. But we're rather disorganized, Doctor, and it must have slipped my mind. Tom! You go out and see her!"

"No, angel-face, I'm hanged if I do! Let her wait. I've got problems on my mind, too. If the taxi-driver can wait for four and a half hours, and in the library they're doing nothing but . . ."

"*Whroo! Whree! Whree!*"

". . . looking up words in a dictionary, then Mrs. Hornby Buller-Kirk can hang about until I finish this tea. Good day, Doctor; don't say anything at all to the lady, if you don't mind, and thanks very much."

With the last knife-turn of a smile Dr. Ashdown bowed slightly and departed for good. In the healing pause which ensued, the tenth Viscount having driven his imaginary flying squadcar far away towards the north side of Telford, Virginia solaced herself with a deep draught of tea.

"Tom," she murmured wryly, "I once thought it would be grand fun to lead a life comparable to spending one's existence in the Crazy House, or whatever they call that place, at Coney Island. But, when it really happens at a quiet romantic place like this, it isn't fun. It's dreadful."

Her husband had got to his feet. Going to the line of four windows, Tom put his head out through one open casement.

As in the Oak Room, the windows here opened out

like small doors. Each had a modern lock with a handle on the right-hand side midway down, each was composed of oblong panes somewhat larger than the large upraised hand of Chief Inspector Masters, and the low sun touched ancient glass with the spectral luminousness of a goldfish bowl. Tom seemed to be peering along the side of the house towards the Oak Room.

"Tom!" said Virginia, her gaze on the door of the dining-room. "What do you suppose they're doing?"

"Detecting, of course." Her husband's voice, since his head was out of a window, sounded muffled. "There hasn't been a yip out of H.M., in the way of a song, for some time. Do you remember the look on his face, and what he said before he left this room, when he learned Masters had tumbled to the solution of the locked room?"

"No, no! I didn't mean . . ."

"He said, 'Caruso, this is pretty bad. Grass will turn red and water will run uphill if that weasel gets the answer to a problem before the old man does.' He was upset, Jinny. But why should he attach any importance to a scratch on the inside of the Oak Room door? And how in Satan's name can the solution depend on the fact that one of Masters' blasted relatives keeps a radio repair shop?"

"*Tom! Dear!*"

"Eh?" said Tom, pulling his head back from the window and facing her again.

"I wasn't referring to Sir Henry and Signor Ravioli. I meant Dad and Miss Cheeseman. In that library. Four hours and a half! I mean to say!"

"But that's nothing, old girl. I can remember times when you and I . . ."

"Darling, please don't talk like that. It's shocking and I won't listen to it. Besides, not continuously—I mean, it isn't even possible!"

"No, of course not, but you want to allow for conversations when . . ."

"Bensons!" said Virginia, her eyes going back to the door. "Oh, Benson, you're a life-saver! Come in."

Benson was already there. As noiselessly he eased shut the door and oozed to attention, one who knew him well would have said he had undergone a great spiritual experience. Yet no muscle moved in the fresh-complexioned face under the spun white hair.

"Benson," said Virginia, "have you just come from the library?"

"From a post of vantage outside and to the left of the door, my lady. Yes, my lady."

"Look, Benson!" exclaimed the astonished Tom. "You haven't been there all this time, have you?"

If Benson's aura did not shimmer with reproach, at least reproach touched and troubled the air.

"Since your lordship distinctly wished me to do so, and at no subsequent time countermanded the order, I should have considered myself unworthy, my lord, had I failed in the trust."

"Benson." Virginia spoke in an off-hand tone. "It's, of course, of no consequence what my father does, but did anything unusual happen in the library?"

"No, my lady. Nothing which I should venture to describe as unusual."

214

Here the butler's guileless eye sought a corner of the ceiling, as Virginia should have observed. It will have been remarked that Benson possessed great dexterity and smoothness in changing the subject.

"Though the matter is scarcely one which concerns my place, my lady, I also venture to offer you a belated word of thanks which I was unable to do yesterday evening."

"Thanks? For what?"

"It was your ladyship, I am grateful to recall, whose diplomacy prevented Sir Henry Merrivale from being present at a proposed exhibition, here at Telford, of a motion picture entitled *A Night at the Opera*. Though I am informed by the servants that the film was not actually exhibited, yet it does not in the least detract from your most generous farsightedness. You are aware, my lady, that next week Sir Henry is to give a concert before the Tuesday Evening Ladies' Church Society of Great Yewborough."

"Mrs. Hornby Buller-Kirk!" said Virginia, suddenly half rising from her chair but sitting down again.

"Yes, my lady. If I may be permitted somewhat to point my meaning: Sir Henry, though a gentleman of strong and original mind, is much influenced by the power of suggestion. Fortunately there is one particular idea, as touches the concert, which has not yet entered his head. Had he been permitted to watch this film, however, I fear . . ."

Tom Brace passed a sinewy hand over his wrinkled forehead.

"What's all this?" he asked. "What are you getting

at?"

Benson coughed.

"When you are better acquainted with Sir Henry, my lord, you will learn of his passion for assuming fancy-dress and donning false beards of inordinate length and luxuriance."

"But he wouldn't stick on a false beard to sing at the Odd Fellows' Hall, would he? Only get in his way!"

"Yes, my lord. On the other hand, there remains the question of the fancy-dress. Er—I mentioned to her ladyship Sir Henry's taste for Scottish songs, particularly those of a strongly Jacobite political flavour."

"Don't we know it!" groaned Tom, glancing at the windows and back again. "He sang 'Lock Lomond' and 'Speed, Bonnie Boat.' Sang 'em both three times. Tommy applauded so hard he gave encores like a shot."

"Precisely so, my lord. Should it occur to Sir Henry that it would become him to sing 'Loch Lomond' at the Odd Fellows' Hall—his person being adorned or otherwise by a kilt, a Highland bonnet, and perhaps a basket-hilted sword—I fear this spectacle could not be viewed by the audience without strong emotion of some kind."

"H'm. Might be something in what you say."

"Thank you, my lord. Nor, I confess, was I altogether happy at Mr. Masters' reference to opera. The bass role in the opera of *Faust*, for example, is not the star part. Yet it is one which might well appeal to Sir Henry, since it would enable him to bound upon the stage, with the entrance-line of *'Me voici,'* in the skin-tight red costume of Méphistopheles." Virginia had been carefully watching Benson with an air which might be described as that of a beautiful and small-girl grandmother.

"Benson!"

"Yes, my lady."

"Benson, you're trying to lead us away from the subject again. You don't want to talk about what happened in the library!"

"I assure you, my lady . . ."

"Please, Benson, confine yourself to answering yes or—wait; not that, but be particular! Your natural delicacy restrains you, we know that, but in this one instance you may feel free to speak. What happened when they *first* went in there?"

A faint lightening of relief touched Benson's features.

"If I may say so, my lady, your ladyship's father was most generous."

"Dad was?"

"Yes, my lady. Miss Cheeseman expressed herself forcibly on the subject of Sir Henry's conduct in general. Though she disclaimed any wish to avenge an affront to her personal dignity, nevertheless the lady insisted that Sir Henry, as she maintained she could prove, can be called a public danger because he has taken to drink."

"But . . . !"

"Yes, my lady. An unfortunate misunderstanding. However, the lady seems to have opened her handbag and read a sheaf of notes collected from the testimony

217

of various villagers at Great Yewborough."

"To what effect?"

"To the effect, my lady, that Sir Henry is each night in a dangerously intoxicated condition. There are those who claim to have heard his brutal bellowings and cursings at ill-paid servants, his shouts to blow the man down, coupled with queries touching the course to be pursued with a drunken sailor, usually concluding with a demoniacal howl for another bottle of rum."

"Tom, this is awful!"

"Easy, old girl! Benson, what did Gramp say?"

Again Benson coughed.

"Her ladyship's father, though describing rather horrible surgical tortures he believed Sir Henry should undergo, and stating that he himself never touched alcohol in any form, nevertheless persuaded Miss Cheeseman that it would be more discreet to forget the matter. Their discussion, however, was interrupted . . ."

"Interrupted? How?"

"So far as one might gather from auricular effect alone, my lady, Miss Cheeseman had also produced from her handbag a photograph or snapshot of her *fiancé*, Professor Hereward Wake. Mr. Harvey commented unfavourably on Professor Wake's personal appearance, comparing the gentleman's face to something which he called a pretzel."

"Go on, Benson! For heaven's sake don't be embarrassed!"

"The conversation then dwelt at some length on poetry, but presently . . ."

"Yes? Presently?"

"There was what in one sense might be described as silence, my lady."

"For a long time?"

"For a very long time, my lady. This was followed by languid conversation in a lower voice, and then, subsequently, more of what a euphemism permits me to describe as silence. Lest your ladyship should feel apprehension in any respect, I must descend to a regrettable popular expression. Despite Miss Cheeseman's stately demeanour, I should say it is far from being the first time she has been there."

Perhaps surprisingly, it was Tom and not Virginia who uttered an exclamation.

"*What?* The Labour M.P. from East Whistlefield?"

"I fear, my lord, that we Conservatives are apt to begrudge our political opponents even the most elementary virtues. It was evident, to continue, that both Miss Cheeseman and Mr. Harvey felt the most extraordinary satisfaction with each other, and later they determined on marriage."

"Good!" Tom said heartily, though Virginia's expression had become one of stupor. "Don't say a word, ginchlet. I proposed to you after only one meeting. And under exactly the same circum . . ."

"Tom!"

"Why not be frank? Runs in both families. Can't be helped."

"Benson," pursued Virginia, getting her breath under the flutter of a struggling smile, "was there anything else?"

219

"Nothing of consequence, my lady." Again Benson's eye strayed towards a corner of the ceiling. "Even in the south wing, I may say, it was possible to hear Sir Henry's vocal accompaniments from the Oak Room, though I could not follow all of them. I trust, my lady, that Sir Henry has not yet sung one of his favourite songs dealing with a big aspidistra?"

"No, he hasn't sung any . . ." Virginia was beginning, when she stopped. "About a big *what?*"

"An aspidistra, my lady. Cassell's New English Dictionary defines the word 'aspidistra' as follows: '*n.*, (Bot.) A liliaceous genus including the parlour palm.'"

"Oh! You're talking about a kind of rubber plant."

"Perhaps, my lady. The parlour palm, in this particular song, is described as growing to an improbable height comparable only to Jack's beanstalk, and is used for various most unlikely purposes. When sung in Lancashire dialect by the incomparable Miss Gracie Fields, the song has often enchanted me in the past. But perhaps, my lady, full justice is not done to its nuances by Sir Henry's *basso profondo* in a lamentable imitation of a cockney accent."

"Benson!"

"My lady?"

Virginian her father's daughter, had begun to be acquainted with Benson and could sense evasion in a witness.

"Benson, you're changing the subject again! Something terrible happened in that library only a few minutes ago; Dr. Ashdown said he heard a fearful shout from there, in a man's voice, and it's too fearful

220

for even you to tell us. What was it?"

"I may give you my word, my lady, that I heard only one shout from the library. This was the powerful voice of Mr. Harvey, suddenly upraised in the single exclamation, 'Tally-ho!' "

" 'Tally-ho'?" repeated Tom.

"Yes, my lord."

"But why 'Tally-ho'?"

"Even now, my lord, I cannot imagine the reason for the choice of terminology. However, I was able to ascertain the cause of it. Mr. Harvey, on looking through one of the open French windows, perceived none other than Miss Cheeseman's *fiancé*, Professor Hereward Wake."

Virginia sprang from her chair. Running for the massive sideboard, over which the portrait of King Charles the Second looked on like a benevolent deity, she gripped the edges of the sideboard before slowly turning round.

"No, Benson!" she wailed. *"No!"*

"Yes, my lady. Having once attended a political meeting at which I heard Professor Wake expound his philosophy of nationalizing everything, I am in a position to testify that it was indeed he. When I opened the door of the library . . ."

"You went into the room?"

A faint reddish bar showed across Benson's placid forehead.

"I am extremely sorry, my lady. Your ladyship will appreciate, however, that the shout was so sudden, and contained such a degree of triumphant savagery, that my action was in a sense involuntary. I . . ."

"Benson, stop!" interrupted Tom, with fierce decisiveness. "Look, Jinny. I don't see this. Why should Gramp have shouted, 'Tally-ho'?"

All Virginia's innocent, little-girl appeal yearned at him.

"Darling, I've already told you the story."

"Story?"

"Yes. Using Benson's narrative style, it has reference to an ancient but celebrated American anecdote about an American in the English hunting field. After a meet, the American asks his English host whether he behaved well. The host says he didn't do at all badly, but adds a word of caution. 'When you sight the fox, old boy, you must shout, "Tally-ho!" and not, "There goes the son of a b . . ." ' "

The last word was drowned in the sharp crack as Tom snapped his fingers.

"Got it!" he said.

"Of course!" wailed the anguished Virginia. "Dad says that thirty years ago, at Princeton, heads would appear at windows and there would be a universal shout of 'Tally-ho' whenever a certain member of the faculty walked past."

Virginia, in one sense of the word, now flung herself at the butler.

"Dad," she said, "had a forty-pound bow and six arrows. Benson, don't tell me! I *know!* He used to be awfully good with a bow or a baseball bat. He drew the bowstring to his ear and shot Professor Wake in the seat of the pants."

"No, my lady."

"He didn't?"

"No, my lady. Such, I fancy, was indeed Mr. Harvey's intention. But . . ."

"Stop!" cut in the brooding Tom, who was a keen rider to hounds. "Maybe they did it in the old days, but I've told you before: *I* never heard anybody shout 'Tally-ho' at a meet."

"Tom, for heaven's sake let Benson tell his story! Benson, you said you entered the library. Please take it from there."

"Very good, my lady. Though I might remark, in passing, that Professor Wake's motor-car, a drive-hire Daimler from Great Yewborough, is now the fourth car in the drive, which appears to be growing somewhat congested."

"The fourth car?"

"Yes, my lady. The first belongs to an infuriated taxi-driver. The second is the limousine of Mrs. Hornby Buller-Kirk. The third is that of Dr. Ashdown."

"But Dr. Ashdown left some time ago!"

"Dr. Ashdown was unable to leave, my lady. From what I gather, the tenth Viscount had let the air out of two tires on the doctor's car, pleading that he, the tenth Viscount, was in reality Superintendent Merrivale of the flying squad preventing the escape of a notorious jewel thief. Dr. Ashdown, not unnaturally, takes a somewhat poor view of this hypothesis."

"Tom! Did you hear that?"

Benson coughed.

"If I may be permitted to deduce the course of events, my lady, I should say that Professor Hereward Wake was obliged to seek entrance to the house by way of the Dutch garden. Professor Wake, it is true, is a man of great personal bravery bearing a striking likeness to the portraits of Mr. Aneurin Bevan. But I am instructed to say that the maid Polly, considering her afternoon too much disturbed, now greets all arrivals at the front door with violent horizontal swings of a broom."

Poor Virginia could only assume a tragic attitude, her arms spread wide.

"I can't bear it!" she protested in her sweet voice. "Benson, you're still evading! You *won't* tell us what you saw when you went into that library, and I can't see how we can make you do it. But, as a special favour to me, won't you make the attempt to try?"

The butler inclined his head slightly.

"As your ladyship pleases. Electrified by the shout of 'Tally-ho,' which I am now informed is tantamount to 'There goes the . . .' "

"Yes, we understand. And then?"

"I took the liberty of opening the door. It is scarcely necessary to remind your ladyship that the library, though lined to the ceiling with great book-shelves bearing on their tops busts of such philosophers as Socrates and Immanuel Kant, is a pleasant and dusky room with deep-cushioned tapestry chairs and sofas. Through three French windows, a pleasing view of the Dutch garden . . ."

"Oh, Benson, you're not writing a guide-book! Just tell us what you saw. Was Elaine Cheeseman there?"

"Yes, my lady. The fair Elaine, if I may be so bold as to use Mr. Harvey's terminology, was seated upon a settee, almost entirely divested of her . . ."

"*Benson!* She wasn't completely—completely . . . ?"

"No, my lady." The butler spoke with firmness and reassurance. "Despite the duskiness of the library and a languorous atmosphere whose dwelling is the light of setting suns, I may say definitely that the lady was wearing her shoes and stockings."

"Damn good idea!" roared Tom, with hearty approval. "A thousand times I've said, Jinny, that amateurs as well as professionals ought to do that. Its effect . . ."

"Darling! That woman! She's *horrible.*"

"Though it would ill become me to contradict you, my lady," said Benson, "I might point out that the lady in question is the granddaughter of Vice-Admiral Cheeseman, the hero of the battle of Cape Ann. I have often observed that in those of gentle blood, such as Miss Cheeseman and your ladyship's self, there is sometimes engendered an imperviousness or even recklessness to appearances, especially on a warm summer afternoon. As for your ladyship's father . . ."

"Yes! Dad! No, you'd better not tell me."

"You may be tranquil, my lady."

"Oh?"

"Yes, my lady. Mr. Harvey, attired at least in trousers and shoes and socks, had for the rest slung over his shoulder a quiver of brightly feathered arrows. It became clear that his shout had been inspired by catching sight of Professor Wake, whom he had doubtless recognized from the photograph, in

225

profile some dozen yards down a straight garden path."

"Face like a pretzel," said Tom. "Well?"

"The shout, my lord, caused Professor Wake to turn his face towards the French window and display a slight but not unbecoming corporation. Mr. Harvey drew the bowstring to his ear. There was a musical hum like the deep twang of a harp . . ."

"What ho!" cried Tom in gleaming-eyed enthusiasm, and rubbed his hands together. "Tally-ho! *Westward, Ho!* Did he wallop Professor Wake in the corporation?"

Benson's aura was one of respectful rebuke.

"Fortunately not, my lord. Or, as I remarked yesterday regarding the attack on Colin MacHolster, there might have been serious consequences. As it was, my lord, the whistling shaft smashed a heavy flower-pot within two inches of Professor Wake's right ear.

"Professor Wake, though a brave man, was observed to turn pale. Without hesitation he swung round and ran hard down the path with his back to the French window. Mr. Harvey, with even more savagery uttering that motto which means 'There goes the gentleman,' instantly loosed a second shaft at Professor Wake's lower dorsal elevation.

"Again he missed, but came quite closer. Since Mr. Harvey had four more arrows and quite obviously meant business, Professor Wake dodged to cover amid the tall tulips. Mr. Harvey, becoming as silent as a red Indian, crept out of the French window and began to stalk his quarry."

Virginia sat down in her chair. She let her head fall on her clasped arms, and breathed. The butler's kindly nature was moved to pity.

"I am sure, my lady, that Mr. Harvey meant no harm. But he was not quite himself."

"Benson, you can't approve of all this!"

"No, my lady."

"And you've no need to say he wasn't himself. I know that. But why on earth did my father behave like that?"

"I should judge the explanation to be fairly simple, my lady. Mr. Harvey, like Miss Cheeseman herself, was in that exalted and rather irresponsible state which, or so I am told, follows a happy—a happy afternoon."

Virginia flung up her head, shaking back the hair.

"But didn't you do anything? Didn't you try to prevent the—the stalking, at least?"

"My lady, I . . ."

"Benson, what was the real reason you did nothing?"

"Miss Cheeseman, my lady, appeared fully as enthusiastic for the pursuit of Professor Wake as did Mr. Harvey himself. The lady sprang up from the sofa, reaching out for two garments which are known, I believe, as a brassière and step-ins, clearly intending to don them and to follow Mr. Harvey in these garments alone. Finding myself face to face with the lady, I thought it best to retreat as expeditiously as possible."

"But . . . !"

"Before you pass a harsh judgment, my lady, I beg

of you to reflect whether none of us, in a similarly exalted state, has ever behaved in a somewhat irrational way."

"H'm," said Virginia thoughtfully, and her eyes dreamed.

"Good for you, old girl!" beamed Tom, and gripped her shoulder.

"But we ought to do *something*. I mean, if Dad is chasing Professor Wake all over the garden, trying to shoot him in the pants with an arrow, and Miss Cheeseman is running after him practically naked, we ought at least to watch him. Benson! Won't you please go and see what happens, and and take notes?"

"Very good, my lady!"

"Benign again, a weight of responsibility lifted and even eager, Benson flickered away in almost indecent haste. Husband and wife were left alone.

"Tom, this is the end!"

"Frankly, Jinny," said her husband, with a sardonic grin, "Gramp doesn't need to be 'exalted' to wallop arrows at professors of economics. Get him going, and he'll do that for the devil of it." Tom frowned. "But Elaine Cheeseman! A gal of experience! That's what beats me."

"Does it?"

"Bet you anything you like it surprises even old H.M." Again Tom frowned, pondering. "Would it surprise him, though? From what I heard, and from what he told you over the phone, he never stated in so many words that she's a dewy-eyed innocent."

"Of course not. All it means is that she never yet

met quite the whirlwind approach but careful tactics afterwards which she's—well, dreamed about."

"Hang it, how do you know that?"

"Tom, darling! Never ask a woman how she knows a thing like that. How do I know there will be sunrise tomorrow? I can't prove it. I just *know* it."

"Well, it does go to show you can't trust anybody in this affair, no matter how innocent he or she seems. But cheer up, Jinny! No good being tragic! When you say this is the end . . ."

"I didn't mean it like that! I meant that there can't possibly be any more trouble, anything worse than what's gone before! We're at the absolute *ultima thule*. So it's impossible for there to be any more . . ."

A heavy male voice, low-pitched yet weighted with an intensity of dangerous furtiveness and nerves, struck across the dining-room at Tom.

"Sir!" it called. "Lord Brace! S-s-t!"

With one accord Tom and Virginia looked at the line of the windows. Outside, visible from the waist up against the pink-gold light of late afternoon, stood the long-absent butler, Jennings.

16

Jennings, tall and lean, gave little sign in his appearance or clothes of having spent a rumpled and hounded night. There was a faint aureole on his flatly brushed black hair. Yet by some trick of the light his long face appeared almost yellow. Seen in half-length at one open window, he was unpleasantly reminiscent of Peter Quint in that rather-too-subtle ghost-story by Henry James.

Moreover, as soon as Virginia and Tom saw him, there fled from their hearts any recollection of events which might have been funny. Jennings, with his furtive and moving dark eyes, was desperate, sincere. He hung there, so to speak, fitfully, as though the least breeze of pursuit would blow him away like a figure of tissue-paper.

Husband and wife hastened to the window. Both spoke at once.

"Jennings, where have you been?"

The butler glanced over his shoulder. He had approached from a northerly direction, past the Georgian wing, and, far beyond that, the wood locally known as Marian's Copse.

"I spent the night with a friend near Cherriton," he said, his voice husky before it found its level. "I—"

His gesture, that of a long big-knuckled hand towards a jaw smoothly shaven though blue, conjured up in one flick everything he meant. He would convey that, like G. B. Shaw's ancient Briton, he at least kept his respectability. Though his speech was far less pedantic than Benson's, he was, in fact, a much better-read man.

"Sir," he continued, "you and the madam have been very decent to me. I've got to go away. But I felt I must see you first, because . . ." He stopped. "You won't give the wire to the slops, I'm sure of that. Here! This address will always find me, if you'd be kind enough to send on my things, and it won't give you or me away if they find it."

His big-knuckled hand darted through the window, holding out a scrap of paper on which there was some writing. Automatically Tom took the paper and put it in his pocket. Tom would compound a felony without hesitation.

"But look, Jennings! Is your name really Prentice Thorne? Are you a forger who can engrave first-class Bank-of-England notes?"

Jennings looked as though he might have burst into a long explanation, but he compressed his reply to two words.

"Yes, sir."

The explanation, however, burst out in another direction.

231

"And I've been with you only a short time, sir and madam. But I didn't come here to do anything I shouldn't. Before God I didn't! I'm a Sussex man; I've always been fond of Telford. I was tempted, that's all. Money did it. Money always does. And I fell. What I wanted to say, though, sir, was this: it's all right! Nothing actually happened."

"What the devil do you mean, nothing happened? And what are you talking about?"

The hand of Jennings, or Prentice Thorne, again went into his side-pocket under the smooth morning-coat. This time what he thrust through the window, and pressed on Tom, was an object hard and heavily covered with soft leather, having a leather thong at the end.

It was a life-preserver. Tom took it, but stared at it as though it might burn him.

"Jennings! Is this what was used to hit Chief Inspector Masters?"

"Yes, sir. And I had the chloral hydrate. For God's sake forgive me, sir; I put it into your black coffee on Wednesday night. Black coffee is bitter. It hides the taste. If you don't use too much chloral, there's no morning-after effect at all. Of course, I gave away the rest of the chloral . . ."

Again Jennings checked himself, glancing quickly right and left. There was a snap as he pressed his hands together and cracked a knuckle-joint.

"You'll see my difficulty, sir and madam. It's the same difficulty as with bank notes. Your trouble isn't the engraving; it's the paper. You've *got* to use a faithful reproduction of the paper, or you're done. It was here in the house, only from another part of it—you'd never guess where—I got the reproduction. I'm not trying to excuse myself, sir. But . . ."

"Jinny, have you the remotest idea what this fellow's driving at?"

"No, Tom, I haven't. Jennings, are you confessing to us that you tried to steal the Cavalier's Cup?"

It was as though a shock of surprise, from an explosion under the butler's long nose, solidified him at the window. He stood motionless, his whitish scholarly face appearing yellow, hand half-raised as though to ward off a blow.

"The Cavalier's Cup? Ah! I see now. Respectfully, madam, I see you haven't guessed what the mystery is."

Tom, maddened, waved the life-preserver in the air.

"The mystery," said Virginia, "is how someone got in and out of a hermetically sealed room."

"No, madam; that's not it at all. Nor the Cavalier's Cup."

"But the cup is worth oodles and oodles of money!"

"Yes, madam. That's why nobody was interested in it."

"*What?*"

Tom, pointing the life-preserver, grimly sought to drive the bird from cover.

"Whatever happened, Jennings, are you confessing you're guilty? Did you do it?"

"No, sir! On my word of honour, no! Except for what I've indicated, as in the analogy of bank notes; and also, sir, I did put chloral into your coffee. But I

233

gave up the chloral; I'd already given up the life-preserver, just in case it might be needed at some time. Only, last night the life-preserver was thrown away, deliberately thrown away. It was many hours before I left the grounds, and I picked it up again."

Jennings stiffened. From along the rear length of Telford, towards the right of Jennings, floated the throaty tin-pan notes of a harpsichord.

"Madam, who is in that room?" asked the distracted butler. "As I came past from Marian's Copse, I thought I saw . . ." He swallowed. "And I can swear there's somebody close to the window now, listening to every word I say!"

"Jennings, you're making us both as nervous as you are!" cried Virginia. "The only person in the Oak Room is a friend of ours, Sir Henry Merrivale. You mustn't mind if he sings."

"Is that so, madam?" *Crack* went a knuckle-joint. Jennings spoke in a curious tone, which then altered. "Sir! Madam! You've been kind to me, and I want to make a full confession before I disappear."

"Then do it!" yelled Tom.

"Sir, forget the locked room. The locked room isn't important and doesn't matter. The really guilty party, sir, is . . ."

Distantly, but approaching rapidly from the north side, small feet pounded the turf. Though the voice was only that of an innocent nine-year-old at play, to an uneasy consciousness its words might have suggested other images.

"Here comes the flying squad car!" it screamed. "Look out for the flying squad car!"

234

The butler's countenance turned from yellow to green.

"Cor stone a crow!" blurted the scholarly Jennings. "Coppers!"

In one sense at least he kept his word. When Jennings shot away, it is no mere metaphor to say that he disappeared. The glass in the windows, like all that at Telford, was clear and limpid and without any flaws or whorls; Jennings' image was whisked off it as instantly as the sweep of an eraser takes chalk from a blackboard.

At the same time, behind Virginia and Tom, rose a loud, domineering, confident female voice, turned to a note of hypocritical ingratiation and cheerfulness which rang as false as hell.

"I am Mrs. Hornby Buller-Kirk," boomed the voice, "Madam President of the Tuesday Evening Ladies' Church Society. You will forgive me for penetrating so rudely into your dining-room, but I am here at the express request of the dear vicar, the Reverend Mr. Swearer."

"Whree! Whree! I'm Superintendent Merrivale of the flying squad!"

Caught between two fires, husband and wife might well have given up in despair. One glance showed them that Jennings, the tails of his morning-coat flying out, was legging it hard for the shelter of the wood to the north.

But husband and wife rallied. They faced the newcomer.

The newcomer was a large, broad, heavy woman in one of those hats which years ago were rendered familiar by the even-then-elderly Queen Dowager. In one hand she held a narrow-edged but very wide roll of bluish paper tickets, on which the two most conspicuous of a number of printed words were "Charity Concert."

Across the visitor's hard, fleshy face, with its mouth drooping at the outer corners, went another smile of false *bonhomie*. She reared up her bust. Evidently she imagined her hosts were a little hard of hearing.

"I am Mrs. Hornby Buller-Kirk," she boomed in a louder voice, "Madam President of the Tuesday Evening Ladies' Church Society. Though I know you both by sight, your habit of keeping yourselves to yourselves, which I always feel—forgive me— to be a little unfortunate in these changed times, has deprived me hitherto of the pleasure of your acquaintance."

"How do you do, Mrs. Buller-Kirk?" murmured Virginia, courteously but faintly.

"Very well. Very well indeed. Hem!" said Mrs. Buller-Kirk, giving herself a settling shake. "It is not needful, after the interest you have so kindly expressed, to remind you that next week our small charitable organization, together with as many guests as we can persuade to attend, will be entertained by a gentleman of widely recognized talents."

"Yes, indeed, Mrs. Buller-Kirk. As a matter of fact, Sir Henry is here now. He's rehearsing."

The visitor looked haughtily taken aback, as though H.M. had no right to be rehearsing anywhere except at home.

"So, Lady Brace? How interesting! Well! The dear

vicar, Mr. Swearer, has asked me to convey to you his deepest thanks. I have here . . ."

Lifting the large roll of tickets, Mrs. Buller-Kirk held them in the air with her left hand. With her right hand she yanked back one end of it, unreeling a whole run of bluish tickets as far as her right ear, in a motion which to inflamed eyes suggested the string of Locksley's good longbow.

But Mrs. Buller-Kirk would not have understood her dignified gesture like this. She was merely measuring a length of tickets, as we have seen drapers measure a yard of cloth.

"I have here," she went on, measuring off another yard, "a few tickets which no doubt you will wish to have for an evening of good, wholesome fun. True, we are not acquainted with the ability of Sir Henry Merrivale as a singer."

"You've—you've never heard him?"

"No, Lady Brace. But, as Mr. Swearer says, no gentleman would so confidently have undertaken a two-and-a-half-hour recital without being sure of himself. And then," said Mrs. Buller-Kirk, unreeling a third yard of tickets, "his name is so famous that he is bound to attract the curious and make our humble entertainment a great success."

"Yes, I'm quite sure of it. But you see, Mrs. Buller-Kirk . . ."

"And upon one thing, Lady Brace, I have most firmly insisted. In these slack times, Lady Brace, too often are we assailed in public halls with the profane, the *risqué*, the suggestive, even that downright hint of indecency which is bad taste, bad manners, and definitely not acceptable to the public. How many tickets would you care to have?"

Desperation shook its warning in Tom Brace's voice.

"How many have you got?"

"All in all, Lord Brace, I should have to consult the Honorary Treasurer. Even in this roll here," out went another yard, "I am uncertain of the exact number. As many as I have measured, perhaps."

"More! Let's have the lot."

"The lot, Lord Brace?"

"Yes. We want to be alone. The whole bloody lot!"

Abruptly Tom became conscious that Mrs. Hornby Buller-Kirk was staring at the life-preserver which he brandished in his right hand.

"Er—fly swat," he said. "Bloody useful, eh?"

Mrs. Buller-Kirk reared up her bust in outrage.

"Lord Brace!"

"Have a drink!"

"Lord Brace," boomed Mrs. Buller-Kirk, "I never touch spirituous liquors, and I must ask you to abstain even from mentioning them. These, and the wicked institution known as the public-house, cause me pain. In addition to this, despite the kindness of your charitable offer to assist a concert held to raise funds for the cause of temperance, I must beg you to moderate your offensive language in the presence of ladies. Both matters, I may say, are in singular contrast to the entertainment you will hear on Tuesday night."

Mrs. Buller-Kirk paused. She could not help pausing. The blare which stopped her, making quiver even her solid bulk, sounded like Don John of Austria shouting to the ships.

> "It shot up like a fahntain till it nearly reached
> the sky—
> It's the biggest aspidistra in the world!"

Tom stood rigid, life-preserver held high. Virginia's arms were outstretched like those of a figure in an allegorical painting.

> "We couldn't keep a-pruning it, it grew so very
> 'igh—
> It's the biggest aspidistra in the world!"

Virginia plunged towards the table and upset the tea-pot.

"Mrs. Buller-Kirk, have a dr—have some tea! Or cake! Have a piece of chocolate cake!"

> "When Father prances 'omewards from 'is pub, the
> Bunch of
> Grypes,
> 'E never takes a drop too much or gets in any
> scrypes;
> You'll find 'im in 'is bare skin plyin' Tarzan
> of the Aypes—
>
> Up the
> Biggest
> Aspidistra

239

In the world!"

Mrs. Buller-Kirk reeled.

"This is not true," she boomed. "My ears are deceiving me, and I am held in the grip of some horrid nightmare. The song I hear cannot, cannot come from the pure throat of Sir Henry Merrivale!"

"Can't it, eh?" shouted Tom. "That's his opening number."

"No! No! No! I beseech you not to deceive me. Indeed, we have planned for the concert a ceremony bountiful and even touching. All Sussex knows of the unfortunate enmity between Sir Henry and Miss Elaine Cheeseman, though I have been unable to ascertain its cause beyond a comprehensible political difference. Miss Cheeseman, granddaughter of the late Vice-Admiral Cheeseman, is a young lady of the highest ideals and the most exemplary moral rectitude. We have decided that she and Sir Henry shall compose their differences; and the platform at the Odd Fellows' Hall shall echo only to the beautiful strains of . . ."

"Tally-ho!"

This cry, it is necessary to state in fairness, did not come from the pure throat of Sir Henry Merrivale.

Virginia Brace, even though she herself believed she was now in the grip of some horrid nightmare, had never dreamed that the pursuit of Professor Hereward Wake would leave the garden. Yet this should have been expected, and such in fact was the case.

Past the line of the four windows, seen as in a

mirror on a monstrous twilight sea, flashed the figure of a man running so hard that details of his appearance were lost. Professor Wake, with commendable sagacity, was heading for the shelter of the wood as Jennings had done before him.

He flashed past and was lost to view. In the centre of the lawn, transfixed, stood the small figure of Tommy, the tenth Viscount, in a trance of fascination, as he watched the figures of two pursuers who—now on the view halloo—raced up and stopped some twenty or thirty feet from the windows.

The gentleman, thoroughly clad in dark blue trousers of excellent cut and polished black shoes, had a quiver of arrows over his shoulder as well as a bow in his hand. He was not otherwise remarkable.

But the lady, though her brassière and step-ins could not be called expensive, having undoubtedly come from Marks & Spencer's, and though her flesh-coloured stockings seemed to be magically upheld since the outline of the step-ins made it evident that she wore no garter-belt, was a different matter.

To a Puritan it might have been pointed out that the lady in question was at least more fully dressed than feminine swimmers whom anyone could see on the beach at Bournemouth or Hastings. But she had so magnificent a figure, its flesh pink-tinted yet gleaming with marbly lights under the sun, that Tom Brace uttered an involuntary exclamation of "Whew!"

And Virginia, who had lost control of herself, went over and slapped her husband's face.

"Tom!"

"Hang it, Jinny, what did *I* do?"

Nevertheless, we spoke of Hastings. Feverishly Congressman Harvey whipped another arrow from the quiver—he still had three left—and fitted its nock to the string. The voice of Elaine Cheeseman rose clearly and beautifully.

"He's heading for the wood, and the ground slopes up there. Hit him on the rise, dearest! Hit him on the rise!"

"Tally-ho!" said Congressman Harvey.

Testing the direction of the wind, then rearing back, Mr. Harvey loosed the shaft for a long shot of fully a hundred and ten yards. Yet this time, though the watchers at the window could see nothing, the effectiveness of the singing missile was proved by a wild yell which rose up from the direction of Marian's Copse.

"You've got two arrows left, Bill! Come *on!*"

"Tally-ho!"

And these two figures, in their turn, raced from sight.

Tommy, the tenth Viscount, stood for a moment motionless. An unthinking observer, not realizing how the mind of a boy really works, might have decided that in his excitement he would have followed the pursuit as automatically as a dog.

But the tenth Viscount had seen something too wonderful, too stupendous, for this. Instead his first instinct was to pour out the story to a sympathetic audience.

"Mom! Pop! Mom! Pop!"

So he raced straight for the open window beyond

which stood his parents. Never before had Tommy achieved, and probably would not achieve again, what he did under the stimulus of incoherent admiration. With one flying leap he landed upright, on his feet, balanced on the window-sill without either falling or crashing his head through the glass.

"Did you see what Gramp did? Did you see what Gramp did?"

"Tommy, come down from there! You'll hurt yourself! Tom Brace, stop that! If you laugh I'll . . ."

"Mom, who was the swell-looking dame in the bathing suit?"

"That wasn't a bathing suit, Tommy. It was—yes, of course it was a bathing suit. Tom! I'll kill you!"

"Will you kindly tell me, Jinny, in what way this is my fault? How can I teach the boy anything if Gramp won't set him a better example?"

"No!" suddenly boomed Mrs. Hornby Buller-Kirk. "No! No! No!"

"Ee!" screamed Tommy, his eyes feverishly alight.

And now, with infinite regret at having to do so, the chronicler must briefly indicate the last event of that peaceful afternoon in old England.

This must be done because the report subsequently spread through the countryside by Mrs. Buller-Kirk, like so many stories by adults about children, was a plain lie. Mrs. Buller-Kirk testified that a nine-year-old demon in a muddy suit, uttering words of the vilest profanity, leaped at her from the window-sill and beat at her with his fists in so insane an assault that she was compelled to fly from the house for her life.

Nothing like this occurred.

Mrs. Buller-Kirk, retreating under the impact of what she saw from the window, had loosened her grasp on fully twelve feet of joined bluish tickets. Nowadays in England they will not give you what you want, in the way of proper materials, even when they have it to give. The long length of tickets, of rather flimsy paper, first floated in curious patterns across the air and then settled down, still writhing in challenge, to the floor.

Thus, to any right-minded boy, the proper course was inevitable.

Tommy —blurting out the word "Snake!"—leaped down from the sill and dived to seize it. Mrs. Buller-Kirk fled. A partial length of the tickets tore off from the main string as Tommy grabbed it. So he raced after the lady to seize the other end.

As the whack of Mrs. Buller-Kirk's flat-heeled shoes died away down the passage, Virginia went off the deep end again.

"But, for God's sake, woman," cried her husband, "in what way is it my fault? Just tell me that!"

"You haven't got to discipline him, Tom Brace. I have! You never do anything, anything at all, a husband and father should!"

"But, look, Jinny . . . !"

"I won't put up with it. I'll divorce you. Yes, I will! *Some* discipline in life is necessary, even if you don't believe that, because you've never had any discipline in your life! You were an only child, and . . ."

"Weren't you?"

244

"That doesn't make any difference. I loathe you! I hate you! It doesn't do any good trying to kiss me, because I won't be kissed. I won't! Well, maybe just once. Oh, Tom, this lunacy must end! And we must stop picking on poor Sir Henry."

"Isn't that another *non-sequitur*, my dear?"

"No, it isn't. Compared to everybody else, he's quite steady-going. But that isn't it. Whoever else was serious, Jennings was serious, fiendishly so, and yet he made no sense. You say Sir Henry is as clever as the very devil. I daresay he has to be, if he can attach any importance to a harmless scratch on the inside of a door. But he's got to help us and end this mystery, or we'll make him. To the Oak Room, Tom. Come on!"

That was how Virginia and Tom, her right hand clutched in his left and Tom's right hand gripping the life-preserver, themselves pelted through the labyrinth of passages until they attained the core of all mystery, the secret shrine of terror: the Oak Room itself.

Without knocking, any more than a butler would have knocked, Virginia turned the knob and opened the rather large, heavy door.

Then up rose the voice of Signor Ravioli, who was sitting on a bench at the harpsichord and pinching his thumb and forefinger together in the air.

"No!" he said.

"Lord love a duck, son, then I'll tell you there's something I'm fed up with! Will you stop goin' on about this crime being committed by a left-handed ghost with asthma?"

"We're-a detectives?" demanded Signor Ravioli.

"Why-a you not tell me?"

His hand flashed across the top of the harpsichord, which was of ancient and fragile inlaid work, and on top of which lay his black hat. This Signor Ravioli jammed down on his head so hard that it flattened out the ears; then he leered.

"There's not one single suggestion," said H.M., his fists on his hips as he stood in the middle of a room fifteen feet square, "that Sir Byng Rawdon ever had asthma in his life. In the second place, we know he was very much right-handed. Didn't you hear the little gal describe how he wore the diamond on his right hand, and scratched that writin' in one oblong of the window?"

H.M. was correct. He stabbed his finger towards the left-hand window of the two in the wall facing the door.

Though the message was very lightly scratched there, almost invisible against the tree-filtered pink-and-gold of the sun, still by turning sideways a spectator could see the tiny sprawling words. "God bless King Charles and—"

But this, to Tom and Virginia in the doorway, was not the most important consideration. The Oak Room was almost overpoweringly hot, since it had been closed up at nearly all times to show the same conditions as those under which a phantom had somehow slipped in and out. Only one glass oblong to the right of the poignant message scrawled by a dying man, the heavy metal handle of the catch was turned so as to drive its steel rod deep into its immovable sill. The right-hand window was locked, too.

Locked! Locked! Husband and wife, creeping in so as not to disturb H.M. or Signor Ravioli, softly closed the door behind them. Tom cast a glance at the two heavy bolts, one at the top and one at the bottom.

"Do you think," Virginia's whisper was barely audible, "we'd better tell H.M. there may not be a concert? I mean, Mrs. Buller-Kirk . . . ?"

"Sh-h!"

Since the panelling of the Oak Room was much darker than such other rooms as were panelled to the ceiling, it wore a touch of gloom even in full sunshine. Except for one difference, nothing had been disturbed since last night's chaos.

The fireplace, with its white-stone hood mellowed by centuries of smokestain along the lower edge was set cater-cornered. That is, as you stood in the doorway, it was in the joining of the left-hand wall with the wall of the windows facing you from fifteen feet away. On the uneven Dutch tiles of the hearth was the lute.

There were three chairs, one of them, overturned on the floor—perhaps cracks gaped between the floorboards here or there—beside a narrow overturned table. On the floor lay a silver ash tray with a scattering of ash and a dead cigar-butt left by Masters. There lay the rapier, its fine cup-hilt and long, thin, wicked blade gleaming darkly under a very light coat of oil used to preserve it from damp, under a patter of oblong shadows thrown by the sun through leaded panes.

Disorder! Fear! Struggle! The harpischord, with Signor Ravioli sitting behind it and facing the door, stood in a position on the right roughly corresponding with the cater-cornered fireplace at the left. But, as noted, there was one change.

The small iron safe, its door open, was against the right-hand wall. On top of this, picked up from the floor, a symbol of lurid gold sharpened by the venomous tongue-points of diamond, emerald, and ruby; against that sombre room blazed the Cavalier's Cup.

Tom and Virginia had seen all this too often before. But again their eyes greedily took in every detail, including the scratch on the inside of the door, until they became aware that for some seconds H.M. had been roaring on.

". . . and that's my final word on the subject. Burn it, this wasn't done by a spook! That's sure, until I get the last detail that'll plug the last little cranny. Until then, are we having a singin' lesson, or aren't we?"

"You want to seeng?" hoarsely asked Signor Ravioli.

"Sure!"

The good music-master bounced to his feet. He removed his hat and flung it on the floor.

"Then-a you make up your mind, eh? All right? And-a you leesten to what I say. You gottem wrong!"

"Son, I'm beginnin' to wonder if you'll ever admit I've got anything right. In the name of Esau, what have I got wrong now?"

"Thees-a words. 'He's dead but he won't lie down.' 'Biggest Aspidistra in World.' You hear what I say?"

"I said I was listening, didn't I?"

"Okay. You read so often, see so often, seeng so

248

often, theenk you know! N-n-n-o! Each-a time you fair, but not-a quite right! Why? See 'em too often! Know 'em too well! That's-a what happen. What-a be next? I tell you! You be on platform, ready to seeng, forget whole damn-a song; then-a where you be? Wan t'ousand time I say: get-a right first time, then—"

Signor Ravioli, despite a gush of words so rapid that he seemed to gargle, stopped with a heave and tremolo of the throat.

Over the visage of Sir Henry Merrivale, a vivid bulk in his white alpaca suit, there had come as visible a change as though he himself had been walloped on the turnip as Masters had been.

"Oh, my eye," he breathed.

"What's-a da mat'?" shouted Signor Ravioli, evidently puzzled.

But in Virginia, though she had never before seen him in this mood, there stirred that feminine intuition which is like a wordless scream. This was the old Maestro.

"You know now, don't you?" she cried.

"Wait a minute!" said H.M., pressing his hands to his temples. "For the love of Esau gimme a chance to think!"

Silence. H.M. remained in that position for some moments. Then he lowered his hands. Though he accepted the presence of Virginia and Tom in the Oak Room, he did not see them as human beings. His fixed, malevolent gaze seemed to move through them in order to fasten upon that harmless scratch, made by the flange of the key to the safe, on the inside of a once-bolted door.

Still the silence lengthened . . . .

Momentarily the sun grew stronger, so that a line of dark old lead in window panel seemed to run with a lighter line like the silver ash tray by the rapier on the floor. H.M. moved. Slowly he moved round, the back of his neck swelling over his collar, so as to peer at the stringed lute on the hearth. In that position he remained motionless for many seconds more.

Round moved his head again, as though on a pivot.

"Dirt!" he said, from deep in his throat. "Far less than tracin' it, you couldn't even tell where it came from. There's too much of it; there's a whole county. For the other thing, who could swear it wasn't busted by accident? There's not even any point to making an enquiry. Haa!" added H.M., and relaxed.

Virginia could not help pouncing again. "You've guessed, haven't you?"

"Me?" said the galvanized H.M., waking up. "Guessed what? No!"

"Sir Henry, it's time we had an explanation of this maddening problem! But that isn't all. Unless Dad is too occupied with Miss Cheeseman to think of anything else, he swears he'll spend tonight here in the Oak Room. Even though you may think it's funny, I don't want him knocked out, too!"

H.M.'s gaze again grew absorbed. His seemed to watch something weighed in a scales.

"My dolly," he said, "my mind it is ashen and sober. But I'll tell you one thing. Neither you nor your Dad has the foggiest idea of what really happened on Wednesday night or last night either."

"Then how are we going to find out what happened?"

"That's easy. Let your old man be the guinea-pig, just as he wants to be, and stay here for a few hours."

"*What?*"

"Oh, my dolly!" said H.M. "He's in no real danger. I'll give you my word on that. The rest of us—all the rest of us; got me?—will take a solemn oath not to come near here. And we'll see what happens, this time, about the hour of midnight."

17

Over sleeping Sussex, on that hushed Saturday night, a multitude of church clocks clanged or boomed or whispered or clashed in eerie throated cacophony on the quarter-hour before twelve.

Congressman Harvey, mainly due to his own imagination, was growing more apprehensive as each quarter-hour passed.

From the rather low ceiling of the Oak Room, on a length of flex, hung its only light, an electric bulb in a parchment shade. Soft illumination induces mental quiet. But there are certain lights whose rawness, whose small but hard-cored glaze, only thickens shadow and suggests what may lie unpleasantly beyond it in the dark.

"Take it easy!" Mr. Harvey muttered aloud. He laughed, and the laugh was too loud. It made him glance suddenly over his shoulder.

Order had long ago been restored to the Oak Room.

Gone was the cup-hilted rapier, which now hung outside a door firmly bolted at top and bottom as well as with the key turned in the lock. The lute rested again on top of the harpischord, both shining with their patina of age like the dark-oak walls which hemmed in Mr. Harvey.

The chairs were all upright again. Inside an again-locked safe, where it remained unseen but safe, rested the Cavalier's Cup. A watcher, had any watcher in the flesh been present, would have known that the key to the safe was burning a hole in Mr. Harvey's right-hand trouser's pocket, lest it might be snatched from him.

Seated in one of the tall-backed chairs with straw-woven backs and bottoms, Virginia's father bent forward at the long, narrow table. On this, beside a silver ash tray from whose edge a balanced cigarette sent up straight greyish smoke because both windows were locked, lay several sheets of notepaper and an envelope.

After that quick glance over his shoulder, he turned back with the fountain pen in his hand, and added another line to what he had already written. Then he looked back at the beginning.

"My dear Virginia . . ."

By some it might have been considered odd that he should be writing a formal letter to a daughter who was now upstairs, in her room, at least within distance of a shout. But Congressman Harvey, being one of those who can never let bad alone, clearly felt he must justify his conduct of that afternoon.

"My dear Virginia," he had written. "It may have occurred to you that your old Dad's behavior, at lest with regard to Miss Elaine Cheeseman, was rather impulsive and not thought-out in advance. Here, I assure you, you are wrong . . . ."

Had he not been the private Bill Harvey, had he been now in the searching public eye as Representative William Tecumseh Harvey of the 23½ congressional district of Pennsylvania, a cold sweat might have broken out on him.

But it didn't. And he did not feel like that. In fact, he wanted the experience of that afternoon repeated as soon as possible. Elaine! Elaine!

"In many ways, Virginia, you are like your late mother. When annoyed or even angry, she would assume a patient smile, assuring her husband that nothing was wrong. Then she would march away in silence to her room, Jinny, try to understand. Miss Cheeseman is a lady of great charm . . ."

Here his pen had made a correction. He had written "of great talents." But, no doubt feeling that this might be open to misinterpretation, he had neatly, carefully altered it.

". . . and will, I hope, shortly become my wife . . . ."

Mr. Harvey, pen poised, again looked up and round quickly.

Every old room has its creaks and sharp cracks. The mere pressure of silence may weight the lungs and squeeze the nerves. Though as with others we may see only a part of Mr. Harvey's mind, it was not all occupied with Elaine even though he had fallen in love. His imagination was fire, was quicksilver. As he saw the harpsichord, it cannot be doubted that a part of his brain ran hotly with scenes and even scents out of a clashing past, when the Royalists attacked uphill at Naseby.

"March to the right!"

The thunderbolt charge of Prince Rupert's Horse, smashing Ireton's line like a china plate. Okey's Dragoons spitting and sputtering with matchlocks behind a hedge, the match-fuses glimmering red through cavalry-dust. The crash as old Noll piled everything against Langdale's mutinous Yorkshire pikes in the centre; then that weird, unmilitary order, "March to the right."

And, at the end of the din, the glimpse which had flung Sir Byng Rawdon into a madness of rage: victorious Parliament men piously slitting the noses of the Royalists' women camp-followers.

In history books you have read how Kentish Sir Byng, who could not attack sleeping men, awakened the Parliament camp with his defiance: "Bestir and arise, ye Roundheads, in the name of the King." That was not true. A very different shout had gone thundering through the ancient night, finer and truer and much deserved:

"The pox smite ye, ye psalm-singing sons of whores!"

Oliver Cromwell himself had been no bigot. He had even possessed a laudably primitive sense of humour, rejoicing in pranks. But Kentish Sir Byng, who had been very gentle towards his Lady and towards King Charles, would not scatter pomander when he met Colonel Harrison or similar canting hypocrites.

> "Here's a health unto his Majesty,
>   "With a fal lal lal. . ."

The harpischord in the Oak Room, of course, did not quiver now to the tingle of ghostly hands. Lady

Marian did not look up, pale-faced. No clumping of boots echoed as another figure stumbled in, with three leathern straps supporting the cup-hilted rapier at his hip.

Stop! This wouldn't do.

Congressman Harvey, holding a Parker fountain pen shining-modern from its conservative black colour to its brass pocket-clip, settled himself and again looked back on what he had written.

"I feel, Jinny, that I must explain to you the facts of life. Though I have no wish to write a long and pompous letter in the manner of Wilkins Micawber . . ."

Purely from force of habit, Mr. Harvey frowned. His pen moved to scratch out that reference to Micawber. Charles Dickens had been a British author.

But he had no time. The church clock at Great Yewborough, though a good distance away, made him jump by its towering imminence.

Bong smote the deep-toned bell on the first note of midnight. *Bong. Bong. Bong.* On it went, as unhurried as the death waiting for us, until it had ominously rounded its allotted number.

Then, a few seconds afterwards, there was a soft but insistent rapping at the door of the Oak Room.

Mr. Harvey, pen poised, his mobile mouth partly open, sat motionless in his conservative dark-blue double-breasted suit, with plain grey tie. He would not have been seen dead in any tie which was even noticeable, let alone conspicuous.

Slowly he turned his head towards the door.

"Who's there?" he called quietly.

The soft, insistent knocking was repeated. Otherwise he had no reply.

Congressman Harvey replaced the cap on the fountain pen with perhaps unusual care; it might have been to make sure his hands were not shaking. But first his alert green eyes went to the bolt at the top of the door, the bolt low down against the door. From there his gaze travelled across to the iron safe which held the Cavalier's Cup.

Yes, unquestionably you would have said that the safe-key burned his pocket, or else that superstition moved and sprang from some unswept corner of his mind. Putting down the pen on the table, he turned over one sheet of notepaper so as to conceal the writing.

The legs of the chair squeaked harshly and piercingly on a board floor as he stood up. He was not aware that he had squared his shoulders and stuck out his jaw. He went to the door, with a wrench of some effort drew back both bolts, turned the door-key with a snap, braced himself as he stood back, and let the door drift open.

Whereupon, after he had braced himself, his look indicated only a silent snort of exasperation at such an anticlimax, and a tinge of humiliation warmed his cheeks.

Just outside, his fussy mop of dark hair almost as heavy as a cavalier's, one hand behind his back doubtless in some dramatic gesture, stood only Signor Luigi Ravioli.

"In the name of sense," said Congressman Harvey, "what are you doing here? I thought you'd be gone home hours ago, after dinner, with that skunk Henry!"

"Sh-h!" hissed Signor Ravioli, pressing his left forefinger against his lips. "Not-a so loud!"

"What ails you?" asked the other, but obediently in a lower tone.

"Don't-a want to hear! All upstairs, yes. But Sir Henry, he's-a here. Drink whiskey in kitchen. Leesten!"

With his back to the door, still in that operatic gesture concealing his right hand, he closed the door. But he was serious, as much so, behind his Chianti nose, as Jennings had been that afternoon.

"Well, come in," invited Congressman Harvey, somewhat unnecessarily. "Not that I need company, mind! Nothing's happened here. Nothing's going to happen. But for the love of Pete don't make any remarks about spooks."

"Pah! No spooks! Talk about spooks so people not theenk about *me*. *I* theenk about me. Use-a misdirection like magician; you know-a what I mean?"

"No."

"Sh-h! All-a time you theenk about where-a you see me before. You-a say you see me before. Okay! You-a see me before, eh?"

"By golly, I'm certain I have!"

"*Ecco!* Here's-a me. Okay. Where-a you see me before?"

"Give me a chance, can't you? I've had a lot of important business on my mind. Incidentally, why are you keeping your hand behind your back?"

"Sh-h! Not-a so loud! Where-a you see me before?"

"All right; I give up. Where have I seen you before?"

"In da can!" said Signor Ravioli simply.

Mr. Harvey's eyes narrowed. Some of his suave manners fell away. Even the pink-tinted fleshly charms of the fair Elaine, all-engrossing to the point of obsession and more important than any other matter save one, were whirled away.

"When you use the word 'can,' my friend, do you mean . . . ?"

"Sure-a theeng! Da coop! Pennsylvania. Stick-a me in can."

"Rockview Penitentiary!" said Congressman Harvey, with sudden illumination. "By golly, yes! I was the guest of the warden, and you were singing Italian songs to a hall full of convicts." Abruptly his gaze darted to the iron safe, and his tone changed again. "What were you in for? Larceny?"

"Arsony? No! No-a set fire to nothing. Ignorant Dutchman, she's say Germans know more about music than Italians. Pah! Stick-a him with stilett'; you-a know what I mean? He's-a not die; he's-a all right. But me? In can!"

Signor Ravioli's voice, though musical and passionate, still kept its low tone as he flowed on.

"That's-a years and years past. What happen? Come-a to England; teach-a da music-sing; be British citizen. War come along. I'm a good British subject; no like-a Musso; everybody know it. But they got-a what you call 18-B. Me? In can again!"

"They kept you there for the whole war?"

"No. Wan fine officer-gentleman he's-a come to Isle of Man and say, 'Luigi,' he say, 'you're all right; out of can.' Good! Ten years more; fine! Then-a get thees job with Sir Henry. Now, oh, *ma donna!* Mees

Cheeseman, she's-a want to chuck Sir Henry in can. Ignorant flatfoot, he's-a want to chuck Jennings in can. You go on-a like today, shoot-a somebody hard in pants, chuck-a *you* in can. Please! You promise not to tell somebody where you see me before, yes?"

"Yes, of course! I won't tell any—here! You're not still wanted by the police, are you?"

"No! It's-a my reputation. You see what-a people say? 'Ravioli, eh? Fine-a teacher! Voice-a like Gigli! But no damn-a good to pupil; always in can.' No; no! You promise not to tell?"

Mr. Harvey was not aware that this afternoon his son-in-law, tacitly at least, had agreed not to betray a wanted man. But his course of action was the same.

"I promise. Word of honour!" he said.

Perhaps Congressman Harvey's nerves in the Oak Room were not as good as he maintained. Behind him there was the faintest flop of noise, hardly a breath against stillness. When he glanced back, he saw that his cigarette, undisturbed and burning to long ash, had fallen from the silver ash tray to the table.

Snatching up the cigarette, he stubbed it out in the tray. Its smoke yet hung flatly and stung the nostrils with sour acridness. The noise had been no more than the fall of that cigarette. But it had all but made his muscles explode like overwound springs. Turning back, he found that Signor Ravioli's eyes were fixed on him with singular intentness.

"Leesten!" said the music-master. "I'm-a no damn-a fool, eh?" And, as had been evident all along, clearly he wasn't. "But I do-a my job. Come-a here, please, and I show-a you something."

"Show me what?"

"I do-a my job. Signor gentleman, come-a here!"

Perflexed, the other took a step forward. At the same instant, noiselessly because its hinges had been oiled, the big oak door behind Signor Ravioli swung open. In the aperture stood a white figure.

Again the reader must not be misled. It was only Sir Henry Merrivale in his alpaca suit. Yet, to judge by the colour, a hot-and-cold crawl of gooseflesh tightened the face of Congressman Harvey.

It was a somewhat changed H.M. It was H.M. rampant; H.M. the powerhouse; H.M. radiating wickedness like a furnace, malignant as the Evil One; charged with energy, ready to pounce. If he saw what Signor Ravioli held concealed, not a muscle moved in his big face.

"Evenin', son," he said.

The music-master, himself uttering a kind of melodious squeal as though his own nerves were not of the best, swung away and backed towards the right-hand wall where stood the safe.

"Why is everybody prowling round like this?" aggrievedly asked Mr. Harvey. "What's up? I'm all right! As I told *il maestro* a moment ago, nothing's going to happen."

"Listen, son. There's only one maestro in this case or any other case. That's me. And don't talk like Masters, either. If you say something can't happen, it'll happen before the words are out of your mouth. What's more, I'm here to make something happen."

"What-a you mean?" demanded Signor Ravioli, with another noise in his throat.

"Son, you've been goin' all day about how you

261

wanted to be Dr. Watson. You've said how you wanted to hear me say something astonishing; then you'd be amazed. Right you are, son! The time's here. Fire away with your questions."

Signor Ravioli made a rush for the still-open door.

"Get-a da hat," he explained.

But H.M., fists on hips, manoeuvred in front of him.

"Never mind the hat. Stay where you are, and ask the questions!"

"*I'll* ask the most important question, if he won't," interposed Congressman Harvey. "I'd like to make sure this was a real locked room; not somebody, somehow, operating from outside. Did the guilty party—on two separate occasions—actually get into this room, move the cup out of the safe, and leave here with the place still locked up on the inside?"

"Uh-huh," assented H.M.

The Oak Room had grown hotter yet. It was as though its smell of old wood, stone, and generations of furniture-polish seeped into the pores of the skin as well.

"In that case . . ." began Mr. Harvey.

But Signor Ravioli was evidently furious.

"Who's-a Dr. Watson, you or me?" he asked Congressman Harvey, with jealous passion. "Anybody ask-a questions, its me. Good! We find-a wan motive for all thees hokey-pokey. Now!" The forefinger of his left hand shot out towards H.M. "What was da motive?"

"Theft," said H.M.

"*Theft?*"

"Sure," agreed H.M., his fists still on his lips.

"You're-a nuts," screamed Signor Ravioli, a sentiment seldom heard on the lips of Dr. Watson.

"Am I? Looky here, Caruso. You were in this room this afternoon when I was rehearsin' at that harpischord. For a little bit I had the right-hand window open, not wantin' to stifle, though I closed it soon after that. And what did we both hear?

"We heard," retorted H.M., answering himself, "the lost butler, Jennings, standing at a window quite close to here, and pourin' out his grievances to Tom and Virginia Brace. Burn it all, he even noticed me and said he noticed me! Properly interpreted, which isn't hard, that story of his supplied every final link we needed. But I was an awful dummy. I never stuck the couplin-pin in the last bit of evidence until . . .

"Anyway, it should have been as plain as print from what Jennings said. Don't wiggle your nose; you heard him say it, too."

"Jennings!" cried Signor. "Jennings, he's the guilty wan?"

"No." H.M. spoke with rounded distinctness. "All Jennings did, as he said he did, was supply the guilty party with certain things the criminal—if you can say criminal—needed and had to have. No more! You'll see it easily if you just unstick your eyelids and remember that the motive for all this was theft."

Despite his own injunction for silence, the music-master danced on the floor.

"You're-a nuts!" he repeated, pointing his left hand towards the iron safe. "There-a nothing been stolen!"

"I know that, son."

"Then what-a you say? Nobody has-a swipe thees

263

Cavalier's Cup!"

"Ah!" said H.M., with such a ghoulish pounce of voice that even a spectre would have shied back. "No, nobody has. But that's the point. That's exactly what led us in the wrong direction from the beginning, and kept us from seeing what we ought to have seen first off. Nobody stole the Cavalier's Cup, just as Jennings said, or ever had the remotest idea of stealin' the Cavalier's Cup."

"Then what did thees guilty wan want to steal?"

Drawing a deep breath like an ogre tucking his napkin into this collar for a good meal, H.M. slowly extended a hand and pointed straight in front of him.

"He wanted to steal that!"

"Me, I not-a see nothing! He wanta-a steal what?"

"There!" insisted H.M., shaking his finger for emphasis.

Signor Ravioli, wild-eyed swung round.

"The guilty party," continued H.M., "wanted to steal a real relic, a holy relic as far as the—hur-rum!—the criminal was concerned. It necessitated, as a very essential part of what the guilty party had to do, all the jiggery-pokery that's flummoxed people.

"In short," H.M.'s big voice rose, "the guilty party wanted to steal just one pane of seventeenth-century glass: oblong, somewhat bigger than Masters' hand when the hand's held upright, the glass scrawled with a historic message written by Sir Byng Rawdon before the fightin' cavalier romantically died in a scrap under the oak tree a little way outside that window."

H.M. paused for a moment.

"Now there's only one person, my fatheads, who both had a burnin' passion to pinch that panel of glass and had the ingenuity to work out a method of doing it undetected. That's the feller who once pinched from the British Museum a beautifully bound, very rare eye-witness account of the battle of Marston Moor in the Civil War, and evolved—as you heard!—a real Arsène Lupin plot to steal it when a friend bet he couldn't do it."

H.M.'s pointing finger swung straight at Congressman Harvey.

"You're the guilty party," he said, "and the only guilty party. Now aren't you?"

18

Mr. Harvey did not move, though he stiffened in the well cut blue suit.

The raw yellow electric light, scarcely drained of harshness by its buff shade, beat down on his smoothly brushed brown hair, his firm jaw, the faint lines drawn round and outwards from his eyes.

He did not deny H.M.'s accusation. His green eyes moved right and left: a look sometimes seen when William T. Harvey, Attorney at Law—who in court never appeared for the prosecution, always for the defence—saw some tricky stratagem by prosecuting counsel, and was first appraising it.

Indeed, he showed more than this. Across his face flickered a brief, appreciative smile, a delighted smile. You could not doubt he was the guilty man. But Congressman Harvey loved the detective duel of wits as much as with a lady he loved, figuratively speaking, the study of a dictionary.

The smile disappeared. Taking several steps back, towards the historic window outside which in moonlight loomed some distance away the famous oak tree, he folded his arms. All he said was, "Close that door!"

Signor Ravioli reeled back, his right hand still hidden behind his back. But about this scene, now, there was not the slightest hint that a black-hearted villain was being unmasked. On the contrary. Once Sir Henry Merrivale had unburdened himself of the accusing blast, he became sombre and even in a sense apologetic.

H.M. closed the door. There was a snap as he turned the key in the lock against intruders.

"Suppose you could prove what you say." Though Mr. Harvey spoke sharply, the flicker of an appreciative smile again came and went. "*Suppose* you could, I say. What do you propose to do about it?"

H.M.'s almost invisible eyebrows went up.

"Nothin'," he said simply. "Oh, son! Aside from the fact that I'm the world's outstanding compounder of felonies, you didn't steal the panel of glass after all. It's still there; look at it! As Jennings said, it's all right and nothing actually happened. My concern, son, is to keep Masters from provin' it when he wakes up tomorrow morning."

Congressman Harvey expelled his breath hard.

"Thanks, Henry," he said.

"Not a bit, son."

"But how in the name of sense did you get on to me?" Mr. Harvey tightened his folded arms, all power and personality, his intellectual interest clearly soaring above the fear of what his daughter would say. "That's what fascinates me, Henry. And it's the main thing. How did you get on to me?"

Now it was Signor Ravioli who burst out.

"Thees-a gentleman do it?" What started as a scream ended in partial paralysis of vocal cords. "Thees-a gentleman bop ignorant flatfoot with blackjack?"

"I didn't want to do it!" protested Mr. Harvey, with apparent sincerity. "I didn't mean to do it! But I had to!"

H.M., looking very hard at his music-master, used the italics of speech to distinguish Signor Ravioli from himself.

"*Maestro,*" he said, "shut up."

"But how he get in and out of room? She's impossible!"

"Sit down on harpsichord bench," H.M. ordered implacably, "and listen." He would not abate his glare until Signor Ravioli had done so. "Though I'll admit," he added, "it was my Dr. Watson who said the first truest words and the last most enlightenin' words we've heard."

"How?" insisted Congressman Harvey.

Slowly H.M. pulled round the tall Jacobean chair beside the narrow table on which lay the fountain pen and the sheets of notepaper. With some effort he lowered his bulk and managed to fit himself into the chair. There he faced Mr. Harvey, who stood away from him, back to the moonlit window, while Mr. Harvey was torn in silence by a number of emotions.

"Y'see, son," H.M. began in his ponderous way,

"good old Jennings stated—though you weren't there and didn't hear him—that your daughter and your son-in-law didn't understand the mystery, that the locked room wasn't important, and neither was the Cavalier's Cup.

"The first clues to this business were all poured out yesterday evening, when a lot of us sat by the fountain in the garden at Cranleigh. But Gigli there made the first very profound observation. Gigli said that the British and the Americans ought to stop tryin' to understand other people, and begin tryin' to understand themselves.

"As an Englishman, son, I'm not goin' to be impertinent enough to say I understand all Americans, because Americans are of too many mixed types. But, oh, my eye! I very well understand Americans of your type. There are lots of 'em, and I'll show you what I mean.

"Now that Cavalier's Cup was a fake relic. It hadn't one particle of historic or sentimental interest. No, it was only worth a staggerin', colossal sum of money. So you, being a Yank, didn't care two hoots and a whistle about it. That panel in the window, where a dying cavalier scratched his last work, wasn't intrinsically worth more than any sheet of seventeenth-century glass. But sentimentally? As a matter of tradition? Historically?

"That's different. To an American of Eng—of Scottish and Irish ancestry, lovin' tradition and history and the Royalist cause in the Civil Wars, hatin' the Roundheads and everything they stood for, that piece of glass would be an unholy joy even if—just as happened with the book from the British Museum—you had to keep it quiet and never show it except in secret. So you, bein' a Yank, would have given anything to own it."

Congressman Harvey drew in his chin.

"Just one moment, Henry! The aspersions you cast on my veracity when I state those great principles and ideals to which my life has been dedicated . . . "

Here Signor Ravioli interrupted him by whacking a note on the harpsichord.

"He's-a telling da truth, Signor Harvey! *Si!* Many Americans just-a like you; only won't admit it."

"Mr. Chairman, I protest against the implication that . . . "

"You be quiet, son!" said H.M. sternly eyeing Congressman Harvey. "There never was anybody who's laid himself so much open to blackmail as you've done. Am I goin' to continue with this, or not? Right! Yesterday evening, when I first heard the lurid tale of Sir Byng Rawdon's adventures and the phantom who slipped in and out of the locked room, I said to myself, 'This has got William Tecumseh Harvey stamped all over it; it's the panel in the window he wanted, not the cup; but how did he do it, and what's the answer to a couple of objections I can see?' "

"Hold your horses, man!"

"Oh, lord love a duck!"

"My own daughter," blurted Mr. Harvey, "hasn't got any idea I'm guilty, has she? Even now?"

"No. That's why I took good care to swear to her you didn't know a thing."

"Today, you see, she told that whole story about the book from the British Museum, and how I had to keep it in secret afterwards. I tell you, Henry, I nearly fainted across the table! Also, I suppose either she or Tom must have mentioned something about it to you tonight?"

"Uh-huh."

"Yes. But how would you have known it yesterday evening?"

"Oh, son! That holograph account of the battle of Marston Moor; we keep callin' it a 'rare' book, because that's the term usually employed, but to be accurate it's unique and its valuable. When it was pinched, years ago, the Museum authorities suspected you and they got in touch with me."

"*Wow!*"

"Sure; that's what I mean. In general, y'see, it's tricky yet not too difficult to nick an ordinary book out of the British Museum. You do it by a substitution process; it wants steady nerves, that's the main thing. But the rare ones, or manuscripts? That's different. The Museum authorities couldn't prove anything, so they had to drop the matter." Here H.M.'s tone grew more apologetic. "I saw through your trick. But it was almighty ingenious; I hadn't the heart to give you away."

"Even though you knew . . . ?"

"It's like this, son. In my philosophy, if somebody swindles or cheats or acts too sharp in a business

271

deal, it's the lowest trick on earth and deserves years in prison. But to pinch a book or a painting or an *object d'art* out of a public institution—where, like heavy-game huntin', the odds are even—that's all right. It shows the fine spark of individualism still burns in a brutish mass."

Congressman Harvey stared at him.

"You damned old villain!" he shouted. Then he recovered himself. "No, I'm not being as inconsistent as I sound. I can't sleep; my conscience is all over me! I do these things, yes. But I don't defend them."

"That's where we're different, son. I defend these things. But I don't do 'em. However!"

"You tell us!" said Signor Ravioli. "You say what-a you theenk last night by da fountain in garden!"

"All right. Yesterday evening—before I learned Jennings was Prentice Thorne, the noted forger—it did seem to me that the conduct of the new butler at Telford was very rummy, and that he was somehow mixed up in the affair. Having gone over that with the little gal, I don't need to repeat it. But, if W. T. Harvey did happen to be the evil genius behind it, it seemed at first glance there were a lot of stumbling-blocks to that theory.

"He wants that panel out of the window, does he? First, then, why does he mix himself up with the Cavalier's Cup at all?

"How would he go about stealin' that panel out of a number of oblong panels in the window, in the second place? Puttin' the method aside for a moment, look at what he's done! He must have had

272

plenty of opportunities to do the dirty work in darkness and secrecy. He can't want a witness. But no! He chooses the one night, the one and only night, when the Cavalier's Cup has unexpectedly come back from the Cherriton Museum—when the cup's locked in that safe there, and his son-in-law is sittin' up in this room—he chooses that night for some kind of flummery with the window!

"And it appeared—I say appeared—there was even worse. When Tom Brace began to worry about burglars, Congressman Harvey was the very feller who made things so much worse, by goin' on about Raffles and Arsene Lupin and Jimmy Valentine, that young Brace determined to sit up all night on guard over the cup.

"So at first sight it seemed there wasn't a reasonable doubt I was loony and Jennings alone must be guilty. Burn me, there didn't even seem an unreasonable doubt of it!

"All the same, as I was sittin' and thinkin' in that same garden, it came to the old man that these seeming contradictions weren't contradictions at all. No, they were the reverse. From evidence just given by the little gal herself, they supplied the key to the door.

"*You,*" here H.M. nodded towards Mr. Harvey, who was watching him intently, "had been in England only about ten days. You didn't intend to stay long. You've still got to get back soon. But what in particular took place on Wednesday, the very day the Cavalier's Cup was unexpectedly hoicked back from the Cherriton Museum?

"Well, your daughter told us. You'd also got an unexpected cable tellin' you to tear straight back to America about an important law case. You were so concerned about it that you upset yourself and everybody else until you got a reservation on the Pan American plane for Thursday. That was real; that rang true. But what did it mean? If you meant to nick the glass from that panel, then you'd ruddy well *have* to do it on Wednesday night!

"It was risky, sure. But there wasn't any other time. The daytime was too dangerous, with people about all over the plane, either on Wednesday or Thursday.

"Now I'm bettin', son, you made this whole particular trip to England with one of your main objects being to pinch that panel you've coveted for so long. But I don't insist on that. We're both lawyers, and I'm goin' on evidence. Was there any further evidence to support this contention of mine?

"There smacking well was! Because, although you did make your son-in-law even more apprehensive about burglars, and did relate a lot of lurid stories, it was to *prevent* him from putting the Cavalier's Cup in the safe in this room." H.M. looked hard at Signor Ravioli. "I say, Boswell! Do you follow that one?"

To the imminent danger of an antique, the music-master smote the keys of the harpsichord another clash.

"Got heem! Remember now! That-a safe is only safe in house. Oak Room here she's natural place to

274

put cup." Now Signor Ravioli bounced. "But-a young lady she's-a tell us . . . "

"That's enough!" snapped H.M., fearful lest his thunder be stolen. "The little gal explained what happened. Tom Brace wanted to put the cup in here. *Tom* did. You," again he glowered at Mr. Harvey, "you, on the other hand, tried like blazes to stop him.

"You argued and argued, according to your daughter. 'My boy,' you said, quoting her exact words, 'why don't you take the cup to your bedroom for the night!' Of course you said that! You didn't want anybody even comin' near that Oak Room while you had a shot at the window. True, next day another cable came to say you needn't go back to America after all. But, at the time, you couldn't have known that; so far as you knew, Wednesday night was your desperate chance but your only chance.

"So, again to quote the little gal, you went on arguing with Tom until you and he, quote, 'got to shouting at each other and pounding the table again.' In the end you dished your own crafty plan. Instead of locking the cup in the safe, and maybe slippin' down here once or twice to make sure it was all right, Tom decided at dinner to sit up all night in this room.

"Cor! That was at dinner, I repeat. But we'll again consider Me," said the martyred H.M., giving himself the capital letter of impressiveness, "still sittin' and thinkin' in the garden. William Tecumseh Harvey's fine Eng—Scottish hand could be seen everywhere. But, if you'd done it, how had you done it?

"Y'see, both Tom Brace and your daughter love

that window as a personal thing. They hang about it. They dream of it. If there's been the slightest hokey-pokey, or so I said to myself, they'd have noticed it like a shot.

"Then, in the garden yesterday evening, *you* turned up. Having already discussed a certain matter with your daughter, I was then handed on a plate, by you yourself, a dazzlin' piece of evidence. I knew it was important, yes, 'cause it hit me between the eyes and made me blink; you saw that. But, bein' awful dense, I didn't see the direction of it. I mean the point about the plumbers."

"Plumbers?" exclaimed Signor Ravioli. "Bang-a da pipe! Make-a da plumb worse than she is before! What's-a plumbers got to do with this?"

"Everything," retorted H.M.

Congressman Harvey, looking as though he did not know whether to utter a wild snort at his own folly or smile wickedly, compromised by tightening his folded arms still further.

"Go on, Henry. The very owls listen to your wisdom."

"Owls are—burn it all, shut up about owls! Who's talkin' about owls? Plumbers! Virginia had mentioned, d'ye see, how you always bragged and bragged all over the place that you'd begun life as a plumber, just because your old man had a bee in his own bonnet.

"Well, you did learn that trade. And, since you pitch in with awful heartiness to anything you do, from—no, never mind; I'll stop there. I told Virginia

276

how the first thing *I'd* ever heard from you, when I met you in the States, was your goin' on about being a plumber. You seemed to have done nothin' else. You waved the soldering-lamp and the plunger as much as you waved the flag, though in fact you don't like workin' with your hands . . . "

"Wait a minute, Henry! I resent that imputation!"

H.M., in heavy distress, peered over his big spectacles.

"Oh, son! Drop your public face for just a second. Admit the horrible charge of bein' a well-born and cultured man. You can stick the public face back on in a second, just as people do here in England. What I'm saying is that yesterday evening in the garden, you dropped your public face so unexpectedly—and for no apparent reason—that it jolted me. Remember?"

"Yes! You needn't rub it in."

"I'm awful sorry, son. But you asked me to tell this. Now, you can drop your public face fast enough when you're hypnotized and swept away by imagination or literature or some female's dictionary. But this wasn't one of those instances, if you'll think back. You were tryin' to remember where you'd seen my good old music-teacher before. I don't know where that was, by the way, and I don't want to know.

"But I asked you very casually, not meaning anything, at all, 'How's the plumbing business?' Oh, my eye! You looked as guilty and strained as though I'd said, 'Aha! You sneaked out and voted Republican, didn't you?' And all in haste you answered, 'Oh, that? There wasn't much to that; forget it. I never was much good as a plumber anyway.'

"Comin' from you, son, that was comparable to sayin' you'd seen a red-white-and-blue turkey with a straw hat on. Lord love a duck, thinks I, *that's important!* That's somehow connected with the secret of how he snaffled or tried to snaffle the cavalier's panel!"

"But-a how?" demanded Signor Ravioli, now melodiously gibbering. "What if he chase-a gas pipe all over house? No gas pipe here! Can't-a crawl through damn-a gas pipe and sock ignorant flatfoot, eh?"

"I'm comin' to that now," said H.M. "That was my state of mind, d'ye see, when last night—or, to be court-exact, in the shiverin' dark hours at half-past three on Saturday morning—the phone rang by my bed. Virginia poured out the tale of what had been happenin' at Telford. I'd already got half the problem. Her account blazin'ly supplied two-thirds.

"Got it? According to Masters, who knows his job about professional crooks, the vanished Jennings was a famous forger. In the little gal's words, he was a man who can imitate anybody's signature. Handwriting! Handwriting!

"Jennings, to be exact, supplied a good part of what had been missing. He was a professional crook. *You,*" again H.M. looked at Mr. Harvey, "you, Bill, I say again don't care two whistles about money. You make it easily; you spend it easily. You didn't pinch that book from the British Museum until you'd offered a smacking sight more than the book was

278

worth. What *else* did Masters say about Prentice Thorne, alias Jennings?

"According to what I heard tonight, in the general post-mortem of talk when all of us except Elaine Cheeseman had dinner here, Tom Brace himself mentioned at the breakfast table this morning what Masters said. If in the future I mention any bit of evidence that trickled out when I wasn't here, just remember I picked it up later, or, bein' the old man, didn't need to hear it. But you heard it. One or the other of you had every scrap of evidence.

"Masters, says Tom, announces that Jennings has been in jail in the United States. He must have intimated that one William T. Harvey might have known Jennings there, because at the breakfast table Tom flat-out suggests *you*," again H.M. considered the culprit, "might have had Jennings as a client.

"You denied it, of course. Then you changed the subject, as deftly but as rapidly as good old Benson himself, while lookin' very hard at a sugar-bowl.

"But it'd already occurred to me. Cor! Just suppose you had once known Jennings? Suppose you came here, burnin' to have that glass panel but not quite sure how to snaffle it without forever alienating the affections of your daughter and son-in-law?

"Here's a former crook. If Caesar Borgia at the harpsichord will remember, I suggested chloral hydrate as a means of drugging the coffee given to Tom by Jennings on Wednesday night. Chloral creeps up on you. Even when you take it knowingly, you think it's not goin' to work; and that's all you remember. It occurred to me first off that both you and Jennings were the kind of wiry, nerve-strung people, sufferers from insomnia, who keep sleeping-draughts handy. Jennings had chloral, as he later admitted. Jennings might succumb to a big money-bribe, as later he confessed he did—Oi! Bill! What's rackin' your conscience at this date?"

"When I defend them in court," said Mr. Harvey, briefly and without a tinge of boasting, "they don't usually go to jail."

"But is that what's bothering you?"

"No! It's Jennings! The only thing I'm honestly ashamed of!"

"In what way?"

"Be human, Henry! I tempted him, and he fell. Mind you, he's very well heeled with cash. If he can get away from this district without being pinched—sorry, I mean 'pinched' in the American sense of arrested—he swore he could reach Canada and start a new life as he's wanted to. But what's happened to Jennings? Where is he now?"

"Haven't you got any idea, son?"

"No, I haven't!" truthfully replied the anguished Mr. Harvey. "Tommy told me he saw Jennings on the lawn this afternoon, talking to Jinny and Tom. But that can't be! You know what kids are: Tommy might honestly believe he saw Henry of Navarre in a white plume, after the lies you fed him. Jinny and Tom denied it, and they're law-abiding citizens."

Caesar Borgia at the musical instrument, his right hand still hidden by the top of the harpsichord, opened his mouth for explosive speech. But H.M.'s look pinned him like an arrow, and Signor Ravioli said nothing.

"Uh-huh," agreed H.M., with *basso profondo* dreaminess. "Tom Brace is English, son. Not bein' a Yank like you, he'd never think of breakin' the law. Jennings has got away off his own bat, that's all. So for the love of Esau let me go back to my sitting and thinking in the early hours of this morning.

"Jennings! The most striking realization, freezin' the hair I haven't got, was the fact that Jennings is an expert forger. For instance, look at that window behind you! It wouldn't be difficult to *duplicate* the glass in just one panel of all those oblongs. 'Cause why? 'Cause, as everybody's seen, the glass here at Telford is smooth and well-blown; it hasn't got any of those flaws or whorls such as you sometimes get in Elizabethan glass of an earlier date. Use another pane of seventeenth-century glass, neatly cut from somewhere else in the house at Telford, and you could duplicate one panel.

"But that's not all you could duplicate. Straightaway I saw the possibility of the real purpose, rather a pretty idea and a brand-new wrinkle in crime—a piece of forged handwriting, done with a very sharp point on glass."

Signor Ravioli, as he had pointed out, was no fool. Clearly he saw what this portended. But he remained frantic.

"Sir Henry! Leesten! That's-a plain, you bet! But-a why this gentleman take-a cup out of safe and put it on table? Once he do it when fine young gentleman sit up here; once he do it when ignorant cop sit here, too. Twice! First, why he do that?"

H.M. shook his big head dismally.

"That's the simplest part, as I saw when I was meditatin' in the early hours of Saturday morning. To make people think what they did think: that the whole attack of the phantom burglar was directed at the cup, and had nothing to do with the window!"

"So-a!" The music-master looked enlightened.

"Exactly. This feller, who could get Judas Iscariot acquitted by drawing attention away from essentials that were in plain sight, very beautifully used misdirection. Just as a certain other person I know, less effectively though, used misdirection to draw attention away . . ."

"But I keep wishing to know," Signor Ravioli was nearing a fit, "how he get-a in and out-a room? Plumbers? Pah! Bang, bang, bang, bang on lead pipe! Water pipe? Gas pipe? What's-a da good?"

"That's not it. But you're getting warm. Quick, now! What do the words 'lead pipe' suggest to you?"

"Sockem-a cop!"

"No! No! You're so obsessed by—hem!—one or two things that have happened to you in the past, Cagliostro, that you can't think of anything except how pleasurable it is when a copper gets walloped. Lead pipe, leaded pipe— What about 'leaded window'?"

Signor Ravioli abruptly craned round to look at the window behind Mr. Harvey.

"Never in our born days," snorted H.M., "have we had two words slung at us so often, or by so many people, as that term 'leaded window.' The trouble is that most people don't even stop for a second to think what it means. They have a hazy picture of manorial houses rich in armorial bearings and leaded windows. Mostly they don't reflect on the really singular point: that a leaded window—its frame, every bit of the joinings between all its oblong glass panels—is really made of lead.

"Astonishin', but true. Lead, and nothing else.

"What's next? There have been plumbers in this house for a week. In this particular case, do the plumbers take away their tools as usual when they leave at night? No, they don't. As Tom Brace mentioned at breakfast, he'd had a flamin' row with the plumbers, and got 'em to leave their tools here overnight, because they weren't engaged in any other job of work.

"Even in that simple process I can't tell you how Tom persuaded 'em; nowadays the only person who's got no rights is an employer. But he managed it. What, among the plumbers' kit, are we certain they've got? A petrol soldering-lamp, my fatheads. It's used on lead pipes; you pump it up first; then, when you switch it on, you get a narrow but fierce blue flame several inches long. Lead softens or gives way like putty.

"When did that snake Masters have his inspiration about how the trick was worked, so that he shouted out he knew? You can remember. It was when he walked straight into a lot of plumbers' tools left at the top of the stairs into the main hall. He stumbled over the tools on his own big feet. He actually kicked the soldering-lamp before he tumbled downstairs on his turnip.

"Now looky here, for a demonstration!"

With an expiring "Haa!" of breath, and a look of martyrdom, H.M. rose up out of the tall chair beside the narrow table. He lumbered over towards the left-hand window. Congressman Harvey, still wrenched between apprension and a wry amusement, stood aside without comment.

"Look at the panel with Sir Byng Rawdon's writing on it!" said H.M. "Where is it? Everybody here has already seen it, so you know."

His finger indicated the panel. Just one oblong-panel to the right of this, or somewhat wider than the breadth of a large man's hand, the heavy metal handle of the window-catch was twisted into its locked position.

"Let's imagine," pursued H.M., "you're standing *outside* this locked window, and you've got a petrol soldering-lamp with the flame roarin'. That flame makes a distinct noise; apart from other consider-ations, you've got to be sure anybody in the room is fast asleep.

"Now anybody at all could work the trick with the soldering-lamp, yes. But only somebody who'd been trained as a plumber, or at least a worker of that kind, could do it just right without possibility of a flub.

" 'Cause why? Well, imagine you're outside. You play that thin, powerful flame on three sides of the oblong: the bottom and the two sides. The lead softens like putty; the glass panel hasn't been fitted into a groove, as ordinary window-glass has. It's only been stuck there in a surrounding of lead. The inside is a part of the outside. When you've half-melted the outside, you've half-melted the inside.

"At the same time—follow me?—you play the flame of your lamp very lightly and quickly across the *top* side of the oblong, not half-meltin' it, but only softening it. So it acts as a hinge for the three loose sides.

"From the outside, push with your finger against the glass. The loose panel, detached at sides and bottom, will swing inwards like a hinge: the panel bein' held by the softened top side.

"There's only one point, which the same I mentioned, where you've got to take care. Half-melted lead won't 'run' in the same sense that water will run. But it's apt to move a bit in a faintly jagged line unless you're awful careful to keep the flame of your lamp straight and steady and even. Keep the flame even, and nobody will notice it afterwards; the movement is too slight. That's where a practised hand with the lamp comes in; and the time you need is very short—measured in seconds, not minutes. If you doubt me, ask anybody who's worked a lot with lead.

"Now look at the window! You see how close the loked metal handle is to the panel? You're outside, the window being only waist-high above the ground.

We knew that too. You're not a big man with a big hand like Masters. You're a small man with small, neat hand like Congressman Harvey.

"Suppose all you want is just a locked room? Right! Pushing the loose pane inwards on its top hinge, you just reach through and turn the locked catch of the window, unlockin' it. You open the window, climb inside, and do any kind of jiggery-pockery you fancy. When you're ready to leave, it's just as simple.

"Climb outside, pull the window shut, lock it again with your hand still through a half-open trap. What you do now can be done in half a dozen ways. But the simplest is to use a child's toy we've all seen. A toy spring-pistol fires at the wall or at a cardboard target a light wooden missile, rather like a pencil, on the end of which is a small rubber suction-cup. When the cup strikes the target, the air-pressure makes it stick there fairly hard.

"All right. Press that toy suction-rod on the outside of the glass panel. Pull it towards you, havin' softened the lead again if necessary, so that the panel moves back into its place, all tightly sealed.

"There's one effect you can partly conceal, but you've got to have great care to conceal it completely. This feller here," H.M.'s big head wagged at the culprit, "worked in a hurry on two occasions. If he'd taken more care, he could completely have covered his traces like the red Indian Chinka-what's-his-name in Fenimore Cooper. But he didn't, and you saw the result.

"When you play a fiercely hot little flame on old lead—which is black in colour from age—you're goin' to oxydize the lead partly. What I mean—it'll turn a bit silvery in colour. You can blacken it again by smearing it carefully, over and over, with ordinary dirt. Nobody can ever tell where you got the dirt; there's too much in the world in every sense. You don't leave a clue.

"But maybe the Duke of Gandia there," H.M.'s finger pointed at Signor Ravioli, "remembers how we were in this room only this afternoon. Hey? All of the sudden a strong sun got very fiery behind some trees, and poured on the window. Along the underside of a panel, *this* panel, there ran a line of light like silver where the sun caught it at the proper angle.

"That was a dead give-away. The joinings of leaded windows, I repeat, are and ought to be black with age. Somebody's been a bit hasty with darkening the window-joinings again, though they weren't large or conspicuous.

"So, my fatheads, you're outside the window; you've just pulled it shut with a suction-rod from a toy pistol. Tommy's got one of those toy-pistol suction-rod outfits. His Gramp bought it for him. Well, you detach the tiny little rod with a flick of your good old wrist. The lead cools and hardens, so there's not one soft bit to mark any sign of entry. The metal catch is solidly locked. Hey-presto! Locked room! Miracle!"

Signor Ravioli, violently agitated, developed once more a tendency to bounce.

"*Corpo di Bacco!* I could do her myself. I like to

287

try, yes?"

"No! Stay where you!"

"You're first man what theenk of theese hoke-poke with leaded window?"

"Exceptin' Congressman Harvey here, yes."

"But how you theenk of it? I mean, sure, you gotta da evidence! Remember evidence. But how your theenk-tank work in such funny way?"

" 'Cause I'm the old man," said H.M. "My whole life," he added with unusual candor, "is devoted to thinkin' how you can hocus things and make miracles."

"I try it, please?"

"No, son. Because you still don't see where this is tending. That's what you'd do, I've said, if all you wanted was a locked room. But our friend here didn't want a locked room. He wanted to pinch the panel out of the window, which was his whole scheme . . . "

"Yes," interrupted Congressman Harvey with some violence, unfolding his arms, "and that's where everything went wrong!"

"So," said H.M., unsurprised.

"Believe it or not, yes! I tried for the first time on Wednesday night, when Tom was asleep in here. Since you've already said so much, you can guess what Jennings had prepared for me. He had prepared an exact duplicate of that oblong panel, the same size down to the shaving of a millimetre, and with an undetectable reproduction of Sir Byng Rawdon's handwriting on it. It was Jennings' best forgery.

"The fact is, Henry, his trouble was not the handwriting at all. His only difficulty, though it didn't prove a real difficulty, was to have a piece of glass which could pass as the original glass . . . "

"Oi! Garibaldi!" H.M. broke in abruptly.

"What's-a da mat'?"

"You remember what Jennings said to Tom and Virginia this afternoon? 'You'll see my difficulty, sir and madam!' " H.M., who never forgot anything, quoted with his eyes shut. " 'It's the same difficulty as with bank notes. Your trouble isn't the engraving; it's the paper. You've got to use a faithful reproduction of the paper, or you're done. It was here in the house, only from another part of it—you'd never guess where—I got the reproduction.' Of course Tom and Virginia thought Jennings was loopy, but . . . "

"He's-a talk about glass!" hissed the music-master.

"Sure," agreed H.M. "He's-a talk about sense all the time. But you were saying?" And H.M. eyed the guilty Mr. Harvey.

"I damn near died," succinctly replied that individual, flinging out his arms. "On Wednesday night, when Tom was asleep in here, I unstuck three sides of the panel—as you said, Henry—and put my hand through, turned the catch, and opened the window.

"But every minute I was afraid the glass would crack. I didn't want a gasoline blow-torch of the kind I had. Not on your tintype! What I needed was an electric blow-torch of the kind they use in radio repair work. In addition to being noiseless, which didn't matter so much, it's got a far hotter and more powerful narrowed blaze, which you can't see at all. You couldn't crack the glass; the lead would be much easier, and . . . "

Signor Ravioli shivered with further enlightenment.

"Ignorant cop! That's-a why Masters say he know because his brother has got a radio repair shop?"

"Bull's eye, son," observed H.M. "But let this confession go on!"

"Well, I didn't have one," said Mr. Harvey. "Even if I'd had one, you need an electric socket to plug it in, and there wasn't one *outside* the house. But that wasn't the first consideration."

Now honestly rattled from Mr. Harvey, full confession which soothes the soul.

"I thought to myself, even as I climbed into the room on Wednesday, 'This isn't like robbing the British Museum or the Library of Congress. This is simply a dirty trick on my daughter and her husband. It isn't going to be so easy to *replace* a panel as merely to get in and out of an apparently sealed room. Maybe I can't work it at all, because the fourth or top side of the panel is going to be a son-of-a-gun. Finally,' I thought to myself, 'if the glass breaks and a historical relic like that is forever ruined, Jinny and— Jinny will never forgive me.'

"I was afraid I might, just might, have left some traces on the window, no matter how carefully I used dirt. I did leave traces, as you say. But, to draw away attention from the window, I slipped the safe-key out of Tom's pocket and took out the Cavalier's Cup. My conscience was all over me. When I slipped out and sealed up the window, I decided to give up all attempt to swipe that panel. Finished! No more!"

"You not do it again?" enquired Signor Ravioli, who was staring at him.

"I swore I wouldn't touch it for a million dollars!"

"Then why you try it again? Fine gentleman!" said Signor Ravioli, expressing his hearty admiration and approval, and indicating that he asked merely for information. "Sock flatfoot like-a nobody's business! Damn-a good! But why you come back on Friday night?"

Mr. Harvey hesitated. For the first time, in this greenish eyes, hovered the look of one who is really hunted and cornered. But he assumed dignity, and folded his arms.

"Such matters, I suppose, we must leave to the late Dr. Freud. No doubt some irrational impulse . . . "

"Irrational impulse in a pig's eye," said the vulgar Sir Henry Merrivale. "Shall I tell you why you did it?"

"Now you be careful, Henry!"

"On Thursday, son, you found you didn't have to go back to the States after all . . . "

"Don't say 'the States!' Just say America!"

"There's a pretty big American continent in Canada, son, and another in South America. However! You didn't have to go back. And what did you discover you'd done with your little escapade? You'd made your son-in-law believe he was half off his rocker, with an old but perfectly unfounded fear that's been lurkin' at the back of his skull for years.

291

You made him fear he might go all the way off his rocker. Your daughter was in a flap, and Tom was in a worse flap. Now, as Virginia told us, you're very fond of your son-in-law . . . "

"*Me?* Fond of a *Britisher?* This is too much! I don't know what the devil you're talking about!"

"Lemme go on, son. Will you?"

"Very well. But if you think for one moment . . . "

"It came to a head on Friday, when—against your wishes, as you admitted in my presence in the garden at Cranleigh—Virginia went for a bloke from Scotland Yard. Son, I don't believe anybody ever took a well-meaning person for what you'd call such a ride as Masters was taking your son-in-law.

"If you'll think back to the scene in the garden on Friday evening, when you turned up there, you can't deny it. I was there when Masters waded through the worst part of it. When Masters got to the point of saying, at his blandest, 'I don't say Lord Brace is off his rocker, only a bit peculiar like an aunt of mine,' what occurred then? You were so upset that Masters himself—remember?—had to touch you on the shoulder and add, 'No call for *you* to be upset about it, Senator Harvey.'

"But there was a call, Congressman Harvey.

"That was where you decided to slip into the Oak Room, this time doin' it purely for the trick of a hermetically sealed room, and move the cup again to provide proof your son-in-law hadn't been dreaming. You decided on something else too, I'm pretty sure."

"Decided on what?" the other asked sharply.

"Well—now. You had chloral hydrate in your possession; you also had a life-preserver. Jennings gave 'em both to you, as he told your daughter and son-in-law, before he did a bunk on Friday afternoon.

"I think, honest-Injun, you didn't intend another go at pinchin' the panel. I'll accept that. But Jennings—who's travelled in some pretty wide company in his time, despite his intentions of goin' straight—still had a life-preserver. Why did you take the chloral and the other kind of sleep-producer from him, afterwards throwin' away the life-preserver where Jennings picked it up again?

"My guess is that you'd had a hazy idea yourself, never quite defined, of lurin' *somebody* to sit up in this room, when it became plain Tom was scared green, to prove the innocence of the son-in-law you—hem!—hate like poison.

"Though you must have had awful qualms about a Scotland Yard man, as you showed, still in your own country you've sailed closer to the wind than that. The process was easy. Tom, as we know, poured everybody a whisky-and-soda before you all retired. It wouldn't have been hard to doctor Masters' whisky.

"Either Masters has got more resistance than Tom, or you had less chloral to give him, or maybe a third reason. I dunno. Anyway, you nipped in again when Masters was unconscious or nearly so. What else would you do? This had to look good! It had to have trimmings. So you opened the door of this room—the locked and bolted one—from the inside. You got the cup-hilted rapier from outside the door. After lockin'

293

and boltin' the door on the inside, you slung down the rapier artistically on the floor.

"Since no crime has been committed and nobody's bothered about fingerprints, none of that need have troubled you either.

"You sneaked the safe-key out of Masters' pocket, did another sleight-of-hand with the Cavalier's Cup, and sneaked the key back in his pocket. We know Masters woke up while you were in the room. But I think, son, I *think* he wouldn't have waked up if he'd been given enough chloral.

"What you protest, that you had to do it, may be true. All the same, Masters' carrying-on about your daughter's husband being loony couldn't have pleased you much. When he did stir up in half-consciousness, you didn't want to hurt him too much, just lay him out. So you took good aim with the life-preserver, and . . ."

Signor Ravioli, putting down on the bench and still hiding what he carried, leaped up and bustled forward.

"Fine gentleman, shake hands!"

"Sir, I thank you," replied Mr. Harvey with easy courtesy, and automatically shook hands before he remembered himself, stiffened, and made frantic wig-wagging gestures.

"Henry! For the love of Pete. Sh-h!"

"So in conclusion we'll fly back to an important consideration like me," said H.M.. "sittin' and thinkin' in the small hours of Saturday morning before Rossini there made me practise. I hadn't heard about the plumbin' tools being always available here at Telford, but I'd heard about the plumbers.

"That's how you did it; and what else would you be bound to do? Over the phone the little gal said one thing that helped no end. The phantom burglar—who hadn't burgled—had taken the lute from the top of the harpsichord—there it is—and for no reason at all stuck it down on the hearth. Why?

"You and I," now H.M. glared at Signor Ravioli, "got here in the morning. What was the first thing, practically speakin', we heard? That the phantom had also made a quite senseless and meaningless scratch—usin' the flange of the safe-key—on the door you can see behind my back now.

"That tore it. You being what you are, and your mind working as it does," pursued H.M., still looking at Signor Ravioli, "you tell me what it must have meant when the phantom burglar deliberately called attention to both the fireplace and the door?"

"Hah!"

"Go on; tell me?"

"She's-a mean," answered Signor Ravioli simply, "that burglar has not get in by either door or fireplace. Must have got in by window. Use-a da misdirection to call attention to door and fireplace; that's all."

"Again whang in the bull's eye. Any detective worth his salt could have seen it must be the window, just as I'd thought. But, oh, what a reelin' dummy I still was! With every thread in my hands, I balked at one thing."

"You bollock at what?"

"Both Braces, husband and wife, love that window and dream over it. Grantin' Jennings was an expert forger, and grantin' he could get a reasonable substitute for the glass—y'see, I still couldn't be sure Bill Harvey hadn't switched the panels, though that's the original panel there—for the life of me I didn't believe there could be a substitute good enough to deceive both Braces. I was wrong."

Here H.M. made a noise like the ghost of Sir Byng Rawdon.

"As with some other people, y'see, they knew the window and the scrawled handwriting too well. They knew it so well that they never really looked at it. I should have guessed it from what the little gal said the very first time I met her. 'In the old days,' she said, 'I would stand at that window looking at the writing, and dream for hours, but nowadays I'm so used to it that I take it for granted.'

"Result? Any kind of tolerable forgery, any kind at all, would have hocussed both the gal and her husband. They'd never have noticed it. And William Tecumseh Harvey, who can size up a juryman in two ticks, knew that blinking well.

"But I, the senile cloth-head, didn't tumble to it until you, Julius Caesar, were at the harpsichord late this afternoon, and you went on again about something you kept saying I was doin' wrong. You were carrying on about my not getting just right the words to 'He's dead but he won't lie down.'

"Remember, Appius Claudius! 'See 'em too often!

296

Know 'em too well! That's-a what happen!' And . . .

"Cor!

"It all fitted together completely. The last bit was in. I looked at the door, looked at the fireplace, looked at the window. I remarked that dirt would do it; dirt would cover up most of the traces. And, if Jennings just took a pane of glass from somewhere else at Telford, cuttin' it to suit the size he wanted, nobody on earth would be suspicious if he said a window or a panel from a window got busted by accident.

"That's all there is. That's every bit to the case. Masters can't prove a ruddy thing, no matter what he suspects; if you stand pat, Bill, especially as you're goin' home soon, he can't do anything. And afterwards," thundered H.M., "all I wanted to do tonight was get everybody except you safely in bed and asleep, so I could tell you this in private. Since it's finished, why are we standin' here like three conspirators, behind a locked door? Pagliacci! Go and unlock the door!"

Signor Ravioli scuttered over and turned the key so as to unlock the door, but immediately he scuttered back again.

"No, it is not finished!" said Congressman Harvey, shaking his fist in the air. "In the first place, Signor Ravioli, what have you been hiding from us?"

"Eh?"

"When you came into this room, you were hiding something behind your back. Since you said you'd spent so much time in the c—in meditation, the wild idea flashed across my mind that it might be a stiletto or some weapon. But I couldn't think why you should want to use one."

"Stilett'? Oh, *Corpo di Bacco!* No! I tell-a you I do my job! I tell-a you that, don't I?"

"Yes, you said so, but . . ."

"Look!"

Reaching into dense shadow thrown by the keyboard of the harpsichord, the music-master seized and dramatically held up what at first glance appeared to be a scroll such as that on which Horace or Ovid might have written their more noble verses.

But this, rolled up carefully, was composed of many sheets of paper pasted together one after the other, and neither Horace nor Ovid had ever been so long-winded. When Signor Ravioli let drop one end of the scroll, it rippled down to the floor and spread out at enormous length.

"Sir Henry, he's-a tell me to write thirty verses. Okay! He's-a drink whisky in kitchen; I compose. Look!"

"I say, son!" Though H.M. had seen the scroll when he first entered, great excitement seized him now. " 'He's a Spook but he won't shut up!' Lord love a duck, you did it? All thirty verses?"

"Thirty? Pah! For genius she's-a easy. Forty-five!"

"In the second place," orated Congressman Harvey, paying no attention to this and making a powerfully forensic gesture, "I will not accept the suggestion that any act of mine was inspired by regard for a Britisher. The English, though they may

298

be all very well in their way . . ."

"That's downright handsome of you, son. What about Elaine Cheeseman?"

"The glorious lady in question, Henry, is altogether different. In spirit she is American. Elaine will fly back with me as soon as possible, where we are to be married by a Presbyterian minister and no Episcopalian vicar. You may ask, no doubt, what my daughter will say. Virginia will say . . ."

"Dad!"

The three conspirators were so engrossed that they had not heard hurrying footsteps outside. But they could not fail to hear when the door was flung open.

Virginia, in silk pyjamas, the traces of tears still marring her face, and red mules on her feet, raced in at the door. She was followed by a stalking, dishevelled-haired husband, also in pyjamas covered by an ancient dressing-gown, and kicking at the floor with leather slippers.

"Dad," Virginia ran on breathlessly, "I was perfectly beastly about Elaine Cheeseman. She must be wonderful, if you say she is, and of course you must marry her."

William T. Harvey stood motionless, staring at his daughter. He was so touched, and also so conscience-stung by what he had nearly done in his wish to nick the cavalier's panel, that his fluent throat closed in choking sounds.

"I couldn't sleep," said Virginia. "Not inviting poor Miss Cheeseman to dinner! Oh, I ought to be *killed!* Anyway, I had to put it right. So I rang up

The Blue Nose and spoke to her . . ."

"But, my dear Jinny," gasped Mr. Harvey, consulting his watch, "it's nearly two o'clock in the morning! She wasn't awake, was she?"

"Of course she was," snorted Tom Brace, with powerful sarcasm. "Nobody ever sleeps in this district. She was reading Byron. She says, Gramp—God knows why—you remind her of Byron."

"Tom!" protested the shocked and hurt Virginia. "Where's your romantic soul?"

"Listen, woman. I was just drifting off to sleep, the first blissful eye-closing I've had since this riot began, when you jabbed me in the ribs and asked if it wouldn't be a fine thing to ring up La Cheeseman." Then Tom relented. "Anyway, Gramp, congratulations. Since nobody's *ever* going to sleep, we may as well have a celebration."

"Hem!" said Sir Henry Merrivale, with a modest cough.

And now H.M., drawn up, was in all his glory.

"Celebration?" he said. "Oh, my son! There'll be more than that. There'll be a real treat for all of you, and I'll tell you what it is. Puccini there has written forty-five verses for a superb ballad called 'He's a Spook but he won't shut up.' Ladies and gentlemen," said H.M., "you're goin' to hear me sing."

"N-n-n-o!" shrieked Signor Ravioli, so agitated that the long scroll fluttered all over the floor like blue tickets in the hand of Mrs. Hornby Buller-Kirk. "Last night! Tonight! All damn-a time! No! I no play accompaniment!"

300

H.M. looked strangely at a point over the Italian's head.

"You won't, hey?" he said. "Y'know, son, I wasn't outside that door when you were talking to Congressman Harvey. No, I didn't hear a thing. I'd never dream, it'd never even cross my mind, to mention in public a certain word about which I'll say nothing except that it's got three letters . . ."

"Can!" gulped Signor Ravioli, and dived for the bench. "You seeng! All forty-five verses! I play!"

"No, please," interposed Virginia in her gentle voice. "Of course it would be a wonderful treat, but we couldn't think of troubling Sir Henry."

"Absolutely not!' agreed Tom, with some haste. "Tell you what. We'll open some bottles of champagne instead. Of course Gramp never touches alcohol in any form, but he might get just a bit wiffled in celebration of . . ."

Slowly, like a heavy cruiser manouvering into position to launch its deadly torpedo, H.M. turned towards them.

·"Y'know," he remarked thoughtfully, "I wonder what's happened to that butler, Jennings! If anybody saw him and didn't tip off the police, if anybody was accessary-after-the-fact to his escape . . ."

"Sir Henry, we should be delighted to hear you sing!"

"Absolutely! We'll open the champagne later!"

"Hem!" said the great man.

Taking the gigantic scroll from Signor Ravioli, he assumed a careless posture by the harpsichord, and tuned up his throat with noises best left undescribed.

"Now is there anybody else," said H.M., peering very hard over his spectacles at William T. Harvey, "who thinks it wouldn't be a rare treat, practically an experience no hearer will ever forget, to hear me sing?"

Snatching up the fountain pen and one of the sheets of notepaper, which he crumpled before thrusting it into his pocket, Congressman Harvey sat down in the chair and gripped its arms hard. But he was a man and he knew how to take his punishment. "Shoot," he said.

TALES OF TERROR AND POSSESSION